# GREEN EYES AND HAM

Also by Mary Penney

*Eleven and Holding*

# GREEN EYES AND HAM

MARY PENNEY



HARPER
*An Imprint of* HarperCollins*Publishers*

Green Eyes and Ham
 For information address HarperCollins Children's Books, a division of HarperCollins Publishers, 195 Broadway, New York, NY 10007.
www.harpercollinschildrens.com

Library of Congress Control Number: 2021951277
ISBN 978-0-06-269693-9

Typography by Julia Feingold
22 23 24 25 26 SB 10 9 8 7 6 5 4 3 2 1
❖
First Edition

*To Carrie Bree—*

*whose very presence has been a master class*

*in unconditional love and compassion.*

*Her friendship through this all has been a steadying*

*light, and the most exquisite place to rest.*

*xoxo*

# CHAPTER ONE

You'd think if your mom was a priest, and you spent nearly every waking moment in a church, you'd never lie.

You'd be wrong.

I never needed to lie until I started public school for the first time ever as an eighth grader, just a few weeks back. I told a lie to protect someone, and convinced myself that was the *good* kind of lie. Even sort of noble of me. But it still ended up hurting people. That's the worst part. You can take back the lie, but you can't take back the hurt.

My mom, Reverend Annabelle Hudson, lies sometimes, too. She dresses it up fancy, and it's usually to get me to do something that I don't want to do.

Like when she told me that *nobody* would see me delivering a giant box of lady diapers to Mrs. Minelli's house. The box was too big to fit in my bike basket, so I had to carry it under my arm. The store didn't have a bag big enough for it.

Three local ~~terrors~~ kids on bikes chased me all the way from the drugstore to Mrs. Minelli's driveway. They rode up right next to me, busting a gut, as they read the details out loud—

"Check it out! 'Now with flexi-wings!'"

"Whoa! 'Absorbs 10X weight.'"

"Church Boy! When's your mama gonna potty train you?"

I just kept my eyes on my front wheel and pretended they weren't there. Which was impossible. I recited the periodic table of elements under my breath until they rode away.

I parked my bike and locked it up on Mrs. Minelli's porch. Then grabbed the bag from my basket that held her *Glowing Red-Hot-Red* lady hair dye.

I pushed the bell and kept pressing until I nearly lost all the blood in my fingertip. Mrs. Minelli is pretty deaf. She's one of my mom's Church Ladies. There's a whole tribe of them. You can't run a church by yourself like Mom does without them. They do all the stuff Mom doesn't have time to do. The Church Ladies would take a bullet for her any day of the week, and probably take a bullet for me, too.

The door flung open and Mrs. Minelli smiled like Christmas had just shown up at her door, even though nearly 100 degrees of August heat beat on us.

"Well, there you are, Ham, my darling! This is just so kind of you." She looked over the top of her bright red eyeglasses to study the diapers, and then to the other arm, where I'd stashed the box of her hair dye.

"Oh, excellent! You found the exact right ones," she said, and led me in. Fortunately, she had air-conditioning, and had it going strong. Mom and I didn't have any at the parsonage where we lived. They hadn't invented air-conditioning yet when the church was built. And my mom's boss—not God, the guy under Him—was a money miser.

"Hammy, would you like some iced tea?"

"Thanks! I'd love some," I said, and waited for the glass of tea so sweet it would make my eyes cross. And, then Mrs. M would bring out a plate of frostbit circus cookies she kept in the freezer. I think she bought a case of them from Costco the year Mom found me. Someday I'd eventually finish the whole lot—but she would never stop calling me "Hammy," even though I was thirteen. None of them would.

"You must think I'm so vain to ask you to do this—" she started, like she always did.

"Gosh, no!" I said, trying to swallow a frosted elephant whole.

"It is vain, I suppose, and may the good Lord forgive me. I don't have pretty silver hair like Mrs. Dort. She's lucky. Mine is dingy. She thinks that the other ladies and I, that we should take all the money we spend on hair dye and feed the poor instead. If she makes one crack about my red hair at church on Sunday, I swear I'm going to deck her!"

"But Mrs. Dort is your best friend," I said, trying to imagine two of the Church Ladies coming to blows in the pews.

"Oh, she is! I love that woman like my own sister. But being friends with someone doesn't mean you always agree with them. You learn, though, which friends are worth saving, and which ones you hide your welcome mat from. She's a keeper, even if she is as stubborn as a horse's backside."

I filed that away in the event I ever had a friend of my own, and took a small sip of tea. The sugar piled up on my tongue.

Mrs. M headed over to the large mirror in her

front room. She held the box up to her face, imagining, I suppose, how the color would look on her. She turned her head from side to side, then studied the hair model on the box.

"Let's take a before and after picture. I've never been a redhead," she said, smiling with excitement. She pulled her phone out of the deep pocket of her sweater and handed it to me. "Will you take it for me? Every time I try to take a selfie, I end up with a picture of the front door."

"Sure," I said, and opened her camera app.

She fluffed her half-brown and half-white hair while she waited for me. "I wish your mom would let us buy you a cell phone," she said, shaking her head. "I don't know how you get along without one. All my grandbabies have them, even Honor, and she's only four!"

I smiled while giant cavities formed in my teeth from the tea. I snapped a front and back head shot, and handed it back to her.

Mrs. M couldn't actually work her phone. At all. One of her great-grandsons had set her ringer to a hip-hop song. He liked to call her during church on Sunday. He thought it was hysterical. I tried to remember to put her phone on silent every Sunday morning. When the older Church Ladies started getting cell phones, I had to learn how to use one so I could help them.

Mom and I didn't have money for anything we didn't absolutely need. Besides, phones were for kids with friends.

I didn't have friends. And didn't want any.

Kids my age were pretty cruel. They thought it was hilarious that a boy lived in a church, and even had homeschool there. Some of them knew the story of how I'd been dumped there late one night when I was a baby. It had been in the newspapers, and I guess maybe their parents had told them about me, probably thinking that their kid would be really nice to me if they knew my story. Instead, it just put a giant target on my back.

On a good day, they'd just shout "Hey, Church Boy!" as they raced by. On a bad day, they'd yell stuff that didn't even make sense to me. It wasn't like I could ask Mom what their insults meant. I'd check the computer for a translation, and sit there while my cheeks burned.

Why would they say such awful things? I did not understand other kids.

At all.

I started to get things ready while Mrs. M continued to fuss about keeping up with modern times. I set out two big towels, one washcloth for her eyes, one stool, and a big comb. This wasn't the first time. I'd dyed her hair before.

And not just hers. Before too long another Church Lady would probably ring the bell, and just happen to have a box of hair dye in her giant purse and—*Oh, Ham, you are here! Would you mind just giving me a quick touch-up? Rev said you wouldn't mind at all if I popped in.*

Another one of Mom's little dressed-up lies. She'd promised I'd just have to do Mrs. Minelli's hair one time until her regular girl at the salon came back to work. I'd been doing it over a year now. Plus a few of the other Church Ladies. They say I'm better at it than a real stylist. I get ten dollars a head, a dollar tip, plus snacks. The diaper delivery service was new.

I loved being around them, and having extra money all my own was great. Sometimes I just wished I could earn money doing something a little less weird for them—like maybe doing yard work or washing their cars. I didn't need anything else in my life that made me seem freakish to the kids in the neighborhood.

But Mom's biggest lie of all was still to come. When the decision was made that I'd have to start going to public school, she told me that it would be "a piece of cake." And, that all the kids would like me once they got to know me.

What she didn't tell me was that I'd end up practically facing felony charges before I even got my first report card. Neither of us saw that coming.

But first, welcome to my world—my nearly perfect life before it all crashed and burned.

# CHAPTER TWO

I was deep in Saturday morning sleep mode under nineteen pounds of meat named Buster, my one-eyed cat, who was exactly the same age as me. We both were excellent sleepers and didn't like being disturbed—ever.

Mom waved a plate of bacon under our noses, which was her only hope of rousing us. She's clever like that.

"Hammy, wake up! Deuce is here. Cinnamon rolls will be out in five minutes—the maple bacon ones!" She tore a piece of bacon in half and fed some to Buster. She laid the rest under my nose like a mustache.

Deuce was the greatest guy in the whole world.

He was seventy-six years old, an amazing athlete, an ex-convict, and the best chef in all of the state. He'd lived across the street from me and Mom here in Muddy Waters since forever.

Buster and I would definitely get up for him, even though Saturday was our only sleep-in day. Sundays were the worst day of the week—church stuff all day long.

"—Kay, we're up, we're up!" I said, and popped the bacon into my mouth. I gently shifted Buster off me, and slid out of our cocoon. My thirteen years old and his thirteen years old were totally different. I wasn't half-grown yet, and he was way past middle age.

Mom threw a clean T-shirt from my dresser at me as she left the room. She'd still like to dress me entirely, but I'd been working with her on that.

Buster hurried out the door after more bacon. Deuce would have also brought half-and-half, and he'd pour him a bowl. Buster loved Deuce as much as Mom and I did.

I pulled my shirt over my head, and dug my fists into my eye sockets. I loosened up my ankles and studied the long scrape on my leg from my run with Deuce yesterday. We had done a trail run and I'd tripped over a tree root. I was going through a growth spurt and had a hard time operating all the new length of me.

"We've got hot buns *and* hot news!" Mom shouted from the kitchen. "Come and get it!"

I shuffled toward her voice, and ran my fingers through my stick-straight hair that liked to pile up on my forehead. Deuce pulled a barstool out for me. He set down a plate of four steaming rolls with squares of real butter melting over them like golden lava.

"Oh man, Deuce, these look great. Thanks!"

Mom reached for the butter plate, and Deuce moved it out of her reach.

"Oh, come on!" she complained, and made a second grab for it. I snaked it and put it on my lap.

"You flunked your cholesterol test," I reminded her.

"I didn't flunk it—" she started.

"Annie, you've got to start taking better care of yourself. When's the last time you got any real exercise?" Deuce asked.

"Two years ago when you turned forty," I said. "The birthday run we all did."

We all stopped mid-chew. Mom and I turned our eyes to Deuce, remembering when there had been four of us. Now there was just us three.

He cleared his throat and wiped his mouth.

"Annie," he said, his voice quieter and gentler. "You've got to do better than that."

Mom sighed and took a drink of her coffee. "I want to do better. I just don't have time right now. There's so much to do. And I know I won't be getting an assistant pastor anytime soon." She reached for the plate of buns and gave both Deuce and me both the hairy eyeball. "I'm having just *one*."

"When's your follow-up appointment with the doc?" Deuce asked. "Weren't you supposed to go back in three months to get rechecked?"

"It was last week," I said. "She canceled it."

"There was a pastoral emergency. I had to," she said. "I'll reschedule."

"Yeah, you will," he said, giving her a stern look. "Take you myself if I have to."

"Fine!" She threw up her hands, then took a giant bite of her butterless bun, still oozy with goodness.

Deuce poured himself a cup of coffee from the French press he always brought over. He thought church coffee was invented by Satan himself to punish churchgoers. "How you feeling today, kid? Up for another run—or do you need a recovery day?"

I nearly had my head in the plate and answered with an enthusiastic headshaking.

"Excellent!" He clapped me on the back.

I swallowed and took a long pull on my juice. "So, what's the news? You said buns and news."

Mom motioned out our front window. I turned to look and saw a giant moving van being unloaded.

"New family moving into the Orchards' old house," she said. "Been too long since that house has been full. I'm going to take them some rolls while they're still warm."

"Met the daughter this morning," Deuce said, scratching his morning whiskers. "Nice kid. She was out crouched in the hedge we share, taking pictures of bugs."

"Prison people?" I asked.

"Yeah, both of her folks will work there. Transfers," Deuce said, and sighed. "Just what I need. Two prison guards living right next door."

Mom patted his hand. Muddy Waters was a smallish-sized town smack in the middle of California. It had an extra-large prison right on the edge of it. Most everyone in town either worked there or had a relative inside. It's where Deuce was locked up for fifteen years, and my mom did a prison ministry. Sometimes I went and helped her with the inmates' kids who were visiting.

Mom and I both knew that the sight of uniformed officers still made Deuce's blood run cold. When he first got out of prison a few years back, he'd planned to stay in Muddy Waters just until he could figure out what he was going to do next with his life. But then he had met Mr. Flynn at his gym, and they'd become the best of friends. They ended up moving in together right across the street from us. Like Deuce, Mr. Flynn didn't have any family, either. They spent a couple of years rebuilding their house from the ground up.

But Mr. Flynn died seven months ago from brain cancer, and now the only thing that kept Deuce in Muddy Waters was me and Mom. I told Mom she should ask him to marry her so we could be a real family. Mom told me she and Deuce didn't love each other like that, but that he'd always be part of our family, no matter where he lived.

"Deuce says the girl is your age, Hammy," Mom added, super casual, but I knew where this was going. She wanted me to hop aboard her welcome wagon.

"Sorry, got plans already today," I said.

"We won't stay long," she started. "Just drop off the—"

I shoved about eight full inches of bacon into my mouth and shook my head no. Pointed to Deuce, then mimed a runner in stride.

"Soon, then," she said. "We want them to feel very welcome." Mom knew better than to argue with me about this. Saturday was my only day off in the week, and I was kind of stingy with it. It was the deal. She had me all the other days of the week. She didn't believe in kids having a whole summer off from school, even if it was homeschool.

It was all I could do not to turn around and take a peek at the girl, though. I knew a few girls my age who came to church, but so far, none of them seemed interested in being friends with me. At least they didn't call me names. I'd give them that.

I had to admit I was kind of intrigued by a girl who took pictures of bugs, though. Or maybe she was just pretending to be busy taking pictures to try to get out of unpacking boxes. My hobby was collecting old vinyl records, especially the ones from Motown. Only Mom knew how much I loved singing along with Diana Ross and the Supremes. I didn't know how much longer I'd have this voice before it started warbling and cracking once I hit puberty. But then, I'd have Barry White to sing along with. He was pretty amazing, too.

I went to the window and watched as Deuce headed

home to change into his running gear. Mom hurried across the street with a tray of fresh coffee and buns. Like everyone did, the new neighbors would fall in love with her right away. Mom looked nothing like a priest today. She had on a pair of old baggy cutoffs and a raggedy 5K race T-shirt. Her long, dark hair was cranked up into a ponytail.

But what they'd probably notice first was the long scar across her face from her mouth all the way up to her eye. It happened when an inmate shanked her. He'd cut her deep. He might have done more to her, but a guard caught it before things got worse.

I used to ask Mom what she'd said to make the inmate so mad at her. She'd never tell me exactly how it happened. She'd just said the guy was scared and confused.

I moved back from the window a bit so no one could see me. The parents and the girl stood in the driveway talking to Mom, and looking happy and friendly. Mom pointed behind her and probably was telling them about her church and inviting them to come to services. But she kept pointing, and then put her arm around the girl. I could see she was steering the girl my way.

Oh no, Mom!! Please don't tell her to come over and meet me.

She looked up at her parents and they nodded. New girl headed my way.

I panicked. I could hide, but Mom would turn the house on its end and shake me out.

I spat a PG cuss word, and hid in the shadows of the drapes while the girl came up to the door.

Before she even knocked, Buster jumped up on the windowsill and meeped at her. He rubbed his head, and then his bottom, against the glass. Very classy, Buster. The girl smiled with sparkly rainbow braces, and tapped on the window near him.

I could hear her voice through the screen door. "Hello, gorgeous kitty! What's your name?"

Buster went into full dance-o-rama mode, then fell off the windowsill in his frenzy. He hurried to the front screen door. He turned and yowled in my direction, giving up my location.

Traitor.

I was left with no choice.

I pulled open the screen door, and the girl dropped down to her knees as Buster shot out. He leaned into her, and acted like no one had ever scratched his head until this moment.

Since she and Buster had eyes for no one but each other, it gave me a quick chance to have a closer look at the girl. She had reddish hair, with a big green streak in it. But no makeup or sticky lip stuff on her mouth.

Buster backed over to me, and wove figure eights between my legs.

The girl stood back up. "Hi! I'm Fey—from across the street. We just moved in."

And at the exact moment she talked, I said, "Hi, I'm Ham. And that's Buster."

We laughed and tried to start over, but both started talking again at the same time.

Fey held up a hand. "Okay—you go first."

"No, you—you go!"

She laughed and reached her hand out to shake mine.

I couldn't ever remember a kid wanting to shake my hand when they met me. It was strange but nice.

"I'm Fey," she repeated. "Your mom said I should come say hi."

"Sorry, she's kind of pushy that way. I'm Ham—and this is Buster."

"Can I hold her? Or is it a him?" Fey asked. "I love cats—all animals really, but we never can have any, because we move a lot."

"I'm not sure he'll let you—" I started, pointless, because Buster leapt up into her arms when Fey held them out. They were now having a love festival.

"Wow," I said. "He doesn't usually let people hold him unless he knows them."

"Animals take to me," Fey said. "I'm lucky that way."

"What grade are you going into?" she asked, Buster's head buried deep under her chin.

"Well, eighth grade, but—"

"Me too! Maybe we'll be in the same homeroom!" Her face lit up.

"Oh, well, no—I'm homeschooled, here, with my mom." I turned and swept an arm back at the parsonage. "Welcome to Mom Academy and First Grace Church."

She cocked her head at me a second. "I've never met anyone who was homeschooled. Do you like it? Have you been to public school at all?"

I reddened. I wasn't prepared to tell her that I'd only made it one week in public school as a first grader. I remember I cried pretty nonstop. Mom came to school with me and sat in the back for reassurance, but that didn't work, either. I wouldn't face the front of the class if she was in the back.

But after listening to the curriculum for a few days, and seeing how packed the classroom was, Mom decided she could do better for me at home. She was very smart and had a PhD in religious studies. I already knew how to read and write cursive by then, anyway.

"I went for a while," I hedged, "but it just wasn't for me. And my mom is a great teacher. I'm learning a lot more here than I ever would at public school."

"I hate starting new schools," Fey said with a big sigh. "I'm always the new kid. My parents transfer to a new prison about every three years, so I don't ever get to make friends I can keep."

"Well, you seem really friendly. You'll probably make a lot of friends right away," I said, a sudden expert on public school relationships.

Fey lifted her shoulders and dropped them. Gave me what I guessed was a brave smile.

"Probably not. I was hoping after I heard about you that I'd have a new friend to know at school."

For a split second, I pictured what she just imagined. We'd be friends at home and school, and all the other kids would see that we were tight. I wouldn't care if they made fun of me as much, because I'd have a friend of my own.

Then I came right to my senses. No doubt she'd meet someone she liked better the first day. Or hear from the mean kids that I was a total loser. She'd probably get wind of that by the end of the day from the neighborhood kids.

"Anyway, I should get back. I just wanted to say hey." She gave me a shy smile and took two steps backward. "Oh! You probably want Buster back." She set him down gently, and kissed his head.

Fey started to walk away, then paused, and spun back around. "If you ever want to hang out or something, you know—" Her face turned red, and I realized she was as nervous as I was.

"Yeah! Sure, I mean, we could, um . . . that would be super fun!" I said.

"Cool." And she smiled like she meant it.

# CHAPTER THREE

Deuce and I both looked like we'd been swimming in our tanks and shorts. We were drenched and out of breath. Well, I was out of breath. He guzzled from his water bottle, then handed it to me. I'd finished my water half an hour ago.

"Drink up."

We'd walked the last quarter mile toward home. He'd kicked my butt today, but I didn't mind. He wasn't like a regular old guy—he was a champ. I worried after Mr. Flynn died that Deuce might get really depressed, and maybe even not want to do stuff anymore. So far, he'd gone the opposite way. He'd redone his whole backyard, put a new roof on his house, and now he was giving his classic Mustang a new paint job. He'd hand polished the exterior chrome for hours until it was almost blinding.

Mom said that sometimes that was *exactly* what grief looked like. Grief can make someone afraid if they stop staying busy, the sadness will catch up and consume them.

I worried about him about as much as I worried about my mom. I couldn't imagine my life without either of them. I wanted them to stay healthy and happy forever. I wondered if adopted kids worried about this more than other kids did. It wasn't like I missed my birth mom, like you might miss someone who moved away forever. I missed her in a different way. It was like there was an old empty file cabinet inside me that rattled around. I'd lost all the files of my life before I'd come here. No files about my birth parents, brothers or sisters, grandparents, uncles, aunts. I was left with nothing but the empty, rusty drawers.

I tried not to think too hard about all the missing information in my family tree. Some days it was easier than others.

Deuce dropped onto his lawn in the shade when we reached his house. I finished off his bottle he'd given me. I was going to drink my body weight in juice when I got home.

"So, what did you think of Fey?" he asked as he rubbed out a gnarly calf.

I shrugged. "She seemed really nice. And Buster is in love with her." I rolled onto my back and pulled my knees up to my chin. We'd run for a couple of hours, and my legs were barking hard.

"Really tough for a kid to have to start eighth grade as the new kid. Hope she makes a friend."

I rolled my head toward him and pulled my knees in tighter. "What's so tough about eighth grade?" Mom and I had already gone through the entire eighth-grade curriculum, and it wasn't so hard.

"Think about it. Eighth graders rule the roost. They're finally the oldest kids on campus. And to make matters worse, they're all being hit with hormones. It's a tough year. Especially hard for a new girl, I'd think. Most kids are already locked in with each other."

Deuce had been a junior high teacher when he first got out of college. He always said he barely made it out alive after seven years at it.

"Huh," I grunted.

"She's such a great kid. I want her to have a good year," he said.

"So do I," I agreed.

I did a few sit-ups while Deuce pumped out a couple dozen push-ups, without even getting winded.

An idea had been rolling around in my head. I decided to run it by Deuce.

"What if Mom could homeschool Fey, too? It wouldn't be too much extra work, since we'd be working on the same material. I bet Fey would be totally up for it."

Deuce finished his push-ups, and turned his gaze toward me. "I don't know. I'm worried about your mom."

I rolled up partway, elbows on the grass behind me. "Her cholesterol, you mean?"

"That, sure, but she's working way too hard. I can't even remember the last time she took a day off for herself. As much as I was glad to see the backside of that sanctimonious assistant pastor she had, at least he'd been able to carry some of the load."

"That's just how she rolls," I said. "You know she loves her job."

"But a person can't keep up a pace like that forever—between the food pantry, the prison, some sort of church service nearly every day, people calling on her all hours of the day, and your education—well, she needs a break. Every time I see her, I want to send her on a beach vacation for a month. Of course, she'd never let me."

One of the things I loved about Deuce was that he most always shot straight from the hip. But I could tell he was circling around something. I sat all the way up to try and catch it.

"Should we try to get her to take the rest of the summer off from homeschool? I doubt my brain will rot in a month."

Deuce gazed off into the distance, chewing on a blade of grass, and then said, "Well, that would be a start."

He stood up then and reached over to give me a hand up. "Hit the shower and then get your legs up for a while. Strong workout, kid. And let's both think hard about what else we can do to make your mom's load lighter."

I nodded as he headed toward the house. But I was left with the feeling that it was *me* he wanted doing most of the thinking about this.

The rest of the summer days raced by, and it wasn't because Mom Academy summer school was so fascinating. It was because Deuce had managed to convince Mom that it would be good for both of us to have a break until September.

I should have known when she agreed to it that something wasn't quite right.

She barely protested, and then threw herself harder into her prison ministry. Her church boss, Mr. Scroogey Tightwad, kept the pressure on her. Whenever she asked about getting a replacement assistant pastor, he'd tell her she'd need more congregants first. It was a game she could never seem to win.

Even though he was a man of God, I wanted to whoop him good.

Once Fey heard that I was on vacation for the rest of the summer, she started coming by almost every morning. At first, I suspected that Mom or Deuce had put her up to it. Like when Mom used to set up playdates for me with other kids from the church. That was always a disaster. I didn't know any of the games or movies the kids liked, and they would get bored with me really quick. I was more used to grown-ups, and the playdate would end up with me hanging out with the parents in the kitchen or garage.

But being with Fey felt different. We'd spend nearly all day together, doing really cool stuff I never thought a girl would like to do. Least none I'd ever met. Fey was obsessed with all the new plants and birds and wildlife in Muddy Waters. She let me tag after her while she photographed all her discoveries. Later, she'd make sketches of what she'd seen in her cool homemade field journal.

I'd even started a field journal of my own. I filled it with notes about what we'd done that day, and some of the funny things she would say. I started sketching her, too, not like a portrait or anything. I'd draw one of her freckly arms, or the crazy way she tied her sneakers. Mom and Deuce had started referring to her as my "friend," which thrilled me, but it kind of scared me, too. So while Fey studied natural science, I studied her. I wanted to get it right. I wanted her to be friends with me, even after the summer was over.

One scorchy afternoon, we were sprawled out in her living room with our journals. Her parents let her stay home alone when they were at work—they knew either Mom or Deuce would look out for her while they were gone.

Her parents had an old turntable, so I'd brought some vinyl with me. Fey seemed to love getting to know the classic Motown bands.

We were listening to the Temptations. They were considered to be one of the most successful pop bands of all times. They had it all—great harmonies, dance moves, style, and flash. Sometimes I wondered if I didn't have some Motown in my family tree—it felt like it lived in my DNA. I couldn't get enough of it. My favorite song was "Papa Was a Rollin' Stone." Fey liked "Just My Imagination" the best, and she hummed along with it.

She studied a plant sample she'd found earlier, and made notes. Buster was draped across her lap. He refused to let me ever come over here without him. I knew she snuck him people snacks when she thought I wasn't looking. But I didn't mind.

Buster wasn't the only lucky one. Fey's parents bought root beer by the case. I'd had two so far today and was working on the third. Soda was not in our grocery budget at home. And Fey's family also kept a giant freezer in the garage full of ice cream, Popsicles, and doughnuts. It was so hot these days, we'd eat the doughnuts frozen.

"Hey, can I ask you something?" Fey said, brushing her cheek with the leaf she was studying.

I'd been trying to draw Buster's head cradled in her elbow, and I looked up.

"Sure?"

"You've never talked about your dad, I just wondered—"

I felt a heat climb up the back of my neck. Not embarrassment, but more like, maybe fear.

"I mean, I know it's personal and you may not want to, and that's totally okay," she said.

"I—uh—well, no, it's not that I haven't wanted to, I just—" I cleared my throat.

"Well, only if you want to tell me," she said.

"I do," I said. I swallowed and realized that I really did want to tell her. I'd only known her about a month, but we'd spent a lot of time together. We were beginning to tell each other lots of things that were private. I knew that was something that good friends did together. At least kids in books and movies did.

She put her field guide down, and waited, rubbing Buster's ears.

"Truth is I don't know who my dad was. My mom doesn't, either."

"Your *mom* doesn't know?" she asked, trying to sort that out.

"Oh, it's not like that!" I said, realizing how terrible that sounded. "I have a birth mother somewhere who isn't Mom. I have no idea who my father is or was."

"Oh! You're adopted. I didn't know that!"

I nodded and took a deep breath. Dared myself to go on. I'd never told anyone on purpose. I was kind of a local legend, I suppose. Being in a small town hadn't helped matters, either. People love a good story, Mom would always say.

"How old were you when she got you?"

"Brand-new—just about a month old."

"Wow. I did a report on adoption last year for school, and I know it is really hard for people to get new babies. It can sometimes take years. But your mom is a priest and all, so she probably got fast-tracked."

"Not exactly," I said. My mouth was dry as dust. I took a long swig of root beer. "Uh, well, she didn't apply for me. She found me."

Fey sat forward, and Buster meowed with annoyance. "She found you? Where?"

I pointed my head in the direction of the church. "Someone dumped me off at the church late one night, and Mom heard me outside crying."

"They *dumped* you off?" Fey's eyes widened. "At night? What kind of person leaves a baby out in the dark?"

I shrugged. I'd wondered that same thing for years. Probably because they didn't want to be seen.

"That blows my mind," she said. "I can't believe they just left you."

I drew a dark line in my journal, then drew over

it, making it darker and wider.

"Well, I suppose, I mean, I guess it's a good thing they dumped me there, and not like at a bowling alley or liquor store."

"Well, of course—" she started.

"Mom always said that they picked the best place they could think of. Maybe even my birth mother hoped that the 'Lady Reverend' would keep me and adopt me."

Fey flopped back against the couch, trying to absorb it all. "Well, she could have dropped you off at the police station, too."

"Yeah, they could have," I agreed. "But if they'd done that, I would have gone right into foster care."

"Right, right, you're right," she said, chewing the end of her pencil. "Did they leave you in a baby carrier on the porch? Was there a note?"

"No, not a baby carrier," I said.

"Please don't tell me they just left you in a box," she said.

I shook my head. Swallowed.

"No? Well, then—?"

"It was Christmas night," I said. "They left me at the Nativity scene on the church lawn—in the manger."

Fey placed both her hands on top of her head like maybe she wanted to keep it from exploding. "They put you in the MANGER with the Baby Jesus?"

"No, not with Baby Jesus. They—or she—took Baby Jesus. But they left me in his place."

"What??" She shook her head, then said again, *"What?"*

I crossed my arms across my chest. A chill just came over me. "I dunno. Like a trade-in?" I tried to make a joke of it. It was a terrible joke.

Mom had never kept the real story from me, but when I was just a little kid, I thought I'd been born Baby Jesus. Honestly, it was a confusing time for me. I kept thinking the Bible stories were about me, which made no sense, because my mom's name was Annabelle, not Mary. And we lived in Muddy Waters, not Nazareth. When I was older and could understand that I'd been abandoned, I'd been pretty horrified. I started going online and reading stories about other places babies had been left. I'd discovered a baby who'd been left in an armadillo burrow, and another in an airplane bathroom. They'd found a baby left in a woman's abandoned purse, one in a Nike shoebox at a mall, and a lot of them in public restroom stalls.

Of all those I'd read about so far, I figured a

Nativity manger was probably better than any of those. Except maybe the armadillo burrow. Armadillos are built like small tanks. I guessed they'd know how to keep a baby safe.

A moment of silence had fallen between us, and I studied my hands. Fey was probably trying to figure out what would be the right thing to say. She was thoughtful like that.

I was trying to decide whether or not to tell Fey what else had been left in the manger with me.

The moment was shattered by the sharp wail of a fire truck siren headed our way. I turned to look out the window and saw, then heard, the ambulance on its tail.

Buster raced from the room to hide from the terrible racket.

When the fire truck and the ambulance pulled right in front of our church, and the medics flew toward the parsonage front door, I shot out the door like from a cannon.

# CHAPTER FOUR

Deuce stood in the open door and caught me by the shoulders as I tore across the front lawn.

"Hold on, Ham! Let them do their job!"

He held me hard as I watched the EMTs run the gurney through the front door.

I turned to look at him, trying to catch my breath. "Is it MOM?"

"Yes, but they'll take care of her," he started.

"What *happened*? Did she fall?"

Fey raced up behind us, panting. "What happened? Is it Rev?"

Deuce kept a firm hand on my shoulder as he explained. "I'd come over to take a look at the leak under the kitchen sink. Your mom seemed a little out of it. She complained that she was a bit sick to her stomach. I noticed she kept rubbing her jaw. I asked her if she had a toothache. She said her jaw was just really sore. Next thing I knew, she broke out in a sweat, and then slumped over the barstool. I barely managed to catch her in time."

He let out a big gust of air, and Fey patted his arm. "Thank God you were there with her!"

"Did your mom seem okay to you this morning, Ham?" Deuce asked.

"Yes! She was fine," I said, one eye still glued to the front door. I wanted to get in there so bad. I tried to pull away again, but Deuce held me back.

"Son, we need to stay out of their way and let them do their job."

Deuce, Fey, and I stood in a tight clump, squeezing each other's hands.

I whipped around at the sound of the gurney coming out the front door.

"Mom!!" She wore an oxygen mask over her face. Her eyes were closed.

Deuce tightened his hold on me.

"What's wrong? What happened?" This couldn't be real.

One of the EMTs hurried over to us as the others

loaded Mom into the ambulance. "Sir, how long do you think she was unconscious?"

"Maybe three to four minutes?" Deuce said. "She was breathing, but she was out. She had complained of a bad pain in her jaw right before she blacked out."

"Okay, they'll hook her up to an EKG on the way to the hospital. Are you family?" he asked, looking at both me and Deuce.

"Yes!" I said.

Deuce nodded.

I wrenched out of Deuce's clamp, and ran over to the back of the ambulance.

"I'm coming, too!" I announced to the uniforms that had just loaded her. "That's my mom!"

One of the EMT ladies put firm hands on my shoulders. "What's your name, son?"

"Ham. And that's my mom—Reverend Hudson!"

"Ham, I'm Emily, and we're going to need all the room in the ambulance to take care of your mom. But you can come to the hospital, and the doctor there will let you know how she is doing."

Deuce appeared at my side, and I grabbed his arm. "We need to get to the hospital. Can you take me?"

"Yes, of course," he said. "Take a big breath. It's going to be okay." He steered me around and headed me toward his house to get the car.

"Wait!" I jerked back toward the ambulance.

"Don't worry, Ham. We've got her," Emily shouted as the siren started back up.

"Tell her not to go to the Light! She tells people when they're dying to go to the Light! Tell her not to even look at the Light!"

Emily gave me a thumbs-up and slammed the rear door, and they sped away.

With me, Deuce, and Fey not far behind.

Two and half hours later, we finally got word from the ER doctor, Dr. Sweeney, that Mom was going to be all right. She said Mom had a "cardiac event," which I think she said because it probably sounded less scary than "heart attack." They were putting a stent in her artery to open up the flow of blood to her heart. Mom would have to make some changes in her life to avoid another one. They were keeping her overnight so they could monitor her.

Dr. Sweeney looked at Deuce. "I haven't been able to reach her primary care doc yet. Is there family history of heart disease?"

"I'm not really sure," Deuce said. "I'm a good friend, not family. I can call her parents. She doesn't have any brothers or sisters."

Dr. Sweeney adjusted the stethoscope that hung from her neck. "Yes, call them. Let me know what you find out. Even at forty-two, she's young for—well, she's young for this."

"Can I see her?" I asked, pleading.

Dr. Sweeney and Deuce exchanged a glance. "Well, she's resting, and she needs that more than anything. Can you promise to be very quiet, and not wake her up?"

"Promise!"

"Okay, come with me, and I'll take you back."

Fey gave me a tight hand squeeze as I headed off. I didn't even know she'd been holding it.

Dr. Sweeney shot me a sideways look as we headed down the hall. "You and I have met before," she said.

"We have?" I said, puzzled. My pediatrician was a man with an office downtown, and I'd never had to be at the hospital before. Well, except when I did visitations with my mom. But never as a patient.

"Yes—I was on call the night they brought you in."

I shook my head. "I've never been a hospital patient before."

She paused a moment, like she was trying to decide if she should go on.

"Oh!" I said, a light dawning. "*That* time. When I was a baby."

Dr. Sweeney nodded.

"On the night I was left in the manger."

"Child Protective Services brought you in with the police. You needed a medical exam to make sure you were okay."

"Was I?"

"Yes, you were fine, but gave me a good fight when I tried to examine you," she laughed, remembering.

"Sorry about that."

"No, don't be. I would have been worried if you didn't fight. And under the circumstances, that would have been understandable."

"Well, thank you for taking care of me that night," I said. "I'm still here, so you must have done a good job."

"I was really happy when I read in the paper later that Reverend Hudson adopted you. I've always wondered how you two were making out."

She paused outside a patient room then, and nodded at the nurse, who moved away from the monitors. Dr. Sweeney stood by the machines, and studied all of Mom's data.

I tiptoed over to Mom, and took all of her in, drawing my first full breath in what seemed like an hour. She looked pale and small. It was awful to see her so completely still.

And quiet.

I said a quick prayer. It wasn't one of my best.

*God—it's me!*

*No disrespect intended, but you can't have her yet. She's not done with all the stuff she wants to do. You saved my sorry life that night when you gave me to her. But I'm still just a kid, and I still need her. Everyone does—Deuce, the Church Ladies, the prisoners, the people in our church.*

*If you save her, I'll do whatever You want.*

*Well, almost anything.*

*Okay, fine.*

*Whatever You want.*

*Amen.*

After a little bit, Dr. Sweeney motioned for me to leave, and the nurse stepped back in as we left. I took one last look before I headed out. I wanted to store Mom up in my eyeballs until I got to see her again. I wanted to see her awake and talking and convincing me she was going to be okay.

Fey was alone in the waiting room when I got back.

"How is she?" she asked, jumping up.

I blew out a giant breath. "She's asleep, but okay. Where's Deuce?"

"He said he was going to call your mom's parents."

"Good luck with that," I said, and shook my head.

"What do you mean?"

"Her parents don't get along with her," I said, shivering in the hospital's subarctic air-conditioning.

"How can they not get along with her? She's like the kindest and most patient person in the world."

"It's not her, it's them. They had big plans for her life, that didn't include her adopting a baby without even being married. Right before she found me, she was headed to the Holy Land for a year to study with some fancy Bible scholars. Once I came along, all bets were off, and she's been tied down here ever since."

"But she's their daughter! Don't they want her to be happy?" she asked. "I mean, studying in the Holy Land would have been great, but so is raising a baby!"

"I know, but they're the kind of Christians who have a lot of money, go to a fancy church, and criticize everyone else. It drives Mom nuts, but she calls them on their birthdays, and holidays. But they always make her cry afterward."

"Have you ever met them?" Fey asked.

"Nope, they don't want to meet me. They told her *she* was welcome to come visit them if she'd come to her senses, turn me back to the authorities, and get back to her religious studies."

Fey gasped. "Did your mom tell you all this?"

"Heck, no! I'm a good eavesdropper. Mom would be horrified if she knew that I knew how her parents felt about me. I overheard her tell Deuce after one of the phone calls."

At the sound of steps coming our way on the blindingly shiny floor, we turned to see Deuce. He looked at his watch. "It's getting near dinnertime. You two ready for something to eat?"

"Did you call them?" I asked. "What did they say?"

"Nothing much. Said that they will pray for her. And that they are both in excellent cardiac health, but heart disease did run in her father's side of the family."

"Are they going to come see her?" Fey asked.

Deuce shook his head. "No," he sighed. "C'mon, I need to feed you two. I've updated Dr. Sweeney about the family history. She said she'll call us right away if anything changes."

"What if she wakes up and asks for me?"

"I promise they will let us know. We can come back after we eat. I just spoke to your folks, Fey. I guess you two left Buster in their house alone, and he's raising bloody hell."

# CHAPTER FIVE

I was on high alert—all pistons firing. I had plans B, C, and D thought out in detail when Deuce sauntered over to have the Talk with me. I knew it would be just a matter of time before someone came to me about it. No big surprise that he'd been elected for the dirty job.

And it wasn't the sex talk.

It was something even worse.

But first, he drove me over to Hook & Press Doughnuts, and sugared me up good. I played it cool like I didn't know it was coming.

"So how do you think your mom is doing?" he asked.

I shrugged, nodded, and twisted in my seat—my

full arsenal of nonverbal communication while my mouth was full.

Deuce continued, so I had time to swallow. "I'm surprised, but happy, that her boss hired that cleaning company for the church and parsonage."

"Me too!" I said, then chugged the rest of my juice. "It's only temporary, but it helps."

"And the Church Ladies?" he asked, stirring more cream into his coffee.

"In full commando mode. They screen all the incoming calls and take care of whatever they can."

"Good. Your mom's main focus right now has to be her health."

I nodded and scrubbed my mouth with a napkin.

"Dr. Sweeney says she'll make a full recovery," he said.

"Yep."

"Still, she can't go back to the crazy way she was living before—it was simply too much for one person."

"I know," I said.

Deuce took a bracing gulp of coffee and then moved his plastic chair closer to the table. "And you know how she is. Once she finishes her cardiac care classes, and Dr. Sweeney releases her back to full duty, we're going to have to watch that she doesn't fall back into her old way of life."

I moved my chair closer to the table, ready to man up for what was coming next.

Deuce cleared his throat and busied himself cleaning his sunglasses with the bottom of his T-shirt.

"Oh hey," he said. "I saw Fey this morning. She was headed over to the school for new student orientation. She's such a great kid—"

"Deuce!" I couldn't take the slow build to the bad news. "I know why we're here. I know what this is about."

He cocked his head at me. "Okay, you tell me."

"You're here to tell me that Mom can't be a full-time teacher and a full-time pastor anymore. And since only one of those jobs pays the bills, Mom Academy has to close. I. Get. It."

"Oh!" was all he said.

"So, you're here to convince me that starting public school next week is in Mom's best interest."

He started to say something, but instead, he leaned back in his chair. Waited.

"I'm guessing that everyone thinks that's the most sensible idea. Well, Mom is probably super torn up about it, but you and the Church Ladies have convinced her it is the only solution. Am I right?"

His head nodded yes and no all at the same time.

I planted my elbows on the sticky tabletop. "I can see how you all came to this incorrect conclusion—believe me, I understand! But public school is just *one* of the options."

"I'm listening . . ." Deuce waited.

I took the underside of my index finger and began to stack up all the crumbs on the table.

"Number one—we can purchase or pirate a perfectly decent school curriculum online. Mom wouldn't have to prepare my lessons anymore. I can take myself through it. That way, I could still be at home and look after Mom."

Deuce stuck his sunglasses on top of his head. "You know she wouldn't be able to keep her mitts off it, or you. Before you knew it, she would be checking your work, critiquing the curriculum, making changes."

I paused, knowing he was probably right about that.

"So, what about you going to a charter school? There are a couple that look halfway decent."

"I don't want to spend all day around a bunch of horrible kids," I said, louder than I meant. I lowered my voice. "It'll just slow me down. I'm smarter than all of them, anyway."

Deuce drummed his fingers on the table a moment.

"I'd agree that you're more educated than most kids your age. But, smarter? Not sure about that," he said, giving me a steady look.

That stung. I couldn't believe he'd said it.

"Look," he said, and reached for my hand.

I pulled away and wouldn't look at him. I couldn't ever remember being mad at him like this.

"Kiddo, I didn't mean to hurt your feelings. I just meant that you don't have enough information about all the other kids your age around here to make that kind of statement."

"Mom always says I'm smarter than other kids," I said, my voice low.

"Maybe you are, but that's not the point. There is more than one kind of smart you need before you go out in the world. And you're never going to learn any of that if you stay holed up in that church until you're eighteen years old."

My face blazed.

He continued. "You know how you always tell me that kids around here never give you a chance—that they judge you and make fun of you without knowing you?"

I blew out a sigh, sending my napkin sailing across the table.

"You do the very same thing, Ham. You pass judgment on all of them. You dismiss them without giving them a chance. Your attitude toward them is really no better than their attitude about you."

"You don't understand how awful they are to me. I don't tell Mom and you everything they've done to me!"

He nodded. "I'm sorry. I know you've had a tough time. And I know a thing or two about being judged and shunned. It's no walk in the park for an ex-felon in a small town."

He was right, but I still glowered at him.

"Small-minded kids grow up to be small-minded adults," he said. "It won't be any easier for you at eighteen to learn to handle yourself when you go off to college. If my opinion is worth anything to you, and I hope it is, I think it's time that you step up to it. Time to stop running and hiding from it."

I screeched my chair backward and hard against the linoleum. "Thanks for the doughnuts and the talk. I'm gonna walk home."

It took thirty-four hours, eleven miles of hot, snotty runs, two extra-cheesy thick-crust pizzas, half a left-over Texas sheet cake, and one new friend named Fey nearly hitting me upside my head before I could get over being mad at Deuce.

I found out later that he'd had nearly as tough a talk with my mom. He didn't take her out for doughnuts like he did with me, but he didn't pull any punches, either. Seems like he'd been holding back his feelings about me being so isolated for a long time. He convinced her that there was more to school than learning math and science. And that she and the Church Ladies couldn't teach me everything I needed, no matter how hard they tried. Or how much they wanted to.

What I needed more than anything now, he'd told her, was to learn how to live in the world, with kids my age.

"But I do live in the world," I argued, but gentler with her than I'd been with Deuce. I didn't want to make her blood pressure go up. "And I have Fey now. I'm getting super regular. I've learned tons from her."

"I know, honey, but she'll get busy with school and projects, and hopefully new friends. It's not enough. Deuce is right." Mom drew my head close to hers and paused a moment before she continued. "I would love nothing more than to take you through the next few years of school, but you need more than I can give you now."

I thought of trying to float my plan C by her, but it seemed pointless. She wouldn't go for me studying for my GED with the inmates in her prison ministry.

She sighed and gave me a long look. "And while I am not going anywhere for decades to come, it really isn't right for me and *this*—" she said, sweeping her arm around the parsonage, "to be all you know of the world."

I wanted to be mad at her, holler, and stomp around. But when your mom just had a heart attack, you don't get to do that.

Which was why on Monday, September 3, I walked through the glass doors of Harvey Mellencamp Junior High armed with my first-ever sack lunch, and a giant case of nerves. Fey pulled me so hard she nearly dislocated my shoulder. She was ecstatic that I was coming with her.

It was the beginning of my end.

The first day of eighth grade.

Sixty-eight more days until I would be grilled by cops.

# CHAPTER SIX

I noticed right off that I was the best-dressed boy in my class. I took a quick glance at Fey and realized that she hadn't dressed up for school. I'd been so nervous, I hadn't noticed. I was definitely not letting Mom iron my school clothes tomorrow.

The only person who seemed to appreciate Mom's efforts was my new homeroom teacher, Ms. Becerra. She'd been at the front door to the class when we'd walked in. She shook my hand and said, "Looking sharp!"

I found out later she'd been in the Marines and served a tour in Iraq. I was glad I found this out *later*. There was enough to be nervous about that first day without a teacher who had experience with large artillery.

Fey and I took seats near the back, and I tried to look as inconspicuous as possible for now. I could feel the stares of the other kids as they checked us out. Seemed like most of them already knew each other. Fey got busy scribbling in her journal and ignored everyone.

"Students! Students!" Ms. Becerra nearly had to shout over the din. "I know this is a very exciting day for all of you as eighth graders, finally! You'll have plenty of time to catch up between classes and at lunch, so let's all settle down and get started."

"Until I get to know your names, I'm going to put you in assigned seating." She glanced at the computer on her desk, and then projected her screen up onto the board. "All right, now, find your name up here, and then move to the appropriate seat." Among the complaints, she held up a hand. "If you can do this quietly and quickly, there will be five minutes of free time before I dismiss you to your next class. Ready, move!"

My seat was nearly upended by a kid with almost a full mustache. "Move it, dog breath."

My assigned seat was still in the back of the room, but on the other side near the windows. I hurried to it like a squirrel being chased. As I dumped my backpack next to me, I realized that I'd left my lunch at my old seat. Mustache had it on his lap and was pawing through it. Not finding anything to his liking, he balled it up and hurled it toward me. It caught me on the side of the head.

"We'll have none of that!" Ms. Becerra said, clapping her hands together. She looked at me, and then glanced quickly at her seating chart. "Ham, is that right?"

I slid lower in my seat. "Yes, ma'am," I mumbled.

"You okay?" She came and picked up my lunch from the aisle, and set it on my desk.

I nodded and she patted me on the shoulder.

She turned to the mustache kid. "Benny, you throw anything in my class ever again and you're headed to a date with the principal. Do you understand me?"

He lifted his shoulders, and then dropped them. "Yep."

She continued to stare at him, and he started to wriggle in his seat. Then he said, "Yes, Ms. Becerra."

"All right, then," she continued. "We have a few new students to our area this year, and I'd like to make some quick introductions."

She studied her seating chart and then looked right at me. "Ham, would you like to start?"

"Yes, ma'am," I said, getting to my feet, dread like concrete running through my veins. I remembered

Mom and Deuce's pep talk with me about first impressions being so important.

I walked to the front of the class and stood next to Ms. Becerra. She looked surprised that I'd come up, but moved aside to make room for me.

Oh no! Was I supposed to stay in my seat? My eyes flew to Fey. She gave me a small tight headshake. No—what? What did she *not* want me to do?

"Ham?" Ms. Becerra broke in. Some of the kids had started to snicker.

"Right! Well, my name is Ham Hudson. I'm from here—Muddy Waters—but I've been homeschooled until now. 'Ham' isn't short for 'Hamish' like you might think. It's short for 'Abraham.'"

Dead silence and blank stares.

"Oh, well, if you don't know who that is, he was probably the most important prophet in the Bible. And Abraham is considered the father of all the religions, not just Christianity."

Fey cleared her throat hard. I startled at the sound and looked over at her. She made a slashing sign across her throat. That I got.

"So that's all, I guess," I said. "Unless anyone has any questions?" That seemed the polite thing to do.

The hands of at least half the class shot up. They

were interested! I bit my bottom lip in nervous excitement.

"All right," Ms. Becerra said. "We can take one or two of your questions." The boy named Benny who'd clobbered me with my lunch sack waved his arm like mad. Ms. Becerra ignored him. Instead she called on a girl. "Mercedes?"

"I have a question for ABRAHAM," the girl started, looking like she was trying hard not to smile, but instead, to sound serious. The girl behind her put her head down on her desk, and her shoulders were shaking.

Mercedes went on. "Well, can I call you Ham?"

"Sure." I swallowed, then tried to give her a friendly smile.

"Do you know a lot about the Bible?"

I looked to Fey. She mouthed, *NO!*

She wanted me to say no? But that would be a lie. I knew nearly everything in the Bible. Maybe Fey just didn't want me to brag.

"If you want to know someone who knows a lot about the Bible," I said, "that would be my mom. She can probably recite the whole thing cover to cover. She's a reverend, so it's kind of a job requirement."

I got a lot of laughs on that one.

Benny couldn't hold it one more second. "Hey! Are

you that kid who lives in the *church* with his mom over on Third Street? I heard once that—"

"Benny! Shut it down," Ms. Becerra warned. She put an arm around my shoulder. "Thank you, Ham. You can take your seat now."

Fey gave me a small encouraging smile as I walked to the back.

"Would any of the other new students like to introduce themselves today?"

Not a sound. Like a graveyard.

Ms. Becerra looked around. I saw a few kids slump down in their seats, including Fey. "No? That's all right. No pressure. But, everyone, please make an effort to meet someone new to you. We have three different eighth-grade homerooms—Mr. Nichols, Ms. Constantine, and mine. Harvey Mellencamp wants everyone to feel very welcome here. And I'm relying on each and every one of you to make that happen. Got it?"

"Yes, Ms. Becerra," the class replied in unison.

"All right, then. Now let's move on. Those of you sitting in the last seat of an aisle, please pick up enough textbooks for your row and pass them out. Quietly, please."

As we all opened our books to the directed section, I couldn't help but notice that Mom and I had done this very same book about three years ago. Looked like we'd be starting with the Greeks, which was fine by me. I could use a little freshening up on gladiators. I could tell it might come in handy in this class.

A small white packet flew my way, landed on my desk, then skittered to the floor.

I leaned over to pick it up. It was a note folded into a small, hard triangle and had my name on it.

I recognized Fey's loopy writing. My first school note! I unfolded it quietly in my lap because Fey had told me you get in trouble if you pass notes during class.

*Hey! Don't sweat it. Some kids are just jerks. The "new kid" smell will wear off soon and they'll just leave us alone.*

She turned back to look at me just then, and I gave her a thumbs-up.

Suddenly there was a loud scratching sound at the back door. Insistent scratching. Followed by a yowl—a familiar yowl.

The entire class turned in their seats. Ms. Becerra hurried to the back door.

As she opened it, a gray-and-white blur shot through the classroom. It ran serpentine through a tangle of desks and legs, and then leapt onto my desktop.

Having found me, Buster purred, chirred, and did his happy dance right on my desk. Trying to contain him only made it worse. He climbed up on top of my shoulders, and then wrapped himself around my neck like a scarf. Which I usually liked.

Though Fey hadn't told me this, I was pretty sure your cat wasn't supposed to be in class with you.

"Check it out!" the kid in front of me yelled. "It's only got one eye."

While the kids laughed and pointed, Buster started to give me an ear wash.

"Oh my God! That cat *loves* the Bible boy!" Mercedes yelled.

Both Ms. Becerra and Fey hurried toward me.

"I'm sorry, ma'am!" I said as I tried to pull Buster off my neck. The harder I pulled, the harder he clung to me. He had all his claws pinned in my shirt collar. He gave Ms. Becerra a good swat.

"BUSTER—STOP!" I hissed.

"Ham!" Ms. Becerra said. "This is your cat?"

The class roared with laughter and taunts.

"The new guy brought his cat to school!"

"Ms. Becerra! Can I take a quick picture?"

Buster got sent to the principal's office.

So did I.

# CHAPTER SEVEN

I found some shade to sit in while I waited outside the school for Mom to come pick up Buster. Every time I tried to set him down in the grass, he would try to crawl up my back. Even though he was relieved to have found me, I think all the laughing and yelling in the classroom had just about done him in. I knew just how he felt. So I held him next to me even though it was over 90 degrees and I'd just about sweat through my clothes. Principal Strickland had said I could wait inside where it was cool, but I'd told her outside was better for Buster. Truth was, I didn't want Mom coming inside after me and then start chatting up the principal. Next thing I knew, my new principal would start coming to our church.

Buster made a nest in my lap. I poured some water from my backpack into my hand so he could have a drink. I scratched his ears while he lapped it up.

Fey and I had walked over to the school last night when it was deserted so she could show me where everything was since I'd missed all the orientation activities. Buster had followed us, so it was easy for him to track us today.

We hadn't been apart in all our thirteen years. I guess I couldn't blame him. But, boy, this was not how I wanted my first day of school to go.

"It's okay, Buster," I said in a soft voice. "I'm not mad. But you can't follow me to school again. You need to stay home and look after Mom for me."

"Cool cat." A voice nearby startled me. I looked up, shading my eyes. A boy with big-mirrored sunglasses stood over me, sipping a Dr Pepper.

"Uh yeah, thanks."

He folded himself down to the ground next to me. "Can I pet it?"

"Sure," I said, swallowing. "His name's Buster."

"Nice to meet you, Buster boy," he said. He scratched him under the chin, which usually made him purr. Instead, Buster pulled in closer to me.

"You new? I've never seen you before," he said,

and pulled off his sunglasses.

He had the most astonishing green eyes I'd ever seen. Like Ireland had lent him their greenest green. My eyes were a boring greenish brown.

"Uh yeah, new to Harvey Mellencamp—my name is Ham," I said, sticking my hand out for a shake. Like Fey had done with me when we first met.

Instead, he smacked my open hand with a low five, and I acted like that was what I meant him to do all along.

"Hey. I'm Micah. I wish I was new. I'm so sick of this place. So—" He paused a moment. "Is Buster like your emotional support animal? They let you bring him to school?"

"Oh! No," I said, my face heating. "He just followed me to school today, so we both got sent to the principal's office. I'm waiting for my mom to come pick him up."

"Too bad. I like cats. Wish he could stick around. He could be the new school mascot!"

"How come you're not in class?" I asked.

"I will be, eventually. I missed the bus, so I had to walk. No big deal," he said. He gave me a nice smile.

It gave me a funny jolt. I wasn't used to boys being friendly like he was.

"Do you know which homeroom you're in?" I asked. "I'm in Ms. Becerra's class."

"No such luck. I got Constantine," he said with a pained expression. "Ms. Becerra is cool. She coaches track. I want to run this year. I started last year, but I got kicked off. Missed too many practices." He lifted his shoulders. "Couldn't be helped. I have to take care of my little brother after school a lot."

A horn tooted and we both looked over. Mom's old van had pulled up at the curb. Never before had the *First Grace Church* decal on the van looked so ginormous.

"Got to run!" I said, scooping up Buster. "Nice to meet you."

He climbed to his feet, and pulled a phone out of his back pocket. "Here, put your number in—maybe we could hang sometime."

"Well, uh, I gotta run now," I stammered. "But I'll find you, okay?"

He gave Buster a pat on the head, and said, "Later, dude!"

He called me a dude! Or maybe he called Buster a dude? Didn't matter. It was nice all the same. I bit back a smile.

Mom slung the side door panel open and put her

arms out for Buster. "Okay, big fella, you're coming with me."

He meowed his displeasure as Mom put him in the back seat and slid the door closed.

"Honey, I'm so sorry, really. I'm sure this was awkward," she said. "We'll have to make sure we keep all the doors and windows closed until he gets used to you being gone all day."

"It's okay," I said. "Thanks for coming to get him."

"So, other than having your cat crash your homeroom, everything going okay? Do you like your teacher?"

"I'll tell you everything later," I said, backing away. "But remember you said that since I was starting school, I could have my own phone? Can we go get one today?"

"Absolutely," she said. "Anything for my brave eighth grader."

I had to concentrate very hard as I hurried back to class so that I wouldn't skip.

Dudes probably don't skip.

# CHAPTER EIGHT

Buster had a perfect attendance record his first week at Harvey Mellencamp.

No matter what precautions Mom and I took to keep him in, he managed to Houdini his way out. I suspected he'd hired his own contractor and had a secret kitty door installed somewhere in the parsonage. If Buster was late to school and missed first-period homeroom, he would head over to the principal's office, in case I was there.

I got to be pretty tight with Principal Strickland's assistant, Miss Emma. She was a bona fide cat person, and loved when Buster came to the office looking for me.

Miss Emma looked like she bought all her clothes

at that girl store Forever 21, even though she was almost as old as the Church Ladies. Her clothes were very colorful and stretchy tight. Principal Strickland, on the other hand, seemed to get her clothes at Forever 61, even though she was pretty young. It was like she and Miss Emma had done a *Freaky Friday* switcheroo.

I was deep in Miss Emma's debt, though. Mom wasn't always home or available when I called about Buster, so Miss Emma let Buster hang out under her desk. Before too long, she'd brought in a special cushion for Buster, and bowls for food and water. She kept cat food and snacks for him now, too. Buster was living the good life under her desk. When Principal Strickland was out of the office, Miss Emma would put him right on her lap and love him up.

Unlike Buster, Micah did not have a perfect attendance record the first week. I was all ready with my brand-shiny-new phone to give him my number. I looked for him by his homeroom door, but never saw him there. It was kind of hard trying to find him, too, since Fey was always with me. I don't know why, but I felt embarrassed telling her I was looking for him.

I didn't want her to worry that I'd want to start hanging out with him all the time instead of her.

I'd noticed that while Fey was nice to other kids, she didn't get too friendly with them.

I never saw Micah in the cafeteria, either, even though everyone ate at the same time. I almost asked Miss Emma to look up his schedule for me, but I guessed she probably couldn't give that out. I could see the big three-ring binders on her desk that held every student's schedule, but since I didn't even know Micah's last name, it would take me longer to find him.

Which is why I ended up heading over to track tryouts on Friday of my first week. Micah had said he wanted to run track, and I figured I'd see him over there at least. I could act like I was going to try out, then realize that I had other obligations on whatever days they got together to practice.

Even though I was a decent runner thanks to Deuce and Mr. Flynn, trying out for an eighth-grade team sport was not on my list of ways to survive the first year of public school. I'd already had nearly a year's worth of teasing from Benny and his friends in my first week. Benny "accidentally" bumped into me every single time he passed me in the halls. I would be safer if I just dropped, tucked, and rolled the minute I saw him coming.

There was a small group of kids standing on the track near Ms. Becerra when I headed over. It was all mostly guys I'd seen around the school and one girl who was putting her long hair in a complicated braid.

But no Micah.

Ms. Becerra blew her whistle and shouted, "Okay, settle down, and listen up." She'd changed from her teacher clothes and wore camo running shorts and big trail-running shoes.

"Here's the deal. There's only eleven of you here, and after today, there could be less than eleven. We don't have enough of you here for a track and field team this year."

Some of the kids groaned at that. The girl stopped braiding her hair and let out a noisy sigh.

"Hold on," Ms. Becerra said, raising her hand. "I'm not finished! We *do* have enough bodies and possible talent here to put together a cross-country team. Harvey Mellencamp hasn't had one before." She looked at each of us, and then said, "So what do you think? I'm not going to sugarcoat it for you. Cross-country is a tough sport. I will expect you each to be willing to run your guts out, then turn them inside out, and keep running."

A few kids nudged each other, looking nervous.

"The good news is"—Ms. Becerra started, looking

each of us over—"there won't be tryouts today. You want to run? You're on the team. You want to stay on the team? You show up for every practice, and you run on the weekends. Buddy up with each other for that. You want to be an asset to this team? Be clear what the word 'team' means. We work together each and every practice. I don't have the time or interest to coach hotshots who only run for themselves."

She studied our small group. "At some point I'll be selecting one of you to be team captain—"

"That will be me, of course," said a voice coming up from behind me.

My head whipped around to see a skinny girl sauntering up to the group. She wore raggedy running shoes and a giant smirk.

And towed Micah in a headlock.

Ms. Becerra handed her the clipboard with a big sigh. "Bijou, Micah, sign in. If you two show up late again, there will be consequences. That goes for every one of you. Cross-country is about discipline, commitment, and teamwork. No room for divas. The team captain I will select will be the person who demonstrates that type of respect for the team."

I tried to catch Micah's eye, but he didn't seem to see me.

"Maybe we all need to start today's practice by

going over how to tell time," she said. "When the little hand and the big hand are on the three—"

"Nobody wears watches anymore, Coach," Micah said.

I made a quick mental note of that and pulled the sleeve of my jacket down.

"You want to run?" Ms. Becerra asked. "You need a sports watch. You can pick up one cheap. How else can you time your splits?"

"We're going to have to do the *splits*?" the kid next to me whispered.

I opened my mouth to answer, then stopped. Didn't want Ms. Becerra to turn her attention to me.

Ms. Becerra pointed to the ground next to her. "There's water in this cooler. Take one. There are running shoes, too—slightly used—in this box if you need them. Take one of these vests to put on. You run cross-country; you wear an orange safety vest. I want to be able to see you all when we go off-road. And this covered box is for everything on your body right now that will slow you down—keys, phones, earbuds, change, snacks."

"Coach! What about bear spray? If we're going to run trails, my mom is going to want me to have it," said the kid next to me who was worried about the splits.

"Do you have any regular camo vests, Coach? I don't like orange." This from the girl with a now-completed hair braid. She had moved over next to Bijou, and they'd had a very complicated hand greeting.

"Coach, did you forget to bring a box of socks?"

"Did you wash these vests? They're kind of stiff."

Ms. Becerra—I mean, Coach Becerra—blessed herself with the sign of the cross, then shouted, "You have sixty seconds to get yourselves ready and on the track for warm-up laps. Fifty-nine, fifty-eight—"

"Uh, Coach, excuse me?" I interrupted, my heart thumping hard against my rib cage. "When are the practices? I'm not sure this would work with my schedule." Micah was still acting like he didn't know me, and I wanted to get out of there before the warm-up started.

"Monday, Wednesday, and Thursday at three fifteen sharp. Be done by about five p.m. If we're going to be later, I'll let you know in advance. When we get close to our first meet, we may have a couple of Saturday practices."

"Um, thanks," I mumbled, and shot a quick glance at Micah, but he was busy pawing through the vest box. "Guess that won't work for me, then."

Bijou shoved past me, her gum cracking like a rifle in my ear. "Wouldn't matter if you could. You won't last a whole practice."

The great comeback to that would probably arrive in a couple of hours. For now, I just turned red.

Micah looked up at that and seemed to see me at last. "Can it, Bij—we need all the talent we can get." He reached back into the box and threw me a vest with a smile. "Game ON, Ham. Let's show her how we do it!"

"C'mon, Becca!" Bijou said to the other girl. "You're with me. Nothin' but cheap talk here."

Micah gave me a bump to my shoulder. Shoulder bumps seemed to be a main form of communication in junior high. Some were awful, and some were nice. Really nice.

"Hey—you didn't tell me you were a runner!" he said.

"Er, gosh, well, hi!"

"Don't worry about Bijou. I've got her in my back pocket. Let's go! Get your vest on."

Uh-oh! I definitely didn't want to run on a team with that rude girl named Becca. I wasn't even dressed for it. Most of the other kids had changed into shorts. I had my sweatpants on. But I did have my running shoes on. I supposed I could—maybe just today. Micah seemed really glad to see me. And we could trade numbers after. It would feel too weird to do that right now. Like he might guess that was the only reason I'd come.

Micah unloaded an incredible and fascinating number of pocket items. Then, he looked up at me, still standing there holding the safety vest.

"Vest up, man! We've got to get out there and show Bijou a thing or two. You look like you could be good. Are you?" he asked, giving me an appraising once-over.

"I've been told I've got some serious fast-twitch muscle," I said, parroting something I'd heard Deuce talk about.

"Whoa!" Micah said. "Then let's go give them some of our dust to chew!"

# CHAPTER NINE

After four warm-up laps on the track, we lost two of the thirteen kids we started with. Coach Becerra told those kids to walk two cool-down laps on the track and then head on home. She didn't want them going into the woods behind the school with us. But she told them to come back Monday for practice and try again.

"Okay, the rest of you, listen up!" She blasted her whistle, and pointed to a tall girl—with impressive calves—who had shown up. "This is Jet from the varsity track team. She'll be helping us out. You're going to follow her on the trail that starts over there," she said, pointing behind the track. "She'll set the pace and I want you all to stay close but keep behind her.

I'll bring up the rear. Everyone clear on that?"

Coach wasn't impressed with our chorus of mumbles.

"*EXCUSE* me?" she hollered.

"YES, Coach!" we hollered back.

"Once I get a feel for your skills and once you're familiar with the trail, I may let some of you practice as the trail leader. But not today, and probably not next week, either. Cross-country is different than running on the streets or sidewalks. It's technical, and I want everyone paying attention. We'll start with this course, which is pretty straightforward, but later we'll be trying some more challenging trails. I need everyone to hold his or her hormones in check. We're not racing each other today, got it? The only thing I want any of you to prove today is that you have lungs, you have legs, and you can follow directions. Got it?"

"Got it, Coach!" we all shouted.

"Then let's do this," she said, and motioned for Jet to take off toward the trail.

Bijou got on Jet's heels right off. I could tell by her legs and her stride that Bijou had some running chops. But so did I. I'd been running trails with Deuce and Mr. Flynn for a long time. But I tucked in behind her, even though I knew I could probably overtake her. Micah stayed close to me, and I was surprised at how strong he was.

"Coach! What's the bad news?" a long-legged kid shouted, huffing next to me.

"What?" she asked, running up next to us.

The kid spit, and then said, "You said at the beginning of practice (*huff*) that the good news was that there (*huff*) weren't going to be any tryouts—that we could all be on the team. (*huff-huff*) So what's the bad news?" (*huff*)

"Come next Friday, you'll all wish you were dead," she said.

To celebrate our first week of eighth grade, Mom and Deuce treated Fey and me to pizza that night at the parsonage. I was tired from practice, but not as tired as most of the kids. Coach had given me a strong slap on the back afterward. She seemed glad and surprised that I'd done so well.

Micah jogged next to me during cool-down on the track. We were both slick with sweat, and still breathing hard from the trail. When we lapped Bijou and Becca, he turned toward them and shouted, "Try to keep up, children!"

He threw his head back and laughed when Bijou

fired a round of insults back at him.

If she'd said those things to me, I would have been mortified. But it was friendly fire, I guessed. He and Bijou seemed to be friends, even though they talked terribly to each other.

Mom waved a triangle of pizza in my direction. "Ham, you're watching your phone like you're expecting a call from the White House. Lord, what have I done? The phone zombie virus is snacking on your brain already!"

I quickly turned it over, like I hadn't been waiting for my first text from Micah.

After practice he and I had exchanged numbers.

"Sorry!" I shoved a big, meaty piece of pizza into my mouth. I tried not to moan at how good it tasted because the pizza that Mom was eating, specially made by Deuce, had a crust made out of cauliflower and pretend cheese on top. She was being a good sport about her new healthy diet, but I knew it was super hard for her.

"Well, I'm very glad you got him a phone," Fey said, eating around a mushroom on her pizza. "It makes it so much easier to find him at school! If you hadn't gotten him a phone, I was going to have a chip installed in his neck." She gave me a teasing look.

"Though, it would have been helpful if you had let me know you were staying after school for tryouts. I waited for you at our usual spot!"

"Sorry, Fey!" I said. "I wrote you a message and forgot to send it. I'm still getting used to it."

I really had. I was so excited about maybe finding Micah at tryouts that I'd messed up. I hated that Fey had waited for me and I never showed up. She told me after she was worried Benny had me tied up somewhere.

"I'll forgive you, but you have to let me pick the movie tonight," she said, studying the mushroom in her fingers before she popped it into her mouth. "There's this amazing new movie about an octopus that makes friends with a photographer!"

I smiled at her. "Cool!" I said, and hoped I'd be able to stay awake through it.

"More pizza, Ham?" Deuce asked, moving the box. "You're probably starving after your practice. I think it's terrific that you're going to run on the team. Why didn't you tell us you were going to try out?"

"Yeah," Fey said. "Why the secrecy?"

All three of them looked at me expectantly.

"I dunno, it was kind of a last-minute thing. A kid I know was trying out, and he talked me into it."

"Who?" Fey asked.

"Um, his name is Micah. He's in Ms. Constantine's homeroom. I met him on the first day of school." I took a giant bite from my pizza and hoped that my cheeks weren't as red as they felt. It embarrassed me how thrilled I was to have made a new friend who was a boy. Just saying his name out loud in front of them made my heart pound. I tried to remember if saying Fey's name out loud made my heart speed up when I first met her.

"Oh! The boy who was outside with you when I came to pick up Buster?" Mom asked.

I nodded, like none of it mattered much at all.

"Well, I think it's a great idea for you," Mom said. "I signed the parental permission form, and put it in your backpack. But you won't ever have practice or meets on Sundays, will you?"

"No, but maybe some stuff on a Saturday," I said, remembering what Coach had said about special weekend practices before a meet.

Just then, my phone pinged, vibrated, and did a little cha-cha on the table. Buster, who'd been snoozing in my lap, sat up and gave it a good swat.

It had to be Micah. Everyone else who might text me was sitting at the table.

"Not at dinner, young man," Mom said.

I grabbed it and shoved it into my back pocket. But not before I saw the lit display with Micah's name and number.

Fey looked over with a question in her eyes. "Who's that from?"

"Just Micah," I said, casual, as if it weren't any big deal.

Which was not true. It was a very big deal. Actually, it was huge. A boy wanted to be friends with me, and he acted as if he liked me for real. And now, instead of sitting there eating pizza, which I l-o-v-e, with three of the best people in the universe—all I wanted was to be alone in my room, lying on my bed, listening to my records while reading Micah's text. And then spend the rest of the night trying to compose the best response ever.

And then he'd think I was so clever and funny that we'd text back and forth all night.

Yeah, that's where my head was.

# CHAPTER TEN

The best part of Sundays in my life was the weekly brunch with Deuce and Mr. Flynn after church services.

Only now it was just me, Mom, and Deuce. Every Sunday when I remembered that Mr. Flynn wouldn't be there, it was like a quiet sucker punch to the gut.

While Mom and I straightened up the church after services, the two of them would be across the street cooking up some seriously good grub. They both loved to watch the Cooking Channel, and Deuce also subscribed to fancy cooking magazines. But it wasn't like snobby food that a kid couldn't eat. They made things like homemade strawberry Pop-Tarts that tasted like something God would serve in heaven. I tried to eat a store-bought Pop-Tart after that, and it was like eating single-ply toilet paper with jelly. Sunday brunch was the best food I ate all week, and I wouldn't miss it for anything.

Eating at their house was like going to a swanky restaurant. Not that I had a lot of experience with that, except from movies. They'd set the table with real plates and matching glasses, and we even used cloth napkins. I know this sounds dumb, but cloth napkins make you happy to wipe your mouth. Mom and I didn't have much in the way of fancy table stuff or matching anything. We were both known to eat right out of a box or can in a pinch.

We still kept a place set for Mr. Flynn every Sunday as if he was still with us. Mom started it the first brunch after he died, and Deuce had kept it up every week since.

"Another waffle, Annie?" Deuce asked Mom.

She leaned back in her chair and groaned. "I could chew it, but I couldn't swallow it. I am full as a tick."

"It's the whole grains," Deuce said, sounding happy. "They pack a punch."

"Well, you should teach me how to make them. These I like."

I snorted. As if.

"It talks," she observed over a foamy latte.

I'd been so busy shoveling food into my mouth, I hadn't said much for a while. Plus, I was working out an afternoon plan in my head. One that Mom was not going to like.

Deuce shook his head. "Technically, I don't think that counted as language."

"Thank you. I stand corrected," she said. "It snorts."

I took a big drink of juice, and then said, "I just meant that there was no point in you learning how to make them. You don't cook, Mom. You don't have a single cookbook or recipe to your name. The last time you used the stove without supervision, you flambéed our best dish towel."

"You'd think those things would be fireproof," she said.

"And I seem to remember a green bean casserole you brought one Thanksgiving that had an actual fork cooked right in the middle of it," Deuce reminisced.

That made her smile. "Mr. Flynn couldn't look at me for days without cracking up, remember?"

This was part of our Sunday ritual every time, too. Somebody would tell a Mr. Flynn story. Mom would usually start. It had taken Deuce a while before he started sharing his favorites.

"He'd always insist we do the fork count anytime you'd been in the kitchen to help," Deuce added. He ran his hand over his freshly shaved head, then laid it to rest across the back of Mr. Flynn's empty chair.

We all were quiet for a moment, remembering.

"Well," Mom continued, "as I've said before, Irish women are not known for their culinary talents, but we have many other redeeming qualities. We can haul giant bales of peat like no one's business."

"Good to know," Deuce said.

"I guess you'll have to just keep cooking for me every Sunday. I generally eat enough here to last me all week anyway." She sighed and pushed herself back from the table.

Deuce popped up like he'd forgotten something. "Oh! Let me fix you two some containers to go. This egg casserole will taste even better tomorrow."

It had been Mr. Flynn's job to load us up with left-overs for the week. Together, Mr. Flynn and Deuce had been the Navy Seals of hospitality. They took it dead serious. Now Deuce carried the torch for the two of them.

"So, what's on the schedule for today?" Deuce asked, refilling our water glasses. They had dipped dangerously below the three-quarters-full mark. "Jesus Rounds?"

Mom clicked her tongue. "Ham, now you've got him calling it that. I am surrounded by smarty-pants today, aren't I? Can a woman get any respect around here?"

I looked at Deuce; he looked at me. "Guess not," I said, my mouth sticky and wadded with waffle.

She leaned toward me with her lipstick-covered napkin ready for a fly-by mother wipe, and I ducked. "Mo-o-om!"

"Some habits are just hard to break." She gave me a moon-eyed look. As if she'd like nothing better than to throw me over her shoulder, burp me, and then put me down for a nap.

"Well, we have a few of our regulars to visit today, and then we've got two in the hospital to pray with."

"Annie!" Deuce said in his stern voice. "Divide that by two. Do half that much today, and then give yourself some rest this afternoon."

"Actually, Mom," I said, and wiped at my mouth. "I need to go to the library. I can't go with you today."

A silence fell. Thick as the syrup in the little silver pitcher in front of me. I could count on one hand the number of times I'd missed Sunday Rounds, aka the

Jesus Rounds. It was one of those mainstays of a pastor's life. And her kid's.

Her mouth opened, but she didn't speak.

"It's super important I go, or I wouldn't ask. I didn't get my literature assignment done."

She drew a deep breath, then folded her napkin. Then refolded it. "You've just barely started public school, and you're already getting behind? I thought you did all your homework yesterday."

"Almost all of it. I ran out of time to go to the library, and the report is due tomorrow."

My report was due tomorrow, but I'd already finished it. In my defense, I did want to go to the library, but not for research. When I'd asked Micah what he was doing this weekend, he said something about his "usual" hanging out at the creek on Sundays with kids from school. They'd all meet up at the library and then walk down from there. He hadn't invited me, but I was hoping he wouldn't mind if I just showed up. He'd texted me twice so far this weekend.

"Working on something interesting?" Deuce asked.

"Yeah—uh, comparing themes in middle-grade literature." I turned back to Mom. "So? Can I go?"

She looked a bit pained about it, but I could also

read something else in her face. She was trying to let go just a little bit.

"Is Fey going?" Mom asked.

"No, she's with her dad. He took her up the coast to the tide pools. She's super excited." She'd asked me to come along, but I'd given her the "need to finish my homework" excuse I'd given to Mom. I hated lying to them, but I couldn't figure out how to tell either of them that I really wanted to hang out with Micah. I was afraid it would hurt their feelings. I couldn't bear the thought of that. So, the little lie about homework seemed kinder.

Go," she said. "But. Just. This. Once."

In my head I did a back flip and stuck the landing. I acted cool on the outside, though. "Anything I can do here before I go?" I asked like I did every week.

"Certainly not," Deuce said. "You're our—my guest. Do you need a lift to the library, though?"

"Thanks, but I'll take my bike. Coach Becerra said cross-training was really important."

Deuce nodded and gave me a thumbs-up.

"Thanks for brunch! It was awesome," I said, backing out the door. I swiveled on my heel, careful not to step on a trip wire that would detonate and change Mom's mind.

"Home by five!" she hollered behind me.

I took a big breath and whooped to myself as I raced across the street.

The thought of spending time with Micah burned right through the guilt I should be feeling about my lie.

Telling a lie on a Sunday was probably even worse than on a regular day. I made a mental vow that I wouldn't lie to either of them again.

But it turns out I would. Big-time.

# CHAPTER ELEVEN

I pulled my bike from the shed where I kept it locked. I'd had my last one stolen from me already. How cold is that? Stealing from some poor kid who lives in a church. Not that I'd ever had anything worth stealing. My bikes, like my clothes, were hand-me-downs. The one I had now, though, I really liked. It was an old cruiser bike that was just wrecked enough to look kind of cool. I noticed some other kids at school had ones like mine.

Just as I was ready to take off, I remembered I didn't have any money on me. I needed some spending money in case the kids liked to buy snacks after the creek or something. I raced back into the house and grabbed my wallet. It was empty. I'd forgotten

I'd spent all I had on an extra-fancy case for my new phone. It hadn't seemed right to make Mom buy a nice case. I knew the phone was already expensive enough.

I kept a ton of spare change in a big pickle jar, so I scooped up a giant handful of coins. It was mostly pennies, so I took a lot of them. I dumped them into my front pants pockets. Which I realized were my church pants. I should have changed out of them, but I didn't want to risk missing Micah. I wasn't sure what time everybody was going down there. I untucked my shirt, though, so I wouldn't look so dressed up.

It was nearly one o'clock by the time I was speeding down the back roads to town. First Grace Church sat on the outskirts of Muddy Waters, closer to the prison. Most of the nicer neighborhoods were on the other side of downtown. As much as the prison helped our town, with jobs and stuff, nobody really wanted to live too close to it. Who wanted to look out the window to see guard towers and electric fences? Mom kept talking about submitting the prison for one of those *Extreme Makeover* shows we watched once at Deuce's house. I think he'd put it on because he'd been trying to give Mom a hint about our house.

But she was more concerned about the way the

prison looked than where we lived. They'd never done a prison makeover before, she bet. I remember she'd said if it wasn't so ugly and depressing, maybe the inmates would feel better about themselves and get back on the straight and narrow.

It was nearly the first thing Deuce did when he got out of the joint. He bought a fixer-upper on our street and tore it all down. After they met, Mr. Flynn started coming by to help Deuce work on it. When they finished the bathrooms and kitchen, Mr. Flynn moved in with him. They'd turned it into a kind of showplace. The house looked just tidy and plain from the outside, but inside was incredible. Sort of like Deuce himself, I suppose. He looked just like a regular old guy in decent shape, but when you got to know him, he'd blow you away with what a terrific human being he was. Just like Mr. Flynn had been.

Speaking of things in need of a makeover, the library in Muddy Waters was an old brick fortress built around the time Moses was carving on his stone tablets. It had been built to last, and not much had been done to improve it. I suppose it was better that they spent their money on books. There were a few computers there now, but you'd usually have to wait your turn to use one. That was one thing that Mom was always willing to spend money on—making sure I'd had the best computer for my education.

We'd had the same librarian since I could remember. He was an older guy named Mr. Dewey, and *no*, he did not invent the Dewey Decimal System, so don't bother to ask. He really shouldn't have been so sensitive about that. He might have figured if he was going to be a librarian, he was going to take some grief about it.

I made sure to lock up my bike in the rack out front. There were only a couple of others. Probably most of the kids got rides from their parents. Mr. Dewey stood behind the front counter mumbling to himself, which he did quite often. But there was no one to shush him because he was the head shusher.

He peered up over his trifocals, or whatever they were. "Good afternoon, Abraham." He couldn't abide calling me just "Ham." He was a formal kind of person.

From under his counter, I heard the steady thump against the wood. That would be Delilah, Mr. Dewey's nearly dead dog. She still wagged her bald tail when someone came up to the desk, but she was too old to get up like she used to.

"How's she doing?" I asked. I leaned over the

counter. "Hi, girl!" She blinked at me and thumped her tail a bit harder.

"Well, we're both here," he said, like he always did. "A little worse for the wear, perhaps. I'm still waiting for that book you ordered," he went on, ignoring the computer in front of him and checking the paper list he kept of all the books that people wanted. "Let's see. What was it? Ah yes, here it is. *Motown: The Golden Years.*"

Mr. Dewey shared a love for '60s music, especially Motown, too. The library had a record player, and now and then, if it wasn't too busy, we'd go in back to the vinyl section, and he'd introduce me to a new song that we'd listen to wearing side-by-side headphones. He loved Marvin Gaye like I loved the Supremes.

"Thanks so much, Mr. Dewey, no hurry." I looked around, and there were just a few people in the main room. And no kids that I could see.

"I heard a rumor that you started public school." He looked pained by the idea. "I hope this doesn't mean I won't get to see much of you and your mother anymore."

Mom had been bringing me to the library and Mr. Dewey since I was in diapers. He'd loved helping Mom with my education all these years. He was always ready with something new to show her.

"Of course not!" I said. I licked my lips. "Hey, I was just wondering if some kids—"

"You missed them," he said, turning away to carry a stack of books to the back desk.

"Missed them?"

"The Nonreaders," he said, and shook his head with an irritated sigh. "If that's who you are looking for. A whole horde of them just got dropped off about an hour ago. They stayed just long enough to get on my remaining nerves." He shuddered under his button-up vest, remembering. "Most of those kids cut their baby incisors right here during Storybook Hour, gumming up my covers." He dumped another armload of books into the cart. "Well, I've done everything I can to plant the seeds of literature. Hopefully, they will find their way back one day. When they are older and quieter, ideally."

He pushed his cart out from behind the check-in area, and headed toward the stacks. I'd always helped him put books back on the shelves. Back then Delilah would make the rounds with us, too.

He paused a moment as he passed me. This was generally when I would grab the cart from him, and off we'd go while he spouted Dewey directions at me.

He gave me an appraising look and then a grunt. "Well, go on with you, then!"

"If you want, I could help you," I started, and prayed he would turn me down.

"Abraham, I am as old as God's mother, but not stupid. The Nonreaders are all headed to the creek by way of Super Frosty. They will be back at 4:59 to slide into the study carrels, burping milkshake, just in time to get picked up by their unsuspecting parents."

"Thanks, Mr. Dewey," I mumbled.

When I made no move to leave, he stopped and waited. "Was there something else?"

I lowered my voice a bit and moved in closer. "Did you happen to notice if there was a boy named Micah with them? He's about this tall," I said, setting a marker with my hand.

"The proverbial plot thickens," he said wryly. "Micah, hmm. Micah, nooo, that one doesn't ring a bell, and I'd be inclined to remember that name."

"He has these super-intense green eyes," I added. "Like green Life Savers."

"If I happen to come upon young Micah, or a pair of 'super-intense' green eyes, I'll certainly let him know that you were inquiring."

"No! Don't do that!"

That earned me a big shush from Mr. Dewey and two older ladies in the magazine section.

"Sorry, Mr. Dewey, I didn't mean to raise my voice. But please don't tell him I was asking for him."

"As you wish. And please don't stand too close to the Nonreaders at the creek. I fear the condition may be contagious."

The creek that ran next to our main street was about the nicest part of our whole town, which isn't really saying much. We pretty much have only two postcards for Muddy Waters—one of the creek, and one of the prison.

There was a wooden bridge that crossed over the creek on Broad Street. Some of the town's old guys liked to fish from it, but I don't know if they ever caught anything. I think it was like a man version of a beauty salon where they could catch up on news. And spit.

If you wanted to get down to the creek, there were a few steep dirt trails that you could take. The creek had a lot of giant old boulders that were good for sitting and thinking.

I worked my way through a thicket of thorny

brush on one of the overgrown paths, and I could tell my hunch had paid off. I could hear a group of kids' voices, guys and girls laughing. They stopped when they heard me crashing through the last few yards like a moose on roller skates. My shiny Sunday shoes were not great on loose-dirt trails.

There was a small group of them, including Becca from the team, Benny, and his sidekick, Royce, who sat in front of me in Ms. Becerra's homeroom. I'd seen most of the other kids around school, but they weren't in my homeroom.

But no Micah.

"Check it out! It's A-bra-HAM," laughed Royce, who was a zit minefield. He had pus-filled pimples the size of Tic Tacs on the back of his neck. I'd had plenty of time to study them, sitting nearly right behind him every day.

"Hey, Cat Boy!" called Benny. He meowed and made little clawing motions, which cracked everyone up. "Where's your little furry girlfriend?"

I tried to think of some funny comeback to that, but I didn't have one. "He's a boy cat" was all I had.

Our heads turned together at the sound of a snapping branch. A familiar figure came through the trees.

"Bijou!" Becca said. "Where've you been? I left three messages at your house!"

Bijou's eyes ignored Becca but found mine and locked on.

I stared back. Tried not to gulp. "Oh hey, hi," I said as casually as I could muster. Even after just a few practices, I knew I was on Bijou's stink-eye list. I had proven to be one of the best runners on the team, and she seemed determined to disprove that.

Bijou wore torn running shorts and a tank top that needed a good spot-cleaning.

"Who invited you?" she asked.

"Bij—check it out! This is the weird kid we told you about, the one with the cat that he brings to school!" Benny started.

"I don't bring—" I started.

"I know who he is," she said, moving in close to me. "He's the preacher's kid who thinks he can run cross-country. Once I'm team captain, and trust me, I will be, you are first on my cut list."

"I think that's up to Coach Becerra," I said, my voice sounding slightly braver than I was feeling.

"What are you doing here anyway? This is my spot and these"—she waved her arm at the kids who had moved closer behind her—"these are my friends."

"I was just looking for Micah, but he's not here." I started to back away.

"What do you want with him?" Bijou asked, stepping even closer to me. We were about the same height, but she somehow managed to look down at me. I took another step back.

"Just wanted to see if he wanted to do something. That's all. Maybe go for a run later. It's no big deal."

"Don't you think if he wanted to hang out with you, he would be? He thinks you're a joke. But Micah's a nice guy and won't tell you right to your face. I'm not as nice, though," she said. Her face was so near mine now that I could smell Mountain Dew and bubble gum on her breath.

Adrenaline rushed into my hands and feet. The need to turn and run was strong. I jiggled the change in my pockets to keep myself grounded.

Bijou looked down at my pants. "You just rob a gumball machine or something?"

Her posse cracked up, elbowing each other and waiting to see what was going to happen.

I tried to laugh. "No, I just hit my change jar before I left home. Didn't have any cash."

"Hear that?" Bijou said. "Not only is this new kid a total wuss, he doesn't have any dough. What's the matter? Doesn't Reverend Mommy give you an allowance?"

I needed to get out of here. I could smell the animal heat coming off them, especially her. "Look, I'm going to take off now. See you guys tomorrow." I took a further step back away from her.

"Wait!" she said. She turned to Benny on her right. "Call Micah and see if he's free for a playdate with our little Ham. Tell him he's here at the creek looking for him."

I put a hand up. "That's okay, you don't need to call him," I said. "I already texted him. He must be busy with his little brother."

Bijou's eyebrow shot up at that. "Yeah," she said, her lips curling over her words. "That must be why he isn't here."

She moved up again and closed the distance between us, squinting her eyes.

"Look!" I said, my voice an octave higher. I would have raised my hands in surrender, but there was no room between the two of us for me to do that. "I don't want any trouble."

"BOO!" she said, her breath a big gust.

I jumped, my nerves on high alert. My right shoe slid in the loose gravel under my feet. One arm flailed behind me for balance, and then the other.

My Sunday shoes slid right off the embankment.

I landed hard in the icy creek water, and banked my head on a boulder.

Nothing but stars after that.

# CHAPTER TWELVE

There was shouting. I groaned, and my eyes flew open. Bijou's face appeared. For a second, I thought I saw fear in her eyes.

She leaned over the bank of the creek and held her arm out to me. I could only stare. Numb.

"Take my hand, you idiot!" she yelled.

I reached for my head, which seemed to weigh about fifty pounds now. I hoped she would just go away. Tried to sit up.

Bijou waded into the creek and grabbed the front of my shirt. The buttons tore away, but she kept a strong hold. She pulled me to my feet on the bank, and didn't let go until she was sure I could stand.

She whistled. "Oh, you're bleeding. That doesn't look good."

Becca whined, “Ah man, why’d you have to push him in, Bij? He wasn’t doing anything.”

She whirled at her. “I didn’t push him. All I did was say ‘Boo!’ and he fell. Not my fault he’s got those stupid shoes on!” Bijou turned back to me, snapping her fingers. “Look at me! Are you okay?”

“Fine,” I lied. I wasn’t. My head felt like a safe had fallen out of the sky and beaned me good. I felt for my phone in my pocket. It would be wet, but hopefully not ruined. As I pulled it out, my key ring came with it, and fell to the ground.

Benny picked it up, and studied my two keys. Then dangled it in front of me. “Hey, I bet this one is your bike padlock key,” he said. “I have the same one.”

I tried to grab it, but he held it away from me.

“Just give it to me, please.” My voice was small and tired.

Bijou reached over and swiped the key ring from him. “Where did you park it? You shouldn’t be riding it with a head injury. Tell me where it is, and I’ll ride it home for you.” She studied the church medallion on it. “‘First Grace Church, 708 Third Street.’ That’s where you live, right?” She twisted the lock key off the ring and shoved it into her shorts pocket. She gave the ring back to me.

“No!” I said, and shook my head. “I’ll just walk it

home myself. Thanks, anyway. Just give me my key back."

"Where did you park it?" she asked again. When I didn't answer, her eyes narrowed. "You parked it at the library, right? Probably went there first, where a lot of kids meet up on Sunday."

"No. No, I didn't," I said.

"You know the best thing about a preacher's kid?" she asked me. "You're terrible liars."

I gave up. I couldn't win here. "It's blue, with baskets," I said as I tried to wipe my phone dry. But there was no dry place on me.

I turned from them all then, and without another word, headed back the way I'd come.

Wishing with all my being I'd stayed at the library with Mr. Dewey and Delilah.

Even Jesus Rounds with Mom would have been better.

I held on to the back of my head, which banged like a bongo drum, as I climbed back up the trail. I hoped to God that it didn't completely explode on the way.

Fifteen minutes later, I limped into Dino's Quick Stop liquor store, my pants making wet, slushy sounds.

I had a knot about the size of a Ping-Pong ball on the back of my head. Every time I put my hand back there, it came back bloody. The back of my shirt probably looked like I'd been shot.

The good news was that now that I had a cell phone, I could call Deuce to come pick me up.

The bad news was that it had gotten soaked and it wasn't working. At least not yet.

There was a line of customers inside getting their adult beverage supplies. The clerk at the cash register didn't look like someone who appreciated being interrupted when he was busy with customers. Especially to be asked if I could use his phone. I hadn't seen a single pay phone in the two blocks I'd walked.

I studied the people in line in front of me. Most of them had their phones in their hands. But not a single one of them looked like a possible good Samaritan.

I pulled out a big clump of wet change from my pocket. I figured I should buy something if I was going to ask to borrow the phone. I had mostly pennies in my hand, so I took another pocket dive, hoping for some quarters. Only now my hand was way too full, and a shower of coins rained onto the linoleum. Nearly everyone in line now gave me their undivided attention.

I heard a familiar voice coming from behind me, sounding a bit breathless.

"There you are! I've been looking all over for you. Dude, you're *bleeding*."

And there he was. The one person I'd been hoping to see all day.

But the one person I absolutely did not want to see me now, soaking wet, bloody, and pawing at the floor for change.

That would be Micah.

# CHAPTER THIRTEEN

"You were looking for me?" I asked. That piece of intel finally penetrated my muddled brain.

He nodded, and helped me pick up the rest of my change. "I got a text from Becca. She told me you'd tangled with Bij."

I shoved the rest of the change into my pocket and grabbed the shelf to steady myself as I stood up. My head was still swimmy.

"C'mon, let's go out front so you can sit down," he said.

He led me outside, and then pointed at a short brick wall. "Here, sit. I'm going to go get some napkins or something for your head."

The sun was out, warm, shining on me on the wall. But I was shivering. I tried to sort my hair out, but it was pointless. God, I hated for him to see me this wrecked.

Micah was back in a flash with a wad of napkins. He leaned over me and placed them on the back of my head. "Hold that there. You're still bleeding."

I grimaced and bit the pain back. "Thanks."

I was still struck that he'd found me at Dino's. "How'd you find me here?" I asked again.

"I was just about at the creek already when I got Becca's text. She told me which direction you'd headed. I just got lucky with Dino's. It was close and I saw you through the front door."

"Wull, thanks for coming to check on me," I said.

"Becca told me Bij had given you a pretty hard time. Tell me the truth. Did she push you into the creek?"

"Nah," I said, shaking my head, which was a bad idea. Pain Central. "I just slipped while she was messing with me."

I tried not to think about her saying that Micah thought I was a joke. But would he have come looking for me if that were true? Wouldn't he have just stayed and had a good laugh with them about it all?

"That girl is something else," he said with a sigh. "You know why she's hassling you, right?"

Because I'm a weird preacher's kid, I thought to myself. "No, not really," I said.

"It's because you're such a good runner. She always has to be the best. Been that way since, I dunno, forever. Once in third grade, she gave a kid a bloody nose when he scored a goal on her in soccer."

"Geez," I said, thinking that maybe I'd gotten off easy.

"Compared to what she's been through, though, my life looks like Easy Street. She's had to learn to come out swinging, I guess."

I tried to see if that fit, or made sense. But it was more than I could handle thinking about right then.

"Uh, could I use your phone? I should call and get a ride home." I was getting that buzzy, sweaty feeling that usually meant I was going to throw up. I couldn't bear any more humiliation in front of Micah.

He whisked his out of his pocket and handed it over. He waited for me to do something intelligent—like dial.

"Oh, here," he said, taking it back. "What's your mom's number?"

"No, not my mom. I want to call my friend Deuce."

I rattled off the number and then Micah handed the phone back to me.

Deuce's phone rang and rang and rang. Fortunately, he didn't have voice mail, so I wouldn't get cut off. I let it keep ringing in case he was in the yard or in the garage under his car hood.

"Yup," Deuce answered at last, his voice deep and scratchy.

It sounded like he had been having a nap. "Deuce! Hey, it's me. Sorry if I woke you up."

Micah nudged me and pointed at the store. He mouthed, *Be right back*.

"You okay?" I could picture him sitting up in his recliner at this point. I hardly ever called him since he lived just across the street.

"Yeah, uh, I just wanted—" My voice started to choke the tiniest bit. I cleared it hard with a cough. "Well, thank you for such a great brunch today."

"Ham, where are you? What's going on?"

I looked around a sec. "Dino's Quick Stop. The parking lot."

Micah was back with supplies. He had a small towel with crushed ice, which he set on my head. I flinched and bit hard on the inside of my mouth.

"Ham, you're still bleeding pretty good back here," he said over my shoulder.

"Bleeding!" Deuce's voice rose. "What's going on? Are you *okay*?"

"Uh yeah, I'm fine, mostly."

Micah took the phone. "Hi, I'm with Ham. He fell into the creek and banged up his head pretty good. Somebody should come get him." He nodded a couple of times. "Mostly he seems okay, maybe a little squirrelly." He took the phone off his ear and held it to his chest. "Do you know what day it is?"

"A really bad one," I said.

He nodded appreciatively and put the phone back up to his ear. "He'll be fine till you get here. Mm-hmm. Yeah, I'll stay with him. I'm a friend of his. Uh-kay. Bye."

He tapped his phone off and slung it back into his pocket. He lowered himself to sit next to me on the wall. Very next to me. I shoved over a couple of inches to give him more room. But then noticed he already had plenty of room. He had sat that close on purpose.

"He'll be right here. Just hang on."

Micah turned then to a small pile of things he'd brought out from the store.

He handed me one of those super-expensive sports drinks, and twisted the cap off. He opened one for himself, too. "Take a drink. Here, I'll hold the ice pack while you do."

It was icy cold and tasted like orange-flavored whiskey, at least what I supposed whiskey tasted like.

I coughed on it and wiped my mouth with the back of my hand.

"Easy there," he said, giving me a clap on the back.

He held up a handful of sports endurance bars and fanned them out like a hand of cards. "You want one while we're waiting? Might make you feel better to eat something." He waved a small bottle of tablets. "Or how about some ibuprofen?" he asked. "Your head must really hurt."

"Nah, thanks." I waved them away. "But thanks for the drink," I said, lifting it toward me again. "And for doing all this for me. I don't have any cash with me now, but I want to split this with you."

"I didn't pay for it, ya goof."

That didn't compute. "What do you mean?"

"I asked the guy for a towel to make an ice pack for you. I told him you slipped by the Slurpee machine. So, he gave me a towel, and when I asked if he had any ibuprofen, he just pointed and told me to 'take what I needed.'"

I turned to him, speechless a moment. "But—but—I didn't slip in the store!"

"I know, technically, you're right, of course. But it sure made him feel more helpful."

He turned and stared at me for a long moment. I

shivered, not just from wet clothes and a sore head, but being this close to him. It was . . . confusing . . . but also kind of sort of really nice. I looked away then. Felt the flame in my cheeks.

"Look, if it will make you feel better, I'll take all this stuff back inside. Well, except for the drinks. I was just trying to help you quick as I could. If I'd waited in line, all the ice would have melted."

I swallowed. I couldn't look at him again. Even though I could feel him still looking at me.

"That's what friends do for each other, you know?" he said, leaning into me a moment.

"Thanks, I really appreciate all your help—I really do!" He called us "friends." It was for real, not just me hoping.

"I think you should have your friend take you to Urgent Care."

"I'm okay," I said, and watched him tear off the wrapped end of a sports bar with his teeth. He spit the plastic bits on the ground, and took a giant bite. He sighed while he chewed, like he'd been really hungry.

He caught my glance and took a long swig off his bottle. "I didn't eat yet today. Mom hasn't been to the store this week. Not even sure she went last week. I gave Mason the last of the cereal."

"Oh, well, it must be hard. She works two jobs, you said."

"Yeah," he agreed. "Today's her sleep catch-up day. Our neighbor is watching Mason for me. I love the little guy, but I needed some time to myself, you know?"

I opened my mouth and closed it. I wanted to ask him more about his life, but was still pretty new at this friendship stuff. Especially with a boy. But I hated to think of he and Mason not having enough to eat at home.

Deuce pulled into the lot just then. He was alone, thank God. I'd been worried that Mom would be home and he'd bring her.

He hurried over to us, and I got to my feet. Well, I tried, but landed back on my butt. The ice pack fell in a melty pile next to me.

"Whoa! Easy does it," Deuce said.

He and Micah each took an arm and pulled me up gently.

Once I was up, he gave Micah a quick nod and a "hi" and then looked around the back of my head. "Ouch! That's going to hurt for a while."

"You should really get that cleaned up," Micah

told him. “Creek water has a lot of bacteria in it.”

“Thanks, I appreciate that,” Deuce said. He stuck out his hand. “I’m Deuce.”

“Hi,” he said, “I’m Micah. And, he might need some stitches, too.”

“C’mon, kid,” he said, leading me to the car. He turned back to Micah. “Can I give you a lift somewhere?” he asked.

“No, but thanks, I’m gonna stay in town for a bit.”

“Well, bye, then,” I said. “Thanks, thanks for all your help.”

“Text me later and let me know how you’re doing, okay?” he said as he headed out toward the street.

“I will, promise!” I called.

“Let’s go,” Deuce said. “Nice and easy in.”

“Do you have a towel I can sit on?” I asked. “I’m all wet.”

“Doesn’t matter, come on now.” Deuce strapped my seat belt across for me.

I don’t remember the ride back home. I was flooded with all that had just happened.

In the course of just a few hours, I lied to my mom, lied to Fey, and left poor Mr. Dewey without any help. That lineup of moral failures led to me getting humiliated by schoolmates and having my head cracked like an egg on a boulder. It was also quite possible that I would not see my bike anytime soon.

This kind of stuff was exactly why I'd never wanted to go to public school in the first place. Why I'd avoided trying to make friends with other kids all these years.

But the truth was that having that alone time with Micah almost made it all worth it. My mind kept looping images of him over and over again. And then, the Supremes joined in, providing a swoony soundtrack.

I couldn't remember ever being so baffled by someone. My mind couldn't sort out all the perplexing ways Micah made me feel. But all the rest of me didn't care about solving the mystery. The rest of me just sat deep in the thrill of it all.

The only thing I was sure about was that I couldn't wait to see him again.

# CHAPTER FOURTEEN

I wouldn't let Deuce take me to Urgent Care. I told him my head looked worse than it was, and it would be a waste of money. He finally gave up trying to convince me but said that Mom would get the final word on that. I did have him take me by the library in the hope that Bijou hadn't gotten to my bike yet. No such luck. It was gone by the time we got there.

Not too surprisingly, Deuce didn't ask me if I wanted to stop at the police station to report the theft. It could be Free Gourmet Cookware Day at the police station, and Deuce wouldn't want to go. He'd had enough of cops to last this lifetime. You couldn't blame him. I think a part of him believed that they still might come for him. That maybe the parole board changed their mind, and he needed to go back and finish his sentence. If that did happen, I had no doubt that he could handle it, and take care of himself back in the joint.

But I also knew that his soul would die there this time.

Mom was still out on Sunday Rounds when we got back. Deuce followed me into the parsonage, set me up on the couch, and went to the kitchen to get ice for my head. Which apparently, we didn't have, as he came back carrying a bag of frozen Tater Tots. He read the fine print with a look of pain on his face.

"Do you two really eat these things?" he asked with a shudder as he set it over some clean gauze on my head. "It would be so much cheaper to make them, and they'd taste so much better."

"We'll get right on that," I said. "Right after we shear the sheep and churn the butter."

"Smart-ass," he said, and adjusted the bag to the right. "How's it feeling?"

"It's fine, really. Look, you can go. You don't have to fuss. Mom will be home pretty soon. And we've got all those leftovers from breakfast. I'm set here." Dr. Buster was on his job, walking back and forth on my chest looking for other injuries. He meowed his distaste at my smell.

"Forget it, champ—I'm not leaving until she gets here. And for the record, I'm not buying your story of what went down this afternoon."

My cheeks gave me away with a fast flush.

"So you might want to work on that a bit before she gets here. It's a pretty lame story."

"I did fall in the creek," I said.

"Not on your own you didn't, is what I'm thinking."

I said nothing and pushed the On button on our ancient remote for the cable-free TV. Deuce took it from me and pushed Off.

"Doesn't quite add up that a boy who goes to the library to work on a paper falls into the creek, gets his bike stolen, and ends up camped out in front of a cheesy liquor store bleeding."

"I told you why I left the library—"

He put his hand up. "Save it, Ham. Your mom is the one you have to convince, not me."

As Deuce predicted, Mom was having none of my story. That's the downside to having an ex-felon friend, and a mom who's worked at the jail for years. They both had very sensitive bullshit-ometers. Mom listened to my first version where I left the library after an hour to get some fresh air down at the creek. Rather than taking my bike, I left it locked up at the library. And while enjoying God's green majesty at the creek, I lost my footing. I'd slipped hard and cracked my head on a big rock. That big-rock part was true at least.

I told her that I'd gone to Dino's to make a call because I was too wet to go traipsing through the library. I'd run into Micah, who was kind enough to help me out. And sometime during all my misadventure, someone stole my bike.

"Well, that was interesting. But I agree with Deuce. You could fly a 747 through all the holes in that story."

Traitor. He'd gotten to her before I had.

"How about we try that again? I'll take the real version this time. And let's show some respect for this being the Sabbath and all." She sighed, and took a sip of the hot tea she'd made for us both when she got home. "Just for fun, let's start with the boy."

"Micah," I said.

Mom nodded. "He's on your team."

"Yeah, and we're friends now."

"How is it that the two of you ended up at the liquor store when you were supposed to be at the library doing homework?"

"That was a total coincidence, Mom, swear."

"Go on."

"I did go to the library," I said. "You can ask Mr. Dewey!"

"And there was no fresh air anywhere there, so you went across town to find some at the creek?"

"Well, it wasn't so much the fresh air," I admitted. "Micah told me that kids meet up at the creek on Sunday afternoons, and I wanted to hang out with them. I mean, isn't that what I'm supposed to be doing? Making friends?"

"I'm good with you making friends, Ham. Not okay with you lying about having homework to do at the library. Why couldn't you just tell me that?"

"I didn't think you'd let me go if it was just to do something fun."

She drew a deep breath and gave me a long look. "Okay, now get to the part where you get hurt while you're out having fun."

Even I couldn't believe all the lies and half-truths I'd told in just one day—to Fey, to Mom, to Deuce.

Life was sure a lot simpler when I went to Mom Academy.

I let out an enormous sigh. "Look, there's this girl named Bijou on the team. She's kind of rough. She didn't like me showing up at the creek. She acts like she owns the property; the kids and everything. She was getting up in my face." I stopped, hoping that would be enough.

Mom took her clerical collar off, and tossed it on the coffee table. "I'm getting the picture. Go on."

I hated telling her this. Made me sound super lame, and like I couldn't be trusted out of my own front yard. "Mom, it's no big deal. Can we just skip it? I'm okay. I stopped bleeding."

"No, sir! I want to know how my boy went to the library and ended up with a head injury."

"Okay, fine! While she was giving me a hard time, getting too close, I backed up and fell off the bank into the creek. Hit my head. End of story. Oh, and she took my bike key and said she'd walk my bike over here later. Said it wouldn't be safe to ride it."

"Excellent! I look forward to meeting her when she gets here," Mom said.

"I wouldn't hold your breath on that."

"If she doesn't return it tonight, I'll give a call to her parents so we can sort this all out."

"No, Mom, you can't do that!"

She leaned over and checked my head under the Tater Tots. "What were the other kids doing while all this was going on with you and Bijou? Was it all girls?"

"No, guys too, a couple of them from my homeroom. They were mostly all laughing and stuff."

"Little sociopaths," she muttered. "I'm going to need to speak to the parents of these children. And your principal, too. We're going to nip this in the bud."

"NO!" My voice rose. "You'll make things worse. I have to ride it out. You going all Mama Bear will make it so much worse for me at school."

"Ham, honey, I can't just sit back and ignore this. You could have been seriously injured. This young lady needs to know that we will not tolerate bullying from her."

"Look! This was bound to happen. I'm the new kid, preacher's kid, and homeschooler. I might as well have a giant *X* on my back. Don't forget, you and Deuce were the ones who wanted me in public school."

A flash of hurt flew across her face.

"Sorry, Mom, I just meant, you know, I know it's not what you *wanted.* It's just what had to happen."

She reached over for my hand. "You don't get to just shoo me right out of your life, though. I am still the parent, and it's my job to protect you."

"Maybe I was 'turning the other cheek' like Jesus said we're supposed to."

"I guess you didn't read the fine print on that verse, which reads, 'Turn the other cheek unless some deranged kid bullies you right into the creek for no apparent reason. And then thy mother has permission to whoop the deranged kid's mother for having such a nasty child.'"

"Uh yeah, missed that part. Please just let it go, Mom."

She blew out a big breath, and then took my hand. "It's not that easy. You're my little Hammy."

"Why don't you bake us up these Tater Tots before they spoil," I suggested. "You'll feel better afterward. And we can heat up some of that egg casserole from this morning."

"You're trying to distract me," she said, gently removing the bag from my head and reading the cooking instructions.

"Yup," I said.

"It's not going to work."

"What if I tell you more about Micah? You're really going to like him!"

She couldn't resist. She settled back into the couch. "So, tell me. Why am I really going to like him?"

"Well, first of all. He was super nice to me, even on the first day of school. He didn't make fun of me when Buster followed me to school. And his mom works all night at two jobs and sleeps all day. So Micah has to take care of his baby brother all the time."

"Wow," she said. "That can't be easy for a boy your age."

I nodded. "I know. I feel bad for him. He has to miss practice a lot. And today at the liquor store . . ." I was about to tell her that he'd not had anything to eat all day, but I stopped. That was tied to his minor looting of Dino's.

"What?" she asked.

"Well, today at the liquor store, he was really nice. And so helpful."

"What does Fey think of him? Does she 'really' like him, too?"

"She hasn't met him yet. He's not in our homeroom."

"Right. Well, I am very grateful that he helped you out of a jam today. Let's have him and Fey over to dinner soon."

I tried to imagine the three of us hanging out together. Didn't quite work in my head. Until recently, I didn't have any friends my age. Now I had two, and I wasn't sure how that all worked.

"Mom? Can you actually get me something to eat? I'm totally starving."

She popped up and sped into action. If you ever need to get your mom off a topic, like this one, just tell her you're super hungry.

While Mom started getting things out for dinner, I sat, quiet, chewing the inside of my mouth. It was really nice that Mom wanted to have both of my new friends over. But I was imagining what it would be like to have just Micah over. After dinner, we could go to my room, and I'd show him my vinyl collection. Maybe I'd play him a few of my favorite songs.

When it was just me and Micah, he was great. Something happened, though, when other kids were around. Like at practice, he was different. Kind of like a wise-ass. I didn't want Fey to meet him when he was acting like that. She'd wonder why I wanted to be friends with him.

But maybe that was just a team kind of thing he did, or maybe all guys did. Maybe he'd be really kind and sweet if it was just me and Fey. The way he was when we were alone.

But what if he wasn't? What if he teased Fey, and acted rude?

By the time Mom hollered at me about dinner, I'd just about convinced myself that having Micah over without Fey was an act of kindness.

The slope was getting a tiny bit slippery.

# CHAPTER FIFTEEN

In the end, Mom and I didn't get to eat the Tater Tots because blood had seeped into the package. We went out for burgers and animal-style fries smothered in cheese and grilled onions, which are my favorite. Then she tricked me by swinging by Urgent Care when we were done. She wanted a "properly trained medical professional" to look at my head and clean out the wound. I did end up getting six small stitches, and she felt way better.

When we got home, there was no sign of my bike, which Bijou was supposed to have dropped off. I managed to convince Mom to show some mercy toward Bijou. It wasn't so much that I wanted to protect Bijou from getting in trouble, because she deserved it. But

I didn't want word getting to Micah and the other kids that Reverend Mom had flown in to save her little fella. I didn't want anything messing up me being friends with Micah, or being on the team.

I had to promise her, though, that if Bijou even so much as raised an eyebrow at me, I would let her know and all bets were off. Deal. And, I assured her I'd get my bike back from her at school. No problem.

Fey and Buster and I got to school early Monday and checked the bike racks, hoping to find my cruiser. I'd called Fey the night before and told her what had happened. I admitted I'd gone to the creek after the library to see if Micah was there. I didn't confess that I'd only spent five minutes at the library, and hadn't really needed to finish any homework. I felt like a bad friend to her about that, and I didn't like it.

Not too surprising, my bike wasn't in the racks in front of the school.

Fey was exasperated. "Man, I wish I'd been with you at the creek yesterday. I've gotten picked on a lot because I'm always the new kid. I used to just let it go. You know, taking the peaceful path and all that. But I've learned that sometimes you need to speak up, or it won't quit."

"How do you know, though, when it's time to

'speak up,' and when you should just ignore it?"

"Experience, I guess," she said. "I know that's not a great answer. It's not easy. But at least now we don't have to go through it alone, right?"

"No, we don't!" I said, knowing that Fey was a better friend to me than I was to her.

She leaned over and scratched Buster behind his ears. Then, she looked up at me. "I think Bijou may be one of those kids you're going to have to take a stand with. It's not like you can ignore her, since you're on the team together."

"I know!" I said, feeling the knot on my head. I tried to finger comb some hair over the stitches. "I'll figure something out. I'll talk to Micah at practice today. He knows her."

"Good. See what he says." She handed Buster to me. He settled into his groove under my chin.

"I don't suppose there's any chance that you'd run on home," I said. Buster nipped at my chin in response. "I guess that's a no," I said, and set him down. He tried to climb back up my pant leg. "Go on, go see Miss Emma. She's got cookies, you know."

At that, he sprinted off, tail high. Happy as a cat can be off to his second breakfast of the day.

As if on cue, Royce and Benny cruised by, Benny

giving me his usual shoulder slam.

"Me-owwww, Cat Boy!"

"Uh-oh!" said Royce. "Looks like Cat Boy found his Cat Girl. Hey, does Buster know you're cheating on him with this chick?" he said, a chin nod to Fey.

I stiffened but didn't say a word.

"Hey, do you know what's funny?" Fey called after them. "Definitely not either of you, so shut your ostium."

Clearly, Fey had more experience at this. I could never think of anything to say.

"Oh hey! How's the head? Heard you fell in the creek yesterday!" Royce called back.

I muttered under my breath, "Sorry about that, Fey. And, what is an 'ostium'?"

"It's Latin for 'mouth.' And, don't worry. I've been called worse than 'Cat Girl.'" She linked her arm through mine. "Trust me, Ham. Intelligence and character will prevail!"

Fey and I settled our lunch trays in a corner away from the multitudes. If Fey hadn't been there to show me the cafeteria ropes, I would have totally blown it the first day. For instance, just because there are two available seats at the table with just a few jocks sitting at it, you MAY NOT sit there. Same rules for the table where the cheer squad sits. All seats are taken, no matter how many empty chairs there are. There was even a cowboy table at Harvey Mellencamp. Looked as if you had to be wearing cowboy boots to sit there.

The trick was to find a table away from anybody that "mattered," according to the unwritten rules. When she led me away from all the perfectly available seats that first day, I suggested we just go outside. But apparently, there were rules for outside eating, too.

Usually the safe seats were very close to the garbage and recycling bins. You almost needed a helmet to eat there safely. Cafeteria trays and recyclables whizzed by our heads. The smell of the composting trash made it hard to get excited about your lunch.

I watched Fey peel back the foil on her yogurt, tear open a bag of Cheetos, and then use them as dipsticks. She had a great style all her own. I took a massive bite of my peanut butter and jelly sandwich.

"Hungry much?" Fey asked with a grin.

I wiped my mouth and took a swig of water. "Starving! Hey, I forgot to ask! How were the tide pools yesterday?"

"*Oh* my God. Totally amazing! Did you know that barnacles produce this fast-drying cement that helps them stay put during the incoming and outgoing tides? And I found one pool that was nearly three feet deep. I saw mussels, anemones, urchins, crustaceans, and even some small fish. I took a bunch of pictures so I could draw them later."

"Pictures?" I asked around a wad of peanut butter. Fey was the kind of person who didn't care if you talked with food in your mouth.

"Here," she said, scrolling through her phone. "Check out this giant urchin. They call them 'edible pincushions.' I love the color of this one."

"Ham, my man!" Micah appeared out of nowhere and draped himself over my side of the table.

The peanut butter lodged in my mouth would not go down. Stuck like some of the barnacles' fast-drying cement.

"Wwffttttchch!" I said.

"How's your head? I wondered if you'd be in school today." He leaned around the back of me and took a look. "I knew it! You had to get stitches."

I grabbed my water bottle and tried to wash it all down. Coughed my way into a full sentence.

"Oh-hi-yeah-stitches-Mom-took-me-to-Urgent-Care-um-do-you-know-Fey?-Micah-this-is-Fey-Fey-this-is-Micah."

"Hey," Micah said. He gave her a once-over and then looked away.

Fey nodded back at him. "You're in my science class," she said.

"Huh? Oh, cool. Did Ham tell you I found him soaked and bleeding at Dino's yesterday?" Micah asked.

"Good thing you were there!" she said.

Micah shrugged and then looked back at me. "What did your mom say when she saw you? Did you tell her what happened? You know, about Bijou and her gang hassling you?"

"Uh yeah, but it was no big deal. She took me out for a burger after my stitches."

Fey's eyes grew wide. She'd already heard from Mom this morning what the "no big deal" sounded like. Mom was still steaming about it when I left for school.

I caught Micah looking at my sandwich. I realized he didn't have a tray. "Oh! Did you eat yet? You can have half my sandwich. I'm not even hungry."

Fey shot me a glance at that.

He had it in his mouth before I even hardly finished my sentence. Fey scooted her carrots toward him. "Help yourself."

Micah shook his head. "Carrots—ugh. How do you even eat those things?"

Fey colored a little, and went back to eating her Cheeto dipsticks.

"Fey was just showing me some amazing pictures of the tide pools she saw yesterday," I said.

Micah reached for my water bottle and took a long swig.

"Fey, show him that one you were just showing me—that big purple urchin. What did you call it? The edible pincushion?"

"Sorry, gotta dash—maybe next time. See you at practice later, Ham. Nice meeting you, Kay!"

"It's Fey—not Kay," I corrected.

"Right. Hey, you going to eat your chips?" he asked, picking them up. He tossed the bag back and forth between his hands.

"No! Take 'em," I said.

Mostly to his backside. He was gone as quick as he had come.

Fey started sorting out her trash. I could tell she was under-impressed by Micah. "So is he a good runner?" she asked.

"He's, well, I dunno. He's good, but he could be a lot better."

"Could be?"

I looked around to see if there was anyone sitting close by. I leaned in a bit. "He's got a tough home life. He is on his own a lot with a little brother. I don't think they have much money or food, to be honest."

Fey nodded. "That's rough. You should probably start packing an extra sandwich, then. You need to eat, too. Especially on practice days."

"Sorry he wasn't very polite. He really is a great person. Just wait until you get to know him better. He's probably just not into sea urchins."

"No big deal," she said, packing up her lunch remains. "I'll take your word for it. Text me later after you get home from practice, okay? We can talk about Ms. Becerra's assignment."

"Great!" I said with way too much enthusiasm. Like that might make up for Micah pretty much ignoring her.

After Fey left, I sat for a moment while my heartbeat calmed itself down. It tended to speed up when Micah was around. Which I didn't quite understand. I kept telling myself that I was just super excited to have a new friend. But Fey had been a new friend to me, and she didn't make my heart break into a sprint. Fey just made my heart feel happy. Micah made me feel nervous—not like getting-a-cavity-filled nervous, but nervous *good*. Like when you're about to open a present.

And while seeing texts come in from Fey made me smile, an incoming text from Micah made me catch my breath. Then my stomach would flap wings I hadn't even known it had. Was this the ways other boys felt about each other? Did Royce and Benny feel this excited about each other?

Or, was it more like the two boys from Ms. Constantine's homeroom that kids whispered about? I'd heard the kids call them "queer" and "gay." They were always together, and didn't have any other friends. They both had matching rainbows sewn on their backpacks, and held hands sometimes when they walked between classes. One was named Sam and the other was Mike, so most kids called them both S'Mike. I wondered if that bothered them.

Some of the kids in my neighborhood who teased me a lot had called me gay and queer before, or "freakin' homo." Even when I was just a little kid. I'd asked Mom what that meant and she'd explained that those words weren't insults, but some people used them like they were. I hadn't really understood it before.

And I didn't understand what was happening to me now. Was I turning out to be a kid who liked boys instead of girls? Or, was I just a kid who had been so lonely that having a boy for a friend made me super excited?

And what if I was a queer? It would be one more thing that would make me different, and I was trying hard not to be so different for once.

When do you know for sure either way? Who could you ask? Who was safe to ask?

The bell rang for next period. I shot from my seat, and I hurried to my next class.

My mind wanted answers. All the rest of me just wanted to remember how he looked when he bit into my sandwich. Or when he'd leaned into me at Dino's and called us friends.

I busied my brain with counting the minutes until I'd see him again.

# CHAPTER SIXTEEN

Micah wasn't at practice yet when I showed up after my last class, but Bijou was.

I guess she'd figured out that Coach Becerra wasn't kidding about being late. She ignored me, but Becca kept throwing looks at me. Bijou already had her orange vest on, and was stretching out her calves. I figured this was all part of her game to become the team captain. Star team member.

I looked around the bleachers and track area as I got ready, wondering if she'd been bold enough to ride my bike to the track. But I didn't see it anywhere. I bided my time, and laced up the new trail shoes Deuce had bought me as an early Christmas present. I could tell Mom was about to have a word with him about it, but instead she just thanked him. And made him promise he wouldn't get me anything else for Christmas. He agreed, but I knew he would anyway. Because he was Deuce and that was just how he rolled when it came to me.

I dropped onto the ground next to Bijou, and leaned into a deep forward stretch.

"I need my bike back. You didn't bring it to my house yesterday like you said."

She looked over and considered me. "Tell Jesus you need a new one."

I leaned deeper into my stretch and blew out hard. "Look, just bring it to school tomorrow, okay?"

"Or, what?" She gave me a look that was part pity and part disbelief.

Coach jogged up to us, with Jet in her wake. She blew her whistle to gather everyone up. She took a quick attendance under her breath, making notes on her clipboard. Everyone was here except Micah.

"Where's Tuttle?" she called, and then sighed hard. "I expect the whole team out here." She planted her hands on her hips and glared at us.

We all looked around like he might be standing in our small group, but we hadn't noticed.

Coach looked seriously peeved.

Jet shook her head when Coach looked over at her. We were down to eleven runners, counting him, if he made it today.

"Jacob!" she shouted to the kid next to me wearing earbuds. He didn't look up, so I elbowed him and motioned toward Coach.

"Hightail it over to the locker room and see if Micah is in there. And while you are at it, leave your earbuds *in your locker.* You got me?"

"Yes, Coach!" he said as he stumbled away from the group.

"Logan! This isn't the baseball team. Take the giant pink wad bulging in your cheek and go spit it out. I'm in no mood to give you the Heimlich today."

Bijou stood closest to Coach, near the front of us. I had stayed in back. She raised her hand like she was a very polite student.

"What is it, Bijou?" Coach asked.

Bijou stood flamingo-style, one leg folded completely in half, her shoe resting on her backside. She had some serious flexibility and balance, I'd give her that.

"That new kid . . ." She turned and pointed at me.

My heart took off in a full gallop. *What?*

"His name isn't 'new kid.' Learn the names of your

teammates, will you? That's Ham."

"HAM is injured, Coach. I heard he fell into the creek yesterday." She shrugged like she couldn't believe anyone could be that clumsy. "I just thought you should know in case he has a concussion. Could be dangerous for him to run today."

All eyes turned to stare at me.

"Ham!" Coach called. "Front and center a minute, please?"

The kids parted like the Red Sea, and I made my way up front.

"Jet!" she said. "Start the rest of them on a couple of warm-up laps."

Once they all took off, Coach pulled her sunglasses up and gave me a long look. "You're hurt, Ham? What happened?"

My hand flew to the back of my head. She looked around the back of me to see it.

"Ouch! Were you running at the creek? Those trails are very unstable."

"Uh—no! I, well—"

Part of me wanted to rat out Bijou. I wanted to tell Coach that she was a terrible person, and wasn't a good teammate. And Coach should never make her team captain. But it was one of those times I had to take one for the team. That's what the kids in the movies I watched would do. The decent kids, at least. And I wanted to be one of the decent ones.

"Ham?" Coach asked. "Can you practice today?"

"Yes! I just slipped. Bumped my head, but it's fine. Got a couple of stitches is all, and I'm good as new. I don't have a concussion."

"All right, then," she said. "And your mom knows you have practice today, and it's okay with her?"

"Absolutely!"

"Tuttle!" Coach hollered as Micah raced by with Jacob on his heels, headed for the group on the track. "You're LATE!"

She sighed and bent over to tighten a shoelace. "I could can that kid, but I hate to lose another runner."

"I'm sure he had a very good reason to be late, Coach." She just couldn't cut him from the team. So far, it was the only place I could count on seeing him.

She arched an eyebrow at that, like she wasn't buying any of it. "C'mon, Ham, let's go. But if you start feeling wonky or fatigued, just fall out today. Got it?"

"Yes, ma'am!"

We fell into an easy trot, toward the track. "So how are you liking Harvey Mellencamp?" she asked.

"Big change from homeschool, huh?"

"It's different, that's for sure," I said. To be honest, I was hating it a tiny bit less. Fey made it easier to bear. So did Micah.

"Just give it some time," she said. "I imagine it feels a bit like when I first went to Afghanistan. It was a whole new world for me. It looked different, smelled different, tasted different. And, I didn't know the language, or the customs."

"Yeah," I said with a small laugh. "It does feel a bit like that."

"Know what made it better?" she asked, her breath coming faster now as we picked up the pace.

I turned toward her then, and shook my head.

"You find yourself a good friend," she said. "Someone you can count on. A buddy who has your back at all times. And you become that kind of friend to them, too. Don't forget that part."

"I've made a couple new friends," I said.

"With Fey?" she asked. "I've seen you two around together. I haven't gotten to know her well yet, but she seems like a great kid. Levelheaded. Don't suppose she's a runner? I'd feel better if we had a couple more kids on the team."

"No, she's not a runner," I said, considering that.

"And definitely not a trail runner! She'd be stopping every ten yards to take a picture of some plant or flower that caught her eye."

Coach laughed. "Yeah, that might be a problem!"

We were silent a minute, and then Coach continued. "And you've made another new friend?" she asked.

"Oh! Yeah, Micah and I are friends now. He's the reason I joined the team, in fact."

"Well, I'm grateful to him for that," she said. "How did you two meet? Do you have a class together?"

"Nuh-uh," I said. "I met him on the first day of school. He was super friendly to me."

"Huh" was all she said.

We were almost catching up with the rest of the team, so I blurted as fast as I could, "Coach, please don't cut him from the team. He can't help being late."

"Not sure I would agree with that," she said. "The rest of us manage to be here on time."

"Look, don't tell him I told you this, but he has trouble at home. It's not his fault."

She dropped our pace to a walk, and gave me a long sideways look. "Is that what he told you? That he has trouble at home?"

I lowered my voice. "His mom works two jobs, and

so Micah has to take care of his little brother a lot. It makes him late for a lot of things, and sometimes he can't even make it at all."

Coach stopped then and turned to face me. "A word of advice? Just watch yourself with him, Ham."

She looked like she had more to say about him, but then seemed to change her mind. She adjusted the settings on her watch and gave me a last look. "You're a good kid. I'm glad you and Fey are friends. She seems rock solid."

And with that, she blew her whistle and rounded up the group to head out for our trail workout. Leaving me to wonder what she'd kept back.

But I only wondered a minute because Micah jogged over with a big smile, aimed right at me. I tried to rein in my smile a bit, so it didn't look like I was breathless happy, just regular glad to see him.

"Hope you put in a good word for me with Coach," he said.

"I did! Told her you and I were friends, and she should cut you a break."

"Thanks!" he said. "Maybe it will help. I can tell she likes you."

"I've got your back," I said, parroting Coach's words.

He draped his arm over my shoulder. "And I've got yours!"

I filed this moment away for savoring and replaying later in private. But my big smile couldn't wait for then, and took over my face.

# CHAPTER SEVENTEEN

Mom was splayed out on the couch with her eyes closed when I got home, one arm dangling toward the floor. She didn't move when the screen door slammed behind me. I took a breath and held it. Prickles of apprehension raced across the back of my neck.

"Mom?" I said.

No response.

I moved closer, and checked to see if she was breathing.

The crucifix on her necklace rose and fell on her chest.

I let out the breath I'd been holding. Mom was just fast asleep in the middle of the afternoon. Which wasn't a bad thing, but a thing I wasn't used to seeing. She still had her prison badge ID on. She must have just crashed when she got home from there.

With her face this still, it made me really notice the shank scar that ran its length. When she was awake, you hardly noticed it because she was smiling and talking. But when she was still like this, it was red, ropy, and long. It reminded me how tough she was, but how dangerous her work was. She'd never give it up, though. It was exactly who she was.

I'd give anything to know exactly who I was.

I hated her going to the prison without me. When I was homeschooled, most of the time she would take me with her. It was one of the many reasons that I hadn't wanted to go to public school. There were so many hours when I couldn't look out for her.

True, there were plenty of guards with big rifles at the prison, but none that could or would watch her as closely as I would.

The problem was that she was fearless. She didn't see bad guys. She just saw broken guys. She wanted to get right up close and let them know that there was hope.

I wished I could tap a pint or so of that kind of courage to take to school with me. I would get right up in Bijou's face, and demand she bring my bike back. I was going to have to be a lot braver with Bijou than I was today, if I ever wanted to see my bike again.

Deuce tapped on the front door, light and polite like he always did. I opened it, then motioned toward Mom with my head. He nodded, and then waved me out toward him.

"She's taking a nap!" I whispered.

"Good for her! Well, don't wake her up. She needs the rest. I've got chile verde enchiladas and tortilla chips just out of the oven. Come on over and eat. We'll just let her rest."

Buster tiptoed across the top of Deuce's sneakers, chirping and purring. Deuce reached down to pet him. "Of course you're invited, too, Buster."

"How did practice go today?" Deuce asked as we walked the well-worn path between our houses.

"Practice was great! Coach Becerra let me be the trail leader today. We went out behind Waller Park."

"So, besides you, what kind of talent is there on the team?"

"A girl—Bijou—she's probably the best so far."

"Same girl you had a run-in with this weekend? The one who took your bike?" he asked, opening his front door for me.

"Yeah, same girl. She's out to get me big-time. She thinks Coach will make her the team captain, and as soon as Coach does, Bijou says she's going to get me cut from the team."

I slid onto a leather barstool at the counter while Deuce shoveled up a plate for me.

"What's the plan for handling things with her?" he asked.

"I dunno yet. I'm going to talk to Micah about it later. He knows her pretty well, I think. I just want her to give me my bike back and then leave me alone."

"Anyone else at school giving you a hard time?" he asked. "Or, just her?'

"Yeah, her goons. Especially these two guys named Royce and Benny." I scooted back as Deuce set a giant steamy plate of chile verde bliss in front of my face. "Man, those smell so good," I said, and took an almighty bite.

Deuce slid a big glass of water down the bar my way.

"What do you think I should do about her?" I asked.

"Seems to me you've got three options with someone like her," he said. "One, you can report her and have the school authorities handle it. Or, two, you can ignore her—or, three, you can deal with her head-on. And what 'head-on' looks like could be many different things."

"You forgot number four," I said, stuffing a whole chip into my mouth.

"And that is?" he asked.

"I quit public school, stay home, and take care of Mom and all the Church Ladies."

Deuce propped his elbows on the bar, and gave me a long look. "I suppose. But you'd miss out on cross-country, being school friends with Fey, and your new friend Micah. Trust me, you can learn how to deal with Bijou and her 'goons' now, or wait until you're older, and a new set of bullies shows up. That's one life lesson that you don't get to skip over. Believe me, I've been there."

Deuce hadn't ever talked to me about why he had been in prison, though I knew he would someday. Mom never would tell me, either. I was willing to wait. But I wondered if I'd just gotten a sneak preview.

---

After eating my body weight in enchiladas, and getting a bit of schoolwork done, I pulled my phone out to check in with Micah. He'd disappeared right after practice. I shot him a message.

ME: **Hey where'd you go after practice I wanted to ask you something.**

HIM: **sorry had to pick up mason from school what's up?**

ME: **Bijou still has my bike—how do I get it from her?**

HIM: **Money works with her**

ME: **not going to pay her for my own bike!**

HIM: **lemme think about it have to go talk later**

ME: **K thx**

I felt like I was always in Micah's jet stream, trying to keep up with him. He was always busy taking care of things at home. His mom was lucky she had a kid like him. I set my phone down and tried to think of what I could do about Bijou. Maybe taking care of things "head-on" like Deuce had suggested. I could tell that was one of the four options he thought was best. Even though he didn't say it outright.

My phone pinged, and I grinned. Was that Micah already?

It was Fey—whoops! I said I'd text her after practice, and I forgot.

HER: **You home?**

ME: **Sorry Fey practice went late then i had dinner with Deuce.**

HER: **Just checking to see how things went with Bijou at practice**

ME: **Told her i needed my bike back and she blew me off**
HER: **Wanna do homework together? i made brownies**
ME: **i've got ice cream come over!**

My phone began to ping-ping-ping with other incoming messages. Last week, Mom had "accidentally" added my name to a church-wide prayer request, so every member of First Grace Church had my cell number now. I didn't like it, but I suppose it was the least of my problems these days. It also meant that if something happened to Mom while I was at school, a lot of people could find me right away. That was the plus side.

The first one was from Mrs. Minelli. It was a picture of a new brand of eczema lotion she wanted to try. She hoped I could shop for her on Saturday. I hoped I could shop for her on Saturday, too. I had to get my bike back. It was pretty far to walk to the big CVS downtown where she liked me to shop.

Mrs. Dort sent me her Saturday shopping list and a picture of a kitten in a bathing cap.

Mrs. Paschal had texted me a message meant for someone else with a recipe for pineapple upside-down cake.

And Mrs. Martinez needed her roots touched up **ASNAP.**

I added all their numbers to my contacts so I could quickly identify them next time.

The last text was from a local number, and it was short.

**if you want your loser bike back bring $40 to school tomorrow—tell anyone and YBS**

My hand started to shake as I read it. And read it again. I couldn't look away from it. It had to have come from Royce, Benny, or Bijou. But how did they get my cell number? I was pretty sure none of them were on my mom's church prayer list. And Fey would never have given it to one of them.

Micah was the only other kid from school who knew my number. But why would he have given it to one of them? He knew the trouble I had with them.

I was still staring at it when Fey burst into my room. "Hey! You want dessert before we start?"

"Fey! What does 'YBS' stand for?"

She unzipped her hoodie, and held out her hand for my phone. "Lemme see."

Fey stared at the screen a second, and then translated out loud. "If you want your loser bike back, bring forty bucks to school tomorrow. Tell anyone and—"

"—you'll be sorry!" we said in the same second.

"Who is this from?" she asked.

"Gotta be from Benny or Royce, or maybe Bijou.

But, no, she probably had one of them do her dirty work."

"C'mon, we need to go show this to your mom. This has gone too far. Bad enough they stole your bike, but now they're trying to extort money from you!"

"No!" I said, grabbing the phone back from her. "We can't tell Mom."

"Why not? She needs to know, Ham."

"I don't want to stress her out right now. She's just getting back on her feet. I'll handle it. Just let me think a minute."

"But how did one of them get your number? I haven't given it to anyone."

"I know. The only other school people who have it are Micah and Miss Emma. I think we can rule out Miss Emma."

"But why would Micah do that? He knows they're messing with you."

"He wouldn't have done it on purpose. One of them somehow got into his phone. Maybe during track practice. That has to be it."

Fey drew a big breath and plopped down on my bed. "Hmm" was all she said.

"What? You don't think he'd do something like that on purpose?"

"I don't know what I think," she said, pulling her

notebook out of her backpack.

"Well, do you think I should reply?"

She shook her head. "I wouldn't. Let's just see what happens at school tomorrow. And I don't want you out of my sight for a second. You got that? We'll meet up between every class."

"Thanks, Fey," I said, remembering what Coach said about finding a friend who always has your back. Fey was winning on that score.

Mom rapped on the door, and stuck her head in. "You two need to come out and eat some of these decadent-smelling brownies. Or, I shall abandon all my resolve and swallow the pan whole."

Fey laughed and dragged me out of my chair. "Yes, ma'am! Coming!"

I put my arm on her before she was out the door. My mouth was so dry from nerves I didn't think I could even choke down a brownie if I wanted to. "What do you think they mean by 'you'll be sorry'?"

"Nothing that the two of us can't handle," she said. "Don't worry, Ham. It's a stupid bluff."

I tried to just shake it off. I nodded and followed her while my mind reeled with images of me being made "sorry."

And I wondered if it wouldn't be worth forty dollars to avoid all that.

# CHAPTER EIGHTEEN

I half expected Benny and Royce to be waiting for me outside school the next morning, waving an empty sack for the bike ransom. But they were already in the classroom when Fey and I showed up. They were acting like their normal idiot selves. Neither of them paid me any more attention than usual. Or less. I was surprised, but not relieved. The day had just started.

Coach—I mean, Ms. Becerra—took attendance, and then started writing discussion questions on the board:

*What tools did the Greeks use to study the starlit sky?*

*How did—*

Principal Strickland's voice blasted through the

intercom with her morning message. I jumped in my seat, my nerves in high gear.

"Good morning, students! I was reminded while driving in this morning how important it is that all our student commuters wear helmets. It's the law! I'm afraid I saw at least three of our students riding without helmets. I will be following up with the three of them today to make sure they have a helmet. I always keep a few on hand; if you need to borrow one this year, please come see me."

Fey caught my eye, and I could tell we were both thinking the same thing. Was one of the un-helmeted riders commuting on my bike?

"Now, on a happier topic, it's time to start making plans for our Fall Frolic!" she continued. "As most of you know, this is an important fundraiser each year for our athletic department. There are committee sign-up sheets on the big board outside my office. I am sure each of you can find a way to help us make it a great night!"

I tried to imagine what a Fall Frolic might be—students rolling around in piles of leaves? Climbing trees? Hay rides? I'd have to ask Fey after class.

". . . make sure you come by and sign up to help. Last year we raised nearly four thousand dollars! I expect each of you Harvey Mellencamp Wildcats to demonstrate a strong school spirit and find a way to contribute!"

It felt like three weeks before class ended. I'd studied Greek astronomy back in fourth grade, I think. It was all new to my classmates, though. Ever since Deuce had given me that talk at the doughnut shop, I tried not to think of myself as smarter than them. I wasn't. I was just ahead of them. And that wasn't really their fault.

But in other ways, I knew that they were way ahead of me. They all knew what a Frolic was, and how that would make money for the school. They already knew how to make friends, where to sit in the cafeteria, and how not to dress for school. And, that raising your hand in class a lot when you knew the right answer would not impress anyone. It was better to let the teacher call on you. They knew plenty that I didn't.

"All set?" Fey asked, hurrying over as the classroom doors flew open. "I'll walk you to your next class."

"Ready!" I said, flinging my pack over one shoulder.

The hallways were flooded with students, and I felt like a salmon trying to swim upstream with Fey.

"Fey!" I had to shout over the din. "What's a Frolic?"

She turned and smiled. "It's a dance! Wanna go together?"

"Sure!" I said, firing another lie right at Fey. But it was one of the good kind of lies. The kind you tell not to hurt someone's feelings.

The truth was that I didn't want to go to a dance with anyone. I didn't know how to dance. Another thing I was going to have to learn. The school dances I'd seen in the movies were pretty fancy. I didn't have a tuxedo. And I'd never seen one come in any of the charity boxes where Mom got a lot of my clothes.

We finally made it through the throng, and Fey pulled me by the hand the last few yards to get around a knot in kid traffic.

"This is it, right?" she said, huffing. "Spanish with Ms. Aycock? I better run—"

Micah was leaning up against the room's doorframe.

"Oh hey," I said while my internal organs did their happy dance at the sight of him. "What are you doing here? This isn't your class."

"Duh. I was waiting for you."

I swallowed. "Cool." I looked over at Fey. "Um,

you remember my friend Fey from the cafeteria?"

"Yeah, hey," he said, not giving her even a glance. "Meet me in the caf after, okay? I want to talk to you about something."

I had lunch every day with Fey. It was our thing.

I turned to look at her. She stood staring at him. And not leaving.

"Well, you know where Fey and I sit. Just come on over," I said.

"Yeah, I could, but I thought maybe we could sit with the kids from the team. You know, team spirit and all."

Fey still stared at him. And not in her usual friendly way. She had that look Buster got sometimes when he saw a bug on the wall. He'd wait for it to move, still as a statue.

"Well, maybe I could stop by for just a few minutes," I said. "But Fey and I always sit together."

He looked at her and then back at me. "So you two a thing, or something?"

A *thing*? I thought. What does that mean?

"We're friends," Fey said.

"Oh yeah, friends," I said.

"Well, whatever, come sit with us or not. Up to you, Ham." He gave Fey a small salute.

"Good to see you again, May."

"*Fey*," I said to his back as he shoved off down the hall.

I turned to apologize to Fey, but she'd left, too.

And neither of them turned to give me one last wave.

I don't remember anything about the rest of the morning except that I nearly gave myself an ulcer worrying about lunchtime. I really wanted to sit with Micah and the team at lunch, and feel like one of the guys. But I couldn't leave Fey all by herself. She hadn't made any school friends yet. I considered just skipping lunch and going to the library to read.

But that wouldn't make anyone happy, especially me.

Fey wasn't in our regular meetup place outside the cafeteria. I found her inside, going through the line. I tried to catch her attention, but she was reading a book and moving along with her tray. When I finally made it through the line, I hurried over to our table. I took the long way around so I wouldn't pass Micah and the team's table.

"Hi!" I said, and set my tray down. "You didn't wait for me."

She looked up from her book and gave me a half

smile. "Aren't you going to have lunch with Micah?" she asked.

"Nah. I'll go over there after we eat and see what he wanted to talk to me about."

She started to say something, and then she stopped. She got very busy unwrapping her sandwich.

"What?" I asked.

"Any chance that the reason he wants to talk to you is to get the forty bucks from you? Maybe Bijou asked him to get it for her. You know?"

I shook my head before she finished talking. "No! He wouldn't do that. We're friends."

She nodded. "Okay, if you say so."

Fey and I usually had so much to talk about that we sometimes talked over each other, but today, it was like we'd run out of words. We both were concentrating very hard on eating. I twisted around a couple of times to see if Micah was still at the table. After my third twist, Fey reached over and put a hand on my arm.

"Ham, just go! I've got a good book. We'll catch up later."

"You sure? You don't mind?"

"Go!" she said, and shooed me away.

I grabbed my tray and headed over to Micah. He,

Jacob, and Logan were talking about team captain, and who they thought Coach would pick. Jacob and Logan both gave me a quick head nod, and Micah shot me a smile. I sat down next to him, and he took a look at my tray. He grabbed a fork and took a big bite of my cake. I moved the plate closer to him so he'd know he could have more. The poor guy never had any food of his own. I regretted that I'd already eaten all of my sandwich.

I glanced at the clock on the wall. There were only a few minutes left until the bell rang. When there was a break in the conversation, I butted in.

"Uh, hey, you wanted to talk to me about something?"

He looked at me like he didn't have a clue what I was talking about. "Huh," he said. "Can't remember."

He shoved a gigantic bite of my cake into his mouth, and then put me in a headlock while he chewed. I didn't know if I was supposed to try and get out of it, or just stay. So, I just turned red and stayed put.

"Hey, guys," he said, and released me. "What if Bij didn't get picked as team captain? What if my man Ham here got it instead?"

Jacob gave me an appraising look. "It's not

impossible, I guess. You're a heck of a good runner," he said. "But there would be hell to pay with her, you know."

Micah smiled at that and finished the rest of my cake.

Jacob cleared his throat. "Heads up! Here she comes." He took a long last swig of his iced tea, and balled up his lunch. "I'm outta here. Logan, let's hit it!"

They both fist-bumped Bijou as they made their escape. She slid into the place they'd left, and stared across at me and Micah.

"So, what?" she asked Micah. "You said you wanted to talk to me."

"Not me," he said. "Ham wanted to talk to you."

I looked at him like he was out of his mind.

He gave me a reassuring smile. "Go ahead. Tell her what you wanted to say."

"Uh, wull, um—yeah, I guess we should, er, can talk," I said, trying to find the right tone.

She crossed her arms across her chest and leaned back in her chair. She gave me a long stare.

My eyes shot across the room to Fey's table, but she was gone. I tried to imagine Deuce's encouraging face right over Bijou's shoulder, and cleared my throat. "You need to return my bike. I need it for my weekend job. And you shouldn't have taken it."

She raised an eyebrow at Micah, and sneered at me. "I didn't take it."

"You took my lock key and said you'd bring it to my house," I reminded her.

"My plans changed," she said. "I didn't take it."

"And I'm not paying you forty dollars' ransom for it," I blurted. "I got your text!"

Bijou looked at Micah, then leaned in over the table and got in my face. "Sounds like you have a lot of personal problems, and none of them have to do with me. Are you done, little man?"

I was more nervous than mad, but she didn't need to know that. "If you don't get my bike back to me, I'm going to tell Coach all about what happened at the creek."

Bijou laughed and pushed my tray up close against me. She turned to Micah. "The kid's mental. I don't know why you even let him breathe in your space. I'm done here," she said, and took off.

The bell rang, and Micah shook his head at me. Leaned in with his bright green stare. "Least you tried. Look, if I were you, I'd bring the cash tomorrow. I can give it to her for you, if you want." He put his hand on my shoulder and left it there for a long moment.

I gulped and nodded but didn't know what to say. Eventually, Micah left with a nod, but I stayed.

I should have been furious at Bijou and what she was putting me through.

I should have been embarrassed at what she said about me in front of Micah.

I should have been frustrated that she didn't seem to have any plans to return my bike.

I was all three of those things, I suppose. But more than anything, I was still feeling the warm print of Micah's hand. It felt really personal, and really private to me.

I didn't know what it meant that he'd put his hand on my shoulder that way. I knew how it made me feel, but I didn't know what it meant.

I wondered if he even did.

# CHAPTER NINETEEN

The announcement came over the intercom on Friday afternoon, during science class with Mr. Ferrini, who loved talking about his retirement as much as he liked to talk about diatomic molecules. We didn't usually have late-afternoon announcements. Everyone stopped what they were doing to listen.

Miss Emma's voice came online. She didn't make the announcements very often, so when she did, they were very loud.

"GOOD AFTERNOON, students. Principal Strickland just called and asked that I make a special announcement of some URGENCY. Someone has padlocked their bicycle to the door handle of Principal's car. She is unable to leave for a very IMPORTANT meeting downtown with the superintendent. She has asked that the owner of this bike report immediately to the staff parking lot to unlock it."

My classmates busted up over this. I tried to imagine why a kid would do that, unless he was super worried about getting his bike stolen, and thought that would be the safest place.

Miss Emma's voice was a whisper then. "Buster, get off my keyboard—oh! *Excuse me*, STUDENTS. The bike is blue with two large wire baskets on either side of the back wheel. A white helmet is attached to the handlebars. Principal says there is a phone number written in large letters on the outside of the helmet."

My heart came to a complete stop, and I swiveled to look at Fey.

Her eyebrows shot up, and she whispered, *"Is it yours?"*

"Students, the number on the helmet is (805) 555-5683. Principal Strickland is in a great hurry and if the owner of the bike does not show up in the next five minutes, she'll have the custodian come CUT the lock off."

I was dead meat. My stolen bike was locked to Principal's car!

Fey elbowed me hard in the side. *"Ham—go!"*

*"I don't have the key!"* I whisper-screamed back.

Fey dropped her head in her hands a second. *"Well, you have to go anyway, so you can get it back. Just tell her what happened. She'll understand—don't you think?"*

I raised my hand, and felt cold sweat running down my back. "Excuse me, Mr. Ferrini? May I be excused?"

As the class hooted and laughed, I made a run for it. I shot across the campus fast as I could. A part of me just wanted to run home, and take cover until all this was over. I could refuse to shower ever again, and Mom would be forced to keep me home because I would smell so bad. When puberty finally arrived, I would grow a long beard, and never talk to kids my age ever again.

Except maybe Fey.

I couldn't imagine never seeing Micah again. I gave myself a terrible side stitch thinking about it.

By the time I blew into staff parking, clutching my side, Principal Strickland looked like she'd lost any patience and understanding she may have had. She was on her phone. The school custodian was trying to cut through the chain and was having a devil of a time. I'd paid extra for a very thief-proof lock and chain.

"Ham!" she said as I hurried toward her. She pulled her phone away from her ear. "Is this your bicycle?"

"Wull, yes, ma'am, but I can explain."

"Please! I've got five minutes to get to my meeting. Unlock it!"

"Ma'am, I would, I swear. But I don't have the key."

She pinched the bridge of her nose. "Tony," she said to the custodian. "Cut it off. I don't have time for this."

As he struggled to get through the NASA-rated metal, Principal gave me a confused and surprised look. "Ham, why in God's name did you lock your bike to my car? Did someone dare you to do it?"

"Oh no, ma'am. I wouldn't do that. I—I—well, I, you see, I sort of lost my bike, and well, I guess whoever found it wanted to put it back in a very safe place." I swallowed hard.

There was a sound of cracking metal, and Tony grunted. "Got it, Principal. You're good to go."

He unwrapped the chain where it was triple looped around her door handle and wheeled the bike out of her way. "Sorry about your lock, kid," he said.

"You can bring your bike to my office, and I'll keep it safe for you until you go home."

"Thank you, sir," I said, my head low.

Principal threw the door open so hard I thought it might fly off its hinges.

She turned back to me as she started the ignition. "We're going to finish this talk later, Ham. I think we're quite a way from getting to the bottom of this. And we will, that I promise you." She sighed hard and peered at me over the top of her sunglasses. "At least you have a helmet. Thank you for that."

"You're welcome, ma'am," I said to a mouthful of exhaust.

I was in the kitchen bent over my helmet, with tiny alcohol wipes from Mom's first aid kit, trying to scrub off the phone number.

Whoever had done it had used an extremely permanent marker. I had planned to hide it from Mom until I got it cleaned up, but she'd seen me ride my bike up to the porch after school.

Busted.

Deuce and Mom sat nearby while Deuce took Mom's blood pressure.

"Well, is it coming off?" Mom asked.

Deuce shushed her. "No talking, Annie, until I'm done here."

"Yeah, I think this will work," I said between swabbing and scraping it with my fingernail.

"I still don't understand why you—" she started.

"Hush!" Deuce said. We all grew quiet at that and waited until he got the reading.

The machine beeped, and the cuff on her arm began to deflate with a whooshing sound.

"Well, it's up a little," he said, folding up the cuff. "Probably because you wouldn't keep quiet. But it is still much better!" He made a note on the clipboard she kept of her daily readings.

I really was pretty proud of how serious she was taking her recovery. As far as I was concerned, keeping her well was my number one priority. Even if it meant my life was a nightmare.

"Well, at least you got it back," she said. "I'm proud of you for standing up to Bijou."

Deuce grunted. "Now, tell me again how your cell number ended up written all over your helmet?"

I kept my eyes down and kept scrubbing it. "I dunno, maybe Bijou didn't have a piece of paper to write my number down. And she figured she'd need to call me about returning it."

"Why would she have your number?" Mom asked.

"Micah probably gave it to her. He was trying to help get my bike back."

"At least your bike is in good shape," Deuce said. "Did she bring it to you at school or just leave it somewhere and tell you where it was?"

I hadn't told them about my bike being locked to Principal's car door. And I hadn't told them about the ransom threat. This was what you called a sin of commission. It's when you don't lie, but you leave out the truth. It's worse than a white lie, but better than a bold-faced lie.

"Yep, she locked it up in a very safe place for me. There!" I said, and gathered up all the tiny, dirty alcohol wipes. "The numbers are mostly off. Well, mostly." I gave it a final wipe, then inspected it from all sides.

"Well, in the spirit of forgiveness, I'll let this go," Mom said. "Deuce keeps reminding me that you kids need to work some of this out between yourselves. You know what? Maybe we should have Bijou and your team over one night after practice for a BBQ?"

I blinked at her, and tried not to show her how horrified I was by the idea. "Yeah, well, maybe? How about after our first meet?" That should give me some time to talk her out of a team party here in the parsonage.

But I'd never make it to our first meet. By then, everything in my life would be just smoke and ashes. I'd be left standing there sucking smoke.

# CHAPTER TWENTY

On Sunday morning, I collapsed into a pew near the back of the church. I was worked over.

I had spent half of Saturday riding my bike to two different drugstores to find the right lady diapers and hair dye, and then did a full tint and two root touch-up jobs for Church Ladies. Afterward, Deuce and I had done an epic trail run. I was determined to become a real asset to the team. Deuce had amped up the challenge factor for me, and I was feeling it.

I stretched my legs out under the pew and prepared to just zone out. Mom had her smiling church face on as she looked out at me from the pulpit, but I knew she would give me the business later. She liked me sitting in the front row, not the back. I'd been the worship leader since I was old enough to totter around the front altar waving my arms like a conductor while people sang hymns. She'd probably call me up to the front later, but for now, I wanted to just keep a low profile in back.

Mr. Flynn and I used to be in charge of the flowers for Sunday morning services. He'd go to the Farmers' Market on Saturday and buy armloads of fresh flowers out of his own money. Sunday morning we'd go into the church early, and I'd run and fetch water for all the vases. He always made it look really fancy. Since he'd died, Mrs. Minelli had taken over. She'd buy pots of mums at the grocery store, and stash them all about. She'd wait until they died before she would even replace them. If Mr. Flynn could see all the half-dead pots of yellow mums, he'd put his head down on the pew and bang it.

Mom and I tried to get Deuce to take over the flowers, but he wouldn't ever come inside our church, unless something needed to be fixed. He always said he was "allergic to churches, but not to God." His church on Sunday was the gym on Fourth Street, where he'd put in a long workout while everyone else was sleeping in.

Even after all these months, I hadn't gotten over

missing Mr. Flynn, not even a single bit. Next to Deuce, he was the best man I ever knew. After all the years Deuce spent in prison, he deserved a happy life. It seemed so unfair that he had to live without Mr. Flynn now. I knew he would never get over missing him, either. But I knew firsthand that life wasn't fair.

Missing Mr. Flynn was like a thorn in my heart. Mom said that eventually the thorn works its way out of your heart. But the place where it was buried will always be sore.

My birth mother was like a piece of buried glass, not in my heart, but in my soul.

Wherever that was in a kid. It still cut me fresh when I thought about her not wanting me, and why she left me after she'd had me a few weeks. Had she been planning on keeping me at first, but after a month, something about me made her change her mind? Was I a terrible baby? And what if Mom hadn't found me, and I had frozen to death out there? What if a coyote or mountain lion had come down from the foothills and carried me off?

After a while, I made myself shut down all the noise of it. All I had were guesses, and what good did those do me? I think I had started to doze off when I was jarred by a body moving into the pew with me, moving to press shoulders with me.

My eyes flew open.

Micah was dressed up like he'd actually meant to come to church, and I instantly regretted putting on my oldest pair of church pants this morning. I'd been too tired to care. Micah's clothes were way nicer than mine. His shoes looked expensive, like something you'd see in a swanky catalog. Mine looked exactly like what they were—hand-me-downs from some other kid. I tucked my feet underneath me. I couldn't quite make sense of his clothes, since it sounded like his family was kind of poor.

He turned sideways, and gave me a grin. Then he handed me a songbook, like he was the home team and I was the visitor. Unfortunately, I didn't need the songbook because I knew how to sing every song forward and backward, and in pig Latin. But that didn't stop me from taking one, and pretending I was following along.

Not only did he look dressed up, but he smelled really good. Not like he'd slapped some drugstore cologne on, but more like he'd just been freshly baked and taken out of the oven. The smell made my mouth water. I swallowed and tried to pay attention to the music.

Impossible.

Being right next to him like this made me want to talk to him so bad, and it was driving me crazy that I couldn't. I hadn't heard from him since Friday. I'd texted him about getting my bike back, but he'd just sent me a thumbs-up emoji, and nothing else.

Micah had a pretty terrible singing voice, but he sang anyway, like it didn't matter. I had the voice of a girl angel, so I tried to sing quiet. Didn't want him to hear me.

I finally got the nerve to lean in close and whisper, *"What are you doing here?"*

He just shrugged. Nudged me with his shoulder.

After Mom finished her sermon, which could have been about penguins or pesto tortellini for all I knew, our usher, Mac, worked his way down the rows with the weekly collection basket. When he got to our row, he reached across, handing it to me, and then discreetly stepped back, like good ushers do. I pulled out my five bucks from my job that Mom made me contribute every week. As I put it in, I watched Micah reach into his pocket. And then like some kind of magician, instead of making a deposit like it seemed he was going to do, he made a nearly invisible withdrawal! The twenty that had been sitting on the top just disappeared.

He handed the basket over to the usher, and sat back, like it just hadn't happened.

It was one of the ballsiest moves I'd ever seen.

He gave me a sideways glance. In the light of the church, his eyes shone like emeralds. They made me feel dizzy.

I glanced around to make sure none of the ex-cons nearby had seen the twenty bucks Micah snatched. They were very protective of their rev.

I shot a glance at Mom, too, but she was busy setting up the little cups for communion.

I couldn't get my head around what I'd just witnessed. Did Micah think the collection basket was like a breadbasket, and you just helped yourself? That had to be it! Maybe he'd never been to church before. I'd talk to him afterward, and he'd probably be super embarrassed at his mistake.

When the service was mercifully over, people lingered in the foyer and on the church steps for doughnuts and coffee. Deuce always made sure this was all set up by the time we came out. If I never had another church doughnut in my life, it would be too soon, but Micah was taking great pains to select just the perfect one. He settled on a blue frosted one with sprinkles. Before he took his first bite, he picked off all the sprinkles, and flicked them away.

"Mm-hmm," he said. "Do you have fresh doughnuts every Sunday? I might become a regular here."

I tried to loosen my tie so I could breathe and talk. Too late I remembered it was a fake one. But not even a half-decent clip-on. The tie was attached to the shirt.

When I gave up and shoved my hands in my pockets, Micah reached over. "Here, I'll get it." He tugged at the knot. "What the heck," he said. "Is this thing sewn on?"

I tried to make a quick joke of it. "Yeah, I forgot. I sew all my ties on so I don't ever have to retie them."

"You're a funny guy," he said. "I like you. And you can sing! Your voice kind of reminded me of Justin Timberlake when he was still on the Mickey Mouse show."

I tried to focus on his compliment about me being funny, and ignore the other comment about Justin on Mickey Mouse. "Coffee?" I offered, desperate to appear more grown-up at this point.

"No thanks, I'm going to get some juice in a sec."

I poured a cup of coffee from the urn, like I did that all the time. Then I drowned it in half-and-half.

I took a slug of it, and tried not to spew it out. Tasted like milky gasoline.

He finished off his doughnut. "Now, that is a good breakfast," he said with a big happy sigh. "Is it cool if I have another one?" he asked.

"Of course," I said. "So you don't go to another church somewhere? Most churches have doughnuts. I think it's a law."

He swiped at his mouth with a small cocktail napkin and shook his head. "Never."

I knew it. He didn't know how things worked at church, and the collection-basket heist was all a big mistake. Maybe I should just let it go.

As if he had just read my mind, he slid the twenty bucks out from his sleeve and shoved it into his front pants pocket. "That will come in handy this week."

"Uh—" I started.

"Good morning!" Mom said, coming up behind me. "And welcome! You're Micah, right? Ham, you didn't tell me you invited him to join us. And I'm so glad you did!"

Micah held his hand out. "Yes! It's nice to meet you."

"Do you live around here, Micah?' she asked. "We'd love to have you come again. We just don't get enough young people. If you need it, we can always arrange a ride for you. Or do you usually go to services with your family?"

I gave Mom a secret warning tug on her cassock.

But Micah was quick and changed the subject. "Reverend, do you have any to-go bags for doughnuts? Or, maybe some kind of foil? I'd love to take a couple of these for my little brother, if that's okay, I mean."

"Absolutely, let me go get you something to wrap them in," she said, and bustled off. As always, she got waylaid, so she tapped Deuce to get some to-go things for Micah.

"Look," he said, "I'm going to split before your mom comes back. I just wanted to check out your deal here."

"I'm glad you came," I said.

"Meet me for lunch tomorrow, okay? Team table? Unless you know, you need to eat with your girlfriend every day. I mean, that's cool if you do."

"No! She's not my girlfriend. I mean, I don't have to eat with her *every* day. We just hang out. She lives across the street," I said, pointing to her house, but he didn't turn to look.

"Well, if she can spare you, I'll see you tomorrow."

"Sure! No problem, I'll be there," I promised.

"Good," he said. "See you tomorrow!"

He grabbed a couple more doughnuts, and threaded them onto his index finger. He jumped down the steps then, humming the song we'd just sung in church.

After Sunday brunch, I made a plan to spend the whole day with Fey. I wanted to try and make up for the fact that I wouldn't be having lunch with her at school the next day. Mom caught me just as I was heading out.

"Hold on, Flash!" she said just as I got to the door.

"You said we didn't have any hospital visits today." I'd been surprised but glad. I think Deuce had convinced her to spread these out during the week, rather than try to get to all of them on Sunday.

"We don't. But I kinda hoped you and I could spend some time together. I feel like I never get to see you anymore."

"Mom, we've been together all morning!" I said, giving her a nice pat on the shoulder.

"Not just the two of us, though. I miss you. When's the last time we spent a day together?"

"Uh, pretty much my whole life?"

"Smarty-pants. You know what I mean."

I sighed and my backpack slid off my shoulder into my elbow crook. "Mom, I really need to spend some time with Fey today."

"Is everything okay with her?"

"Yeah, but, well, cross-country takes up a lot of my time, and I don't want her to feel like I'm ignoring her."

She nodded in approval, but added, "When you say 'cross-country,' do you mean Micah?"

My backpack clunked to the floor. I grabbed it and hefted it back on with purpose. I was getting a whiff of a Mom Talk in the making. "Well, practices and training eats up a lot of time, but I guess Micah, too." My face started to flush at the mention of him, and I willed my cooling system to kick on.

"Will you sit with me a minute, Hammy?"

It sounded like a request, but I knew it wasn't. I moved over to the couch and sat down on the edge of it, carefully, like it just might detonate with any sudden moves.

"Let's talk about Micah. I know he's very important to you. And that means," she said, "he is important to me."

"Okay." I gulped. "I've already told you a bunch of stuff about him."

"Not quite everything," she said.

"Well, what else do you want to know? I've told you he has sort of a tough time at home, with his mom working all the time, and he's been so nice to me. I mean, he got all dressed up today and came to church. Even Fey hasn't done that!"

Mom curled her legs up under her and extended her arm across the back of the couch.

"How about we talk about him stealing from the collection basket?"

I held my breath. Uh-oh.

"Mac reported it to me after church. He always keeps an eye on the new people. It's not the first time someone has done it, and it won't be the last."

I dropped my eyes to my lap.

"Mac said he had a pretty slick sticky-finger routine."

"You're not going to bust him for it, are you?" My windpipe was in a near knot.

"Not this time," she said. "Right now I'll just pray to Big J about it. I imagine Micah has his reasons for stealing."

"He does, Mom! Good reasons, too. He's probably going to spend the money on food for him and his little brother."

"Is that what he told you today? He knows you saw him do it?"

I just nodded. And waited.

She waited, too.

"He's a nice kid, Mom. I know it probably doesn't sound like it to you, but—"

"Right now I'm more concerned with how it sounds to you, Ham."

"I know you think he should probably ask an adult for help, rather than stealing."

"And what do you think?" she prodded.

"I think I like him a lot, Mom. I *really* like him." I held her eyes then.

She studied me a minute. "I know you do, son. I understand that you *really* like him."

I blew out a big breath. "Then can you please understand that I don't want to talk any more about this?"

"Okay, for now," she agreed. "But here's the deal. I need to get to know him better. I want you to have him over. We still haven't done that. Got it? And at some point, I'd like to meet his mom, too."

"Please, *please* don't say anything to him ever about the money he took today? I would die if you did."

"I'm not planning to. But if he comes back to church, and I hope he does, I want you two sitting in the front row. Deal or no deal."

"Deal," I said. And with that, I made my escape.

# CHAPTER TWENTY-ONE

Fey and I had signed up to paint decorations for the upcoming Fall Frolic. We were on the back patio at her house, where we'd laid out big rolls of paper and our supplies. We planned to make giant leaves painted in all sorts of colors. Fey was making sure all the leaves she drew were native to the area. I was responsible for the lettering. Buster kept throwing himself on the paper, and ended up getting a lot of paint on his backside. Before long, all three of us were decorated in fall-colored paints.

I looked up after finishing a mammoth *F*, and found Fey staring at me.

"What?" I asked. "Does it look okay?"

"Looks great! I was just thinking about the dance.

You've never been to one?"

"Nuh-uh," I said, mixing more paint. "Well, sometimes at the weddings my mom does, people dance afterward. But that doesn't really count, does it?"

"Do you like to dance?" she asked.

I looked up and shrugged. I was trying hard not to think about the dancing part.

"I have kind of a confession," she said. She picked up Buster and buried her face in his warmth.

"What is it?" I asked.

She looked up over Buster's ears. "I don't know how to dance."

"Oh, me neither," I said.

"Ruh-roh!" we said in perfect unison, then both laughed.

"But you've been to dances before, right?" I asked.

"Yeah, but I usually just serve the punch or something. I probably should have told you I didn't know how to dance before I asked you to go with me."

"I still would have wanted to go with you," I said, and smiled.

She blushed. "So, should we try and learn?"

"Like take lessons, you mean?" I shuddered at the thought.

"No, not lessons. But, well, how did all the other

kids learn to dance?" she wondered aloud.

"Maybe their parents taught them?"

Fey shook her head. "No thanks. I've seen my parents dance. Those moves should not be passed on to a new generation. So, I looked online and there are dance videos that teach you basic moves."

"Awesome," I said. "When we're done with this, let's go watch some. It can't be that hard, can it?"

"Famous last words, right?" she said with a laugh. She bent over the banner, and drew the outline of another leaf. She went on talking but didn't look up. "I'm so glad I met you this year, and super glad you decided to go to public school."

"I didn't exactly *decide* to go to public school," I corrected. "I really didn't have any choice, with Mom getting sick and all."

"But aren't you a little bit glad it worked out this way? I mean, look at you, you're running cross-country and meeting all kinds of new people."

"Well, the classes are kind of boring, because Mom and I were way ahead of eighth grade already. I could have just skipped a year of school while Mom got better. I wouldn't have lost anything by doing that."

"You would have missed the Fall Frolic," she teased.

I flicked my paintbrush at her for that and left a spray of green freckles on her face.

"Hey, no fair!" she yelled, but not in a mad way.

She put her thumb over the top of her bottle of root beer and gave it a good shake. I ducked just in time to avoid a full soda bath.

"Ha!" I laughed, and wiped my sticky arm off with the bottom of my T-shirt.

"Well, this is turning out to be such a fun year for me," she said. "You know this is the fifth school I've been to? It was easier to make friends in the early grades. After sixth grade, kids aren't as nice to the new kid. Last year was awful," she admitted.

"What happened?" I asked.

"Nothing!" she said. "Nothing is what happened. Everyone already had a best friend. It's not that I don't mind my own company. It's just really nice to have a real friend at school."

"Yeah," I started, and stopped. I needed to tell her about wanting to eat with Micah and the team sometimes, but how could I?

"But," she said, reading my mind as she often seemed to do, "that doesn't mean you won't have other friends."

I nodded, but still couldn't find the right words.

"Look, I know Micah wants to hang out with you sometimes, too. It would be nice if the three of us could be friends, but I don't think he likes me much."

"It's not that," I said. "I'm sure he likes you. He mostly likes guy friends, I think."

"Except for Bijou," she said.

"Well, right," I admitted. "But I'm not sure they're friends much. I think they've just known each other a long time."

I hesitated a minute, wondering if I could talk to Fey about Micah. The idea of trying to explain the feelings I was having for him scared me. I hadn't even figured it out for myself yet. What would she think? I just knew that I really wanted her to like him.

"You know, Micah came to church this morning."

"Really?" she said, sounding very surprised. "Did he come with his mom and brother?"

"No, he just came alone. I think whenever his mom is home, she is sleeping. He never talks about a dad, and I'm guessing he isn't anywhere around."

Fey picked up her field guide to check on another leaf shape. "It's weird, isn't it? You'd never guess that about him. He seems like the kind of kid who has everything going right for him. Well, he's lucky to have you for a friend. Just be careful, will you?"

"What do you mean?"

She paused a minute as if to choose her words very carefully. "I'm not even sure I should tell you this."

My heart began to thrum. "You can tell me," I said. "I want to hear it."

Fey sighed. "I heard some girls in gym class talking about him. They were talking about how really cute he was. But I guess they've known him for kind of a long time. They said that he was always stirring up trouble for people."

"Huh" was all I could come up with to that.

"But you know, you can't ever let people decide what someone is like. You have to discover that yourself."

I flashed on him stealing money from the collection basket, but that wasn't stirring up trouble. That was him trying to make life better for Mason.

"It's just that you're so nice, Ham. I don't want him to take advantage of you."

"I'm pretty sure Micah is not that kind of kid," I said.

"Good! Anyway, don't feel bad about making other friends. That's a good thing! Maybe I'll meet someone, too. I'm just glad to hang out with you when I can. Now c'mon, let's go inside and learn how to dance."

*Dear Principal Strickland,*

*I know you are very busy at work, so I wanted to save you from having to meet with me about my bike being locked to your car. I sure am sorry about that! I hope you weren't late to your meeting.*

*I lost my bike at the library. I must have left the key in the lock, and whoever took it was trying to teach me a lesson about keeping it safe. I bet they figured if they locked it to your car, the principal of Harvey Mellencamp, you'd make sure it was returned to the rightful owner.*

*If it weren't for you, I wouldn't have gotten my bike back! I need my bike for my weekend job delivering things to the older ladies at my mom's church. It you ever need anything from the drugstore, you can just ask me. It will be free of charge, and I will deliver it right to your front door. I also can do root touch-ups.*

*In summary, I'm very glad we were able to clear this up without a meeting.*

*Very sincerely yours,*

*Ham Hudson*

# CHAPTER TWENTY-TWO

Coach Becerra jogged out of the gym toward the track. Buster hurried behind her. I tried not to smile. Having found me at the track a couple of weeks back, Buster liked to come and look for dropped popcorn under the bleachers.

After nearly a month of practices, we knew the drill once Coach arrived. We all quickly lined up and grew quiet. She grabbed a bottle of water from the cooler that Jet wheeled out. She gave us all a long look as she put the cap back on and wiped her mouth with the back of her hand.

"Well, well! Everyone is here, and everyone is on time. Is it my birthday or something?

Micah, you're not dressed. Aren't you running today?"

"I can't, Coach. I had a terrible leg cramp last night, and my calf still bites. But I didn't want to miss practice. I thought I could just stay and watch all the gear. I've got homework I can do."

"Fine, thank you. Jet, will you show Micah some good stretches for his leg?"

Jet gave her a quick salute.

"All right, then, before we warm up, I wanted to announce that I've made my decision about team captain."

I shot a glance over at Bijou. She straightened up. I could tell she was ready to receive her crown. If Coach made her captain, my life on the team was about to get bad. Very bad.

"I told you all at the beginning of the season that our captain would be the person who showed the most respect for the sport and the team. And part of that is attendance. The only team member who hasn't missed a single practice is Ham."

Micah clapped his hands and hooted.

Bijou erupted. "Coach, I haven't missed a single practice!" She turned and shot me a look of death.

"Settle down, Bijou!" Coach said. "You have been to every practice, but you've been late three times. You were warned."

Coach made a motion with her hand in my

direction. I looked around to see who she meant.

"Ham, come on up," she called.

I moved toward her, but tripped and stumbled over Logan's foot on the way up.

"Sorry!" I said to him.

"Congratulations!" Coach said to me, and shook my hand. Then she turned toward the team. "Ham Hudson will be team captain of the Mellencamp Mountain Lions cross-country track team. Not only has he demonstrated good sportsmanship, but he is a strong and dedicated runner."

The team, with the exception of Bijou, clapped and those around me slapped me on the back. I was stunned.

Bijou blew up. "Coach! I told you it wasn't my fault. Mr. Nunez kept me late in class every time."

"I understand that," she said. "And I spoke to Mr. Nunez about why he was making one of my best runners late to practice. He had good reason. Enough said."

Bijou folded her arms across her chest, and I could almost imagine the conversation in her head. I guessed she was deciding whether to walk off the team, or bite the bullet.

After a few moments, she raised her arm in the

air. "Coach Becerra?" she asked, her voice calmer.

Coach dropped her clipboard to the ground and drew a breath before she answered. "Yes, Bijou?"

"I'd like to request that I be made assistant captain. I think I've earned that."

Coach looked surprised, then considered it a moment. She looked out at all of us. "Is there anyone else here who would also like to be considered for assistant captain?"

The team went silent as stone.

"Well, Ham, is that okay with you? Does that seem like a good partnership to you?"

*What I was thinking*: No! NO! NOOOO! Are you kidding?

As if Bijou needed more reason to see me fail, or disappear, or get hurt on the trails.

*What came out of my mouth*: "That's fine, ma'am."

My happiness at being made captain took a rapid nosedive. Why couldn't Micah or anyone else have raised their hand when Coach asked for others who might be interested? Probably because Bijou would have made them pay.

Coach nodded. "All right, Bijou, your job as the assistant captain is to support and protect our team captain, then. You have his back here, on the trails, everywhere. Understand me?"

"Yes, Coach," she said. "But if something happens to him, I mean, I'm the captain if he's not around, right?" she asked.

"Ham, do you foresee any reason that you wouldn't be around to lead the team through our season?" Coach asked.

"No, ma'am."

"Fine. So, Bijou, again, your job is to help support and protect the captain for the duration of the season. Are we clear on that?"

"Yes, ma'am," she said.

"Our first meet is November fourteenth. That is a month away. By then, I expect this team to be the strongest that Harvey Mellencamp has ever seen. Starting today, I want everyone's mind in the game."

She reached into her pack on the ground and dug out a brand-new safety vest that read *CAPTAIN* across the back. She handed it to me and I pulled it over my head, dazed. Micah started a big hoot and holler until everyone joined in.

Except Bijou. She leaned over and retied both her shoes.

The whistle finally shrilled. "Let's go! Captain, lead us out! Bijou! You and Jet bring up the rear!"

My arms and legs dissolved to jelly. I wondered if I'd be able to run at all. I drew in the deepest breath I could find. I led the team around the track for two warm-up laps and then toward the big park behind the school. Adrenaline without oxygen was a lethal combo. I gave myself a god-awful side cramp. I pushed into it under my vest and tried to get it to let go.

Coach ran up beside me. I could feel her looking at me. "Bre-e-a-t-h-e, Ham."

"Try-ing . . . ," I panted. "Got a cramp."

"Do you want to drop to the back for a bit? I can get Jet up here."

I shook my head hard. "No! But . . . maybe . . . you-should-have . . . picked . . . someone . . . else . . . for . . . cap-TAIN!"

"Nope, you're the right guy."

She swiveled around, running backward and yelling at the team.

"We're going to work on our breathing today! I want everyone to close your mouth, and take a deep breath IN through your nose—good—now open your mouth—blow it out hard. Good! Again! C'mon—big breath IN through the nose—now blow it out! Big breath in—blow it o-u-t. Keep going!"

Six repeats later, the red-hot cramp in my side

loosened its wicked teeth. Relief flooded through me. My arms and legs returned to muscle and sinew. I wiped the sweat from my forehead, and fell into the natural rhythm of running.

Coach sidled up to me, still running backward. She looked over at me.

I gave her a thumbs-up and a smile.

She nodded and grinned back.

I felt a surge of gladness race through me.

This wasn't the first time in my life that I had kids running behind me. But before, they'd been chasing me to bully me or make fun of me. This was the first time in my life that kids had been running behind me because I was their leader. It was nearly more than I could take in.

I smiled so long and hard through practice that my teeth were covered in trail dust.

# CHAPTER TWENTY-THREE

There was no one in the whole student body or faculty at Harvey Mellencamp Junior High more excited about the Fall Frolic than Mom.

Deuce came in at a close second, tied with Fey.

I was not in the top ten.

I would have been more excited if I'd known if Micah was going to be there. But every time I asked him, he just shrugged like a school dance was too lame to even consider. I told him that Fey and I were going together, and we could pick him up if he needed a ride. I wondered if he didn't have money for a ticket. I couldn't think of a single way to offer to buy him one without embarrassing him, or embarrassing me with my desperation to have him there.

So I waited, and hoped. It wasn't that I wanted to

go with him, instead of Fey, but I just needed to know if I'd see him there, and maybe we could hang out a bit. Maybe he could get to know Fey a little bit better, and then maybe finally the three of us could all be friends. It would make my life so much easier.

Deuce and Mom were in the kitchen cleaning up after dinner. Deuce had made smoked baby back ribs and brought them over. For Mom, he'd baked a lemon garlic salmon. Buster had gotten to sample both, and he was laid out on my bed giving himself a luxury spit bath while I got ready.

Mom had asked me three times what I was going to wear to the dance. I told her I was all set. I knew she was dying to come pick out an outfit for me—most likely a pair of church pants, a button-up shirt, and a sweater of some kind. She also wanted me to get my hair cut for the dance, but I liked how my hair was just fine. It finally had started to look like the other boys' hair, not too long and not too short. Not too combed and not too messy. It was just right.

I'd overheard Mom tell Deuce before dinner that she thought I was starting to get "hormones" because all of a sudden, I needed privacy and got prickly when she asked too many questions.

Deuce chuckled. He told her that I was right on

schedule, and that was just how boys were with moms.

My phone pinged, and I reached for it. It was probably Fey asking if I wanted to practice our new dance moves before we left for the school. Whatever Fey did, she did all the way. She ran on a never-ending loop of study/practice/repeat. I liked that a lot about her.

But the message was from Micah! My stomach sat up and fluttered its wings.

HIM: **i might go to the dance my mom has the nite off and im not doing anything**

ME: **great need a ride?**

HIM: **naw i can catch a ride with bij.**

I let out the breath I'd been holding. I'd prayed that Bijou wouldn't be at the dance. To her credit, she'd been decent since I was made captain, but I still didn't trust her as far as I could throw her. And the idea of her and Micah showing up at the dance together made me feel . . . I dunno what it was, but I didn't like it.

ME: **k will see you there soon**

I pulled a shopping bag out from under my bed. I'd bought new stuff to wear to the dance, with money I'd earned from the Church Ladies. I'd hidden it from Mom so she wouldn't be tempted to iron any of it or embroider *Team Captain* on my shirt pocket. I'd bought new jeans that were already faded and ripped in some places, and a dark blue T-shirt that was kinda big on me. The girl who worked at the store had insisted it was the right size. On top of that, she'd talked me into a bomber jacket. She'd told me I'd "kill" at the dance in this outfit. I also bought some black tennis shoes that were more for style than running. She'd tried to convince me to buy some guy perfume, and finally coaxed me into taking a small sample for the dance night.

The front doorbell rang, followed by a chorus of high-pitched ladies' voices.

I took a final look in the mirror before I went out. I looked sort of grown-up, and it startled me a little. I wondered, as I had a million times before, if I looked more like my birth dad or my birth mom. Or, if I had brothers or sisters I looked like, too. I used to worry when I was younger that one day, I would accidentally run into someone who looked just like me. What if they'd try to get me to come back and live with them? And, worse even, what if Mom was relieved, because then she could have her own parents back in her life and more time to be a priest.

In my head, I knew that would not be true. But like a lot of things in my life—like Micah, for instance—my head and heart didn't always have the same opinion about things.

Mom rapped on my door then. "Ham, you about ready? The Ladies are here to see you off."

I caught a quick glance at Mom's face before the Church Ladies surrounded me in a group clutch. She looked surprised, but not horrified at least. It was probably killing her, though, not to be able to run over and tuck my T-shirt into my pants.

"Oh, Hammy!" Mrs. Dort cried, squeezing my shoulders.

Mrs. Minelli moved in to smell my neck. "You smell so good, Ham. Are you wearing cologne? Tina, come over here and smell our boy!"

Mrs. Paschal worked her way to the front of me, and handed me a plastic food container. Inside was a huge sunflower with a giant pin stuck through it. "Darling, I know you're so busy with school, so I made Fey a little corsage. In case you forgot to get her one."

Oh right, a corsage! I'd seen that in a movie about a school dance. Was I supposed to get Fey a corsage for a Fall Frolic?

Mom hurried over and spanked the back of my jacket for pretend lint. "Isn't that lovely!" Mom said. "Fey will love it, I'm sure. Thank you, Yvonne!"

"Uh yes! Thanks, Mrs. Paschal."

"Looking sharp, kid," Deuce said. "You excited?"

I shrugged, then smiled. "A little, maybe." I leaned in closer so only he could hear. "Can we get out of here now?"

"Sure thing," he said. "Ladies, if you will all excuse us, I need to get Ham and Fey over to the gym. Nice to see you all!"

Mrs. Minelli patted a five-dollar bill into my hand. "In case you two have snacks after the dance."

I was smothered in hugs and kisses and a few photos before the Ladies let me go. Most of them had changed my diapers and bathed me when I was little, so they all felt very entitled to ~~manhandle~~ ladyhandle me. Mom looked dazed and like she might start bawling any minute. "Have a great time, Ham" was all she said, but then reached for a tissue to blow her nose.

Deuce and I escaped to the cool relief of the porch. My mouth dropped open when I saw what was parked in our driveway.

I turned to look at him. "You're taking us in the Mustang? We're not going in the pickup?" I asked.

Deuce put an arm around me and pulled me in a bit. "I sure am," he said.

"But you hardly ever drive it—I mean, you mostly

just work on it." And what I didn't say was that I knew he and Mr. Flynn had liked to take it out for a Sunday drive each week.

Deuce cleared his throat and jangled his keys. "Well, I do for special occasions, and this is one of those times."

"Wow" was all I could say. The streetlights bounced off all the chrome and fenders.

Fey came scurrying across the street. She had on a green shiny dress and new boots. She'd put her hair into a big curly bun on top.

Deuce gave me an elbow.

"Fey, you look so nice!" I handed her the corsage. "One of the Church Ladies made it. You don't have to wear it, if you don't want," I said. "It's kind of big."

She smiled and studied it a moment. I half expected her to reach for her field guide to recite its origins. "It's so cool! I've never had a corsage before."

Deuce opened the passenger door of the Mustang for her. "Thank you, kind sir," she said with a happy grin.

"Nothing but the best for you two."

From the driver's side, I climbed into the back seat. I'd sat back here before, but only when it was parked and Mr. Flynn had been working on it.

Fey swiveled in her seat, and gave me a big smile.

"You look nice, too, Ham!"

Deuce turned the ignition, and the Mustang fired right up. It was a classic beast. We arrived at the gym too soon. Deuce pulled up right in front, and even in neutral gear, you could feel the Mustang ready to rear up and take off.

He got out to let me out from the back. Door, he mouthed, nodding in Fey's direction.

"Right," I said, and hurried over to the passenger door. Fey already had her door open, but I held it for her and closed it behind her.

"I feel so grown-up and so fancy," she giggled.

And me? What was this feeling? I think I felt like a regular kid. I even looked normal. Just weeks ago, I couldn't have dreamed of a night like this—me and my first-ever friend, Fey, headed to a public school dance in the coolest car in Muddy Waters. What else could a kid possibly want?

I knew exactly what else. I wanted a chance to see Micah tonight. I drew a deep, steadying breath. My cell was in my coat pocket, and my fingers played lightly over the keys like a piano piece while my heart provided the bass.

# CHAPTER TWENTY-FOUR

The school gym was ablaze with lights and throbbed with music and excitement. Students, teachers, and parents stood around out front. It wasn't quite eight p.m., so the doors probably weren't open yet. As soon as Deuce had pulled up in front, heads had turned. Some of the adults came toward us, making a big noise about how cool the Mustang was. Deuce had to roll down his window so he could answer their questions. I could tell he didn't mind.

"Call me when you're ready for pickup," he hollered as we waved and hurried off.

"Nice ride, Hudson!"

"*Cool* wheels—is that your grandpa's car?"

And then, of course—"Where's your kitty, Cat Boy?"

I just blew it off. Honestly, I was getting used to it. And besides, I wasn't just Cat Boy anymore. I was a team captain.

Fey and I worked our way through the throng. I spotted Micah right off. I had developed a radar for his presence. He had his hands shoved in his pockets near the front door. He was alone.

I steered Fey toward him but hoped she didn't notice.

"Oh hey!" I said.

"Hi, Micah," Fey said.

"Whose car?" he asked, pointing with his chin to the curb where Deuce was still parked with his Mustang fans.

"My friend Deuce," I said. "You remember, you met him at Dino's that day."

Micah turned toward Fey then, and nodded in her direction.

"Uh, did Bijou decide not to come?" I asked, trying to keep my voice neutral.

"Nah, she's here. We're both working at the team booth tonight. Coach told us she would comp us dance tickets if we helped out. She knew from Fey that you two already had your tickets. I better get back. I just came out to see if you were out here yet."

"Oh!" I said, feeling a heady buzz at the thought he'd been looking for me.

"Cool jacket," he said, then turned to Fey again. This time he looked her over. "And that's some corsage you got there," he said, nodding toward the mega-flower pinned to her dress.

Fey blushed, and jutted her chin out a bit. "Isn't it pretty?"

"Did you make that for her?" he asked me.

"Well—I—uh . . ."

"Never mind." He just shook his head and clapped me on the back. "Don't forget to come buy some raffle tickets," he said over his shoulder as he left.

I looked down at Fey's corsage, and then scanned the crowd of kids nearby. None of the other girls were wearing corsages. "Really, if you want to take it off, it's okay."

"Are you kidding? Of course I am going to wear it." She tucked her arm in mine and gave me a big smile. "And I'm going to press and save it in my journal so I will always remember tonight. Micah is just jealous," she said.

The idea that he might be gave me a little thrill. And I wondered if it meant Fey thought Micah liked me in *that* kind of way.

The doors flew open then, and we pulled out our tickets and moved to get in line.

We were quickly shoved through the door by the mob of students eager to get inside.

I couldn't believe it was the same boring, smelly gym where we had school assemblies.

"Wow! Everything looks great!" I said, and it was true. There were tons of hay bales all around, and big leaves hung on strands of twinkly lights above us. The music was loud, and it was almost impossible to talk without shouting.

"Look!" Fey said, and pointed to our banner, which hung right over the DJ stand.

"Fey!" I shouted close to her ear. "Can we go to the cross-country table first? I want to buy some tickets." I also wanted to make sure Micah wasn't mad about me coming with Fey.

"Sure!" she shouted back, and we scoured the gym for the right table. Different teams and clubs were hosting raffles to help raise money.

"There! See where Ms. Becerra is standing?" Fey steered me over in the right direction.

Micah and Bijou were seated behind the booth while Coach chatted with nearby teachers.

Micah had the cash drawer on his lap, and Bijou was tearing off tickets. Becca was standing near the table redoing her ponytail.

Seeing Micah with the cashbox made me uneasy. I hoped he wouldn't help himself to some of the proceeds. Coach was right next to him, but he was kind of fearless. That might not stop him. I just didn't want him to do anything stupid that would get him kicked off the team.

I braced myself as I always did around Bijou. For the occasion, she had found clothes even grungier than what she wore to school. She had ringed all around her eyes with purple eyeliner. She looked scary.

"Ahoy, Captain," she said with a fake friendly smile and a salute. "How many?"

"Five," I said, and pulled out the five-dollar bill that Mrs. Minelli had given me.

Micah snapped it out of my hand quickly. "I'll take that!"

Fey leaned in around me. "Two tickets, please," she said.

Bijou ripped off two tickets for her. "Here you go, Mrs. Captain, and wow—nice corsage there." She then elbowed Becca, who was now watching us.

The music cut off then, and the DJ picked up the mic. "All right, Mellencamp Mountain Lions, time to cut loose! Everybody ON THE FLOOR!"

The speakers blasted with the song's opening.

*Been working so hard*

*I'm punching my card*

*Eight hours, for what?*

Fey thrust her money at Micah and grabbed my hand. "Omigod, Ham! It's the *Footloose* song!"

We'd watched the movie *Footloose* about four times while trying to learn to dance. We both liked it because it was about an outsider who manages to win everyone over.

I hesitated a moment, and Bijou seemed to catch a whiff of my nervousness.

"Get to it, Captain! I've seen you run, but can you bust a MOVE?"

Fey pulled us out to the floor, turned toward me, and started to dance. She waved her arms overhead and bounced to the music. She had the best grin on her face.

I felt paralyzed for a second, like a kid on a cliff with a bungee cord and second thoughts. Fey and I had practiced for hours—I could do this. *Right?*

Bijou and Becca came at me then onto the dance floor in force, pushing between me and Fey, and twirling me at warp speed.

"Wooo-hooo!" Bijou yelled.

Becca grabbed my waist and chicken walked

around me while Bijou pulled my arms overhead.

I felt dizzy, and I kept losing Fey. The dance floor was total chaos. Kids danced in groups, instead of with one person. This was also not in my eighth-grade orientation packet. How the heck were you supposed to dance with so many people?

Bijou and Becca stuck to me like static cling. They wouldn't let go, and I couldn't shake them.

Fey came up behind me and shouted into my ear. "IGNORE them. Let's just have fun!"

Bijou and Becca seemed determined to cut Fey from their dancing bumper-car games. I got between them to grab hold of one of Fey's hands. I wanted to get us away from them.

Instead, I pulled Fey right into a tight tangle of Bijou's and Becca's footwork.

Fey fell forward, a belly flop in slow motion, and then hit the floor. The music stopped just as she was fully flayed out.

Becca, Bijou, and all the kids around us stepped back and encircled Fey. I dropped down to help her back on her feet.

"Fey! Are you all right?"

She raised her head, took a big breath, and gave me a shaky smile. "M'kay."

Fey scrambled to get her feet under her as I pulled

her up as gentle as I could. Corsage petals littered the gym floor. What was left of it on her dress had been pancaked.

Bijou slid up next to us, and patted Fey's dress down where the layers were all ruffled up. "Man, that looked like it hurt. You sure you're okay?"

I glared at Bijou and Becca hard until they backed away. They raised their hands up like they were innocent bystanders, only trying to help. Fey limped slowly from the floor. She seemed to be trying not to put too much weight on her right foot. I helped her sit down on a bottom-row bleacher.

"You've hurt your ankle!" I said.

"It's fine," she said, but winced when she tried to slip her boot off.

"You all right here a sec? Let me go get you something to drink," I said, though thirst was probably the last thing on her mind. Her face was bright red, and I wasn't sure if it was from all the dancing or from embarrassment.

She nodded, pulled the carcass of her corsage off, and studied the damage. She stroked the remaining petals like it was this that hurt the most.

I returned in a flash with a bottle of water. "Here," I said, opening it for her, and waited until she took a long sip.

She wiped her mouth with the back of her hand and mouthed, *Thank you!*

Seconds later, Bijou hurried toward us with Coach in tow. "Here she is!" Bijou said, pointing to Fey.

Coach squatted down next to her. "Fey, I heard you took a spill. You all right?"

"Just turned my ankle is all," she said with a one-shoulder shrug.

"Right or left? All right if I take a look?" Coach asked.

Fey nodded. "It's no big deal."

"Humor me, then," Coach said. She pulled out her cell and turned the flashlight on. "It's swelling up a little. Let's get some ice on this. Bijou! Run and get me a bag of ice from concessions."

Bijou ran off with Becca in tow.

"What happened?" Coach asked, the flashlight still on Fey's ankle. "Did you slip on something?"

"Just me being clumsy," she said.

"It's all my fault," I said. "I had her hand and was trying to pull her away—"

Fey shook her head. "Not your fault, Ham, really. And it's fine."

"Can you put weight on it, Fey?" Coach continued.

"Yeah, I walked over here on it. Probably just a tiny twist."

Bijou arrived with the ice, and Coach turned Fey and had her put her leg up on the bleacher bench. I took my jacket off, and Coach folded that under her leg. She molded the bag of ice around the top of Fey's ankle.

"I know this is very cold," Coach said, "but it's the best thing." She checked her watch. "Keep this on for ten minutes, okay? I'll be back to check on you in a little bit," she said, giving Fey a gentle shoulder squeeze.

"Thanks, Ms. Becerra!"

Fey turned to look at me. "Wipe that guilty look off your face. Really, it's no big deal. I'll be good as new in just a few minutes."

I shook my head and exhaled hard.

"Aw, c'mon, Ham, this is the *Fall* Frolic, after all!" she teased.

"Har-har," I said. "I just wish it had been Bijou or Becca who had fallen, instead of you. I shouldn't have tried to pull you."

I hated that being my friend meant that Fey got some of the backwash meant for me. First Benny and Royce teasing her at school, and now Becca and Bijou here.

She looked up and over my shoulder. Her expression changed—chilled was more like it.

I turned to see Micah sliding in next to me on the bench. And he kept sliding until we were nearly attached.

"Hey!" he said, and then looked past me over at Fey. "Bij just told me you fell—you doing okay?"

She tucked in some hair that had come loose from her bun. "I'm fine."

"Can I borrow your date a sec?" he asked her.

She stroked the flower in her lap. "Sure, I guess."

"I don't want to leave," I said. "She's hurt." Though the honest, sickening truth was that I did want to leave her, for the chance to be alone with Micah.

But I wouldn't. It wasn't right.

"Whatever," he said. He leaned in close. "Just wanted to let you know that there is a very good chance you may win the cross-country team raffle tonight!"

I turned toward him, puzzled. "What do you mean? Aren't people buying tickets?"

"Oh yeah, we're selling plenty. But I've got a feeling you will win. Wait and see," he said, nudging me. He flashed me a slow smile.

His breath smelled like root beer, and I drew it in, capturing it. Still, I shook my head, not understanding what he was saying.

"Gotta get back! Take it easy, Fey!" He was gone

in an instant, leaving me breathless.

"What was that all about?" Fey asked.

"Something about the team raffle—not sure what he meant."

But an hour later, when the DJ announced the raffle winners, it was "HAM HUDSON" who was congratulated for winning the cross-country team raffle—a $100 gift certificate from Roadrunner Shoes.

My stomach dove. It went splat on the gym floor.

Micah had somehow fixed the raffle so I would be guaranteed to win. And he'd been so pleased with his plan that he couldn't resist telling me in advance.

Which made me what? Co-conspirator? Riding shotgun to his crime spree? First Dino's, then the collection basket, and now this. And maybe other stuff that I didn't know about.

I was getting in deeper and deeper with him. I had to figure out a way to help him stop stealing.

He'd even stolen my heart right out from under me.

# CHAPTER TWENTY-FIVE

Fey and I waited outside the gym for Deuce to pick us up. After the ice had come off her ankle, Fey wanted to keep dancing. Coach told her she could as long as it didn't hurt. We learned to find a less hectic area to dance. Fortunately, Bijou and Becca steered clear of us after that.

"That was some frolic!" Fey said, laughing. She lifted up my hand and whirled herself under my arm. "I'm starving, are you? I ate about a half dozen cupcakes, and I'm still hungry."

I shoved my fists into my coat pocket and felt the gift certificate folded up in there. After they'd announced my name, I'd asked Coach if she would draw another ticket. I'd told her it just didn't seem right for someone on the team to win. She'd laughed, thumped me on the back, and told me I needed to practice being a winner.

I did not feel like a winner at all. I felt like an accessory to fraud.

Micah had witnessed the conversation between me and Coach, and shook his head like I was completely hopeless.

"Ham! Wait up!"

I turned. Micah was in front of the gym by the door, and waved me over.

"Be right back," I said to Fey. "I'll just be a sec!"

Micah pulled my sleeve and led me over to the side of the gym. "Why did you try to give back your winning ticket?"

"Did you fix the raffle to make me win? You said before the drawing that I was going to win. How did you know that?"

He shot me a grin. "I might have thrown in a few extra raffle tickets with your name on them," he said. He looked quite pleased with himself.

"Did you pay for them?"

"No! Why would I do that? Besides, you deserved to win. You bought more tickets than any other kid. I just wanted to make sure you did win. Didn't want some entitled jerk who only bought one to get the prize. Besides, it's not like you and your mom are rolling in the dough. That prize will come in really handy."

*"MI-CAH!"* I whisper-screamed. "That's cheating! If Coach found out, you and I could both get kicked off the team."

"We're not going to get caught. I 'accidentally' threw away all the ticket stubs so she wouldn't be able to figure it out."

I leaned up against the wall and closed my eyes. He was unbelievable.

"Hey," he said, tugging on the front of my jacket. "Why are you getting so bugged about this? I did it because I *like* you."

"I like you, too, but what you did is wrong!"

"Fine. Here, give me the gift certificate," he said, holding out his hand. "I'll give it back to Coach."

"But what will you tell her? And does Bijou know what you did?"

"Of course not! I'm not stupid."

No, not stupid, I thought. Just reckless, and a cheater. That he did it because he "liked" me did not make me feel any better.

"Look," he said. "I'll figure out something to tell

Coach. I'll tell her you want to donate it to some kid who needs shoes. Seriously, though, Ham. Don't be such a preacher's kid, okay? It's boring!"

That stung, and I colored. "Just promise you'll make this right."

I didn't want to get kicked off the team. In a very short time, it had become really important to me. And Coach had trusted me when she made me captain.

"I will!" he said.

"Look, I gotta go. Deuce is on his way."

Micah peered around the corner of the gym, and then turned back. "He's not here yet. So, seriously, what is the deal with you and Fey? You two are always together. I never get to see you without her."

"We're just really good friends. It's not like that."

He tilted his head to look at me, then gave me a slow shoulder bump. "Good," he said. His voice was quieter now, and he stared at his feet. He looked up at me then, and gave me a long look.

I swallowed and looked back at him.

Neither of us said a word. But my heart thudded like a dryer full of shoes on spin cycle.

Micah shuffled his feet and slid one over, so it was right up against mine.

I didn't dare breathe. It was just two feet lined up

next to each other, but it felt like so—much—*more*.

"Ham!" Fey called. "He's here!"

Our feet jumped back, almost guiltily.

I reached into my pocket and handed him the gift certificate. "Promise me," I said.

"Dude," he said, and gave me a slow-motion fist bump and a soft smile.

I found my way to the car, dazed.

Mom was in the passenger seat of the Mustang. Her face lit up with a big smile and she waved when she spotted us. She popped out to let us into the back seat.

"Hey, you two! How was it? Was it fun? Did you get to dance a lot?"

Fey and I collapsed in the back seat, nearly falling on top of each other.

"Well," Fey said, breathless. "I fell on the dance floor, but once that was over, it was great! And guess what? Ham won a raffle and a hundred-dollar gift certificate for running shoes!"

"Wow!" Mom said.

Deuce caught my eye in the mirror. "Congrats! That's great. I'll take you shopping so you can get a second pair. It's nice to have a spare so you can let your shoes dry out between workouts."

My fingers curled in my pocket where the gift certificate had been. "Well, uh, I actually gave it away."

"You gave it away? To who?" Fey asked, staring at me.

I was silent, trying not to actually squirm in my seat.

"Did you just give it to Micah?" she asked, her voice incredulous.

"Yeah, but I told him to give it back to Coach. It didn't feel right that I won since I'm on the team."

It got very quiet in the car. I couldn't meet Fey's glance. She knew Micah had come over and talked to me about the raffle before I was announced. Had she heard him? Did she suspect something?

"Hey! I'm starving like an animal," I said to break the silence. "Fey is, too. Can we stop somewhere to eat?"

"Sure," Deuce said. "In-N-Out Burger work for everyone?"

Mom reached back without turning, and gave my knee a squeeze. She was probably thinking that I'd been a good Samaritan, giving my prize to someone who maybe needed it more than I did.

Fey shivered and pulled her sweater over her front. She stared out her window.

* * *

Later in the week Mom hosted a dinner for all the Church Ladies to thank them for their extra work since she'd had to cut back her hours. Deuce had made lasagna, salad, and garlic bread in advance. All Mom had to do was "heat and greet," he'd said. I begged off so I could work on what I told her was homework, but it really wasn't. She sighed hard but said okay.

"They'll be disappointed," Mom said. "But I understand. Your schoolwork is important. You're an excellent student, and I'm proud of you."

Nothing worse than getting a compliment from your mom after you just lied to her.

Every once in a while, Mom would look over my homework assignments and the stuff we were studying. She never said, but I could tell it was hard for her to have my education out of her hands. We both knew that I was repeating things I'd already learned, but we tried to make the best of it. We didn't really have a choice. Something in her life had needed to go.

And that had been me.

I planned to escape to the attic during her dinner party. I knew if I stayed in my room, every time one of the Church Ladies had to use the bathroom, they'd stop and knock at my door to say hello. I didn't feel like being interrupted all night. So before they arrived, I pulled down the attic ladder from the trapdoor in the hallway and headed up. As I turned to pull the ladder back up, I saw Buster hurrying toward it.

"Coming up, Buster?" I waited until he was safely up, and watched him head to his usual special place. He'd find it right off every time, tucked away in the corner.

Buster loved the manger where my birth mom left me.

He leapt right in, and began to paw at the towels in the bottom until he had it just right. He snuggled down and started his spit bath, purring like a John Deere tractor.

The attic was where the artifacts of my life lived. The rest of the Nativity scene was locked in the big shed behind the church, but Mom wouldn't risk having the manger out there. To her, it was the Ark of the Covenant.

It surprised me every time when I saw how tiny it was. Mom had kept both the towels that I'd been wrapped in. She always told me I had been perfectly "swaddled"—safely and securely. I used to study the towels, looking for some kind of clue to my former life. One towel had a big ad for Corona longneck beers on it. The other towel was plain and a faded rose color. I reached under Buster and pulled it out. Just like Buster couldn't help jumping into the manger every time, I couldn't help but want to smell the rose-colored one. I was sure that this one was my birth mom's personal towel. I imagined it hanging in her bathroom, and her grabbing it the night she decided to give me away.

I used to think that she had to have left a note, pinned to me, or something. Mom swore she hadn't. That always got to me. Why hadn't she left a note? It seemed like a thing a mother would do. For a while then, I was convinced that she had left a note, and Mom just wouldn't let me see it. Maybe the note said who she was, and why she gave me away.

When I'd beg Mom to show it to me, she'd pull me close to her and say, "Ham, there was no note. But she did leave me one very important message."

I'd stop, waiting to hear the rest.

"Her message was *where* she left you. She didn't leave you at the fire department, or a hospital, or even right up on our porch. She left you in the manger where Baby Jesus was."

She'd pause then, making sure I was paying close attention. "Her message was that, to her, you were the best and most loved baby on earth."

I'd finish, "And she was putting me right into God's hands that night."

"Exactly," Mom would say. "And why she had to give you back to God is just one of life's great mysteries."

And that was the story I had to live with.

I reached over and gave Buster a good scratch behind his ears. He turned his neck and leaned into my hand with all he had.

The mystery of what my birth mom did lived inside me. Even all these years later, my mind still wanted to wring the truth from it somehow. It was like an algebra equation that couldn't be solved:

*I was the best and most loved baby in the world* + *The mother of the best and most loved baby in the world gave him away* = "An equation for which we don't have a closed-form solution," my algebra teacher would say.

This unsolvable equation left me feeling like there were two of me. There was the mysterious baby boy left in a manger by my birth mom, and then there was the homeschooled church boy who had grown up with Mom. But I didn't want to be either of those anymore, and I sure didn't want to be both of those.

I wanted a third part that was just me, a regular kid, someone other kids would like. And that part had to be up to me.

It was time to turn up my own game. I wanted to be the best runner and team captain Harvey Mellencamp had ever seen. I wanted Micah to see me that way, and not see me as a boring preacher's kid. I wanted us to be tight friends . . . and maybe something more, but I couldn't quite get my head around that. And the problem with that was he didn't seem to care about Fey, and seemed tired of the fact that I was always with her.

The more that Fey saw of him, the less she seemed to like him. What if Fey decided she didn't want to be friends with me because I'd picked a kid she couldn't stand to hang out with?

I just had to make this work. But how could I possibly choose between them?

I didn't know that sometimes life takes the wheel and makes the choice for you.

# CHAPTER TWENTY-SIX

The last place I expected to find Micah that Thursday night was sitting in my living room when I got home. I was late because Coach had wanted to talk to Jet and me after practice about some upcoming trail runs. And I was dead sure I wasn't hallucinating because I was so surprised to see him that I tripped right over Buster, barely missing a face-plant on the floor.

Micah's laugh was real. Buster's hiss was real.

"Oh hey—" I said, trying to right myself.

"Hey, dude," he said. "Where've you been?"

The question almost made me laugh because Micah was the one who was so hard to find.

"Let me get you something to drink," Mom said.

"More iced tea, Micah?"

"Please! Thanks, Reverend."

Micah gave me one of his star-studded smiles as Mom headed into the kitchen. "So what's up?"

I had so many questions I didn't know where to start! Like—

What are you doing here with my mom?

Why weren't you at practice?

Why have you barely texted me this week?

What did Coach say when you gave her back the gift certificate?

But I settled for a casual, "Just got together with Coach and Jet to talk about our meet coming up."

"Bet she's mad at me for missing practice today," he said, reaching into his front pocket. He pulled out a ChapStick and rubbed it over his lips, over and over again. I could not look away.

I vowed to buy some ChapStick immediately.

"Want some?" he asked, holding the tube out toward me.

"Uh sure, thanks," I said like I used it all the time. Never had.

"Hope Coach doesn't bench me for the meet. You don't think she will, do you?"

I shook my head as I rubbed it over my lips. It

was warm from being in his front pocket, and it slid smooth across my mouth.

"She'll be mad, but we need you for the meet. I wish you'd tell her about how you have to pick up Mason from school some days when your mom doesn't get home in time."

He leaned in toward me and pointed at my mouth. "You have a little blob right there."

My finger flew to my mouth. I rubbed some more, embarrassed.

"No, here," he said, his finger on my mouth.

We didn't hear Mom come in at first. She looked at us both a second, not saying anything. I handed the ChapStick back to Micah underhanded, like we'd been doing something illegal.

She placed Micah's tea in front of him, and handed me a Gatorade.

"Thanks," we both said in perfect harmony. I blushed.

Mom headed back to the kitchen and pretended to be busy at the sink, like she wasn't listening.

"I can't tell Coach or anyone about my mom being gone all the time." He added three whole packets of sugar to his tea, gave it a vigorous stir, then looked up at me. "Promise you won't tell, either. The last thing

I need is somebody calling Social Services about us. They could pull me and Mason out of there because she's not supervising us enough."

"I won't tell Coach," I said, and hoped he didn't ask me if I'd told my mom already. Or Deuce. Or Fey. God, I was a total blabbermouth.

"How was practice anyway? Hope you kicked Bijou's butt."

"I'm not trying to kick her butt. She's my teammate. But it went okay. She's been mostly decent to me since the bike thing." At least at practice, anyway. I avoided her everywhere else.

Mom still hadn't come back in, which surprised me. I could hear her rummaging through the fridge, hoping as she usually did that shelves full of delicious food would magically appear.

"I haven't hardly talked to you since the dance," I said. I'd looked for him in the cafeteria at lunch, but he was always stapled to Bijou. I'd eaten with Fey but kept trying to catch his eye.

"You could talk to me every day if you'd eat with the team at lunch." He made patterns in the small hill of sugar he'd spilled on the coffee table. "But right—Fey."

Buster started doing fast figure eights between my

legs. For an instant, I wished I had a big pit bull. Dogs were cool. Cranky, jealous one-eyed cats were not.

"Your cat doesn't like me," Micah remarked. "He tried to bite me when I first got here."

"I'll have him put to sleep," I deadpanned, and then felt ashamed of myself immediately. I reached down and scratched the top of Buster's head. "Sorry, buddy, I didn't mean it."

Micah's eyes crinkled, and he laughed. "You're funny."

Mom came back in with a big plate of cheesy nachos topped with olives and red peppers that she'd heated in the microwave. She looked quite pleased with herself. Per usual, she'd nearly nuked the life out of them.

"Careful," I warned Micah. "She blasts the cheese until it runs like molten lava."

He grinned, and blew on his chip a couple of times before cramming it into his mouth.

Buster vaulted up on my lap and started doing a happy march in my crotch. He was a big melted-cheese fan. I set him down as fast as I could.

"Ham, why don't you go hop in the shower?" Mom asked. She put a few chips on a napkin and handed it to me. "This will hold you until you're done."

Go? Me? Why would I leave when Micah was there?

"I'll shower in just a bit," I said, giving her an eyeful of what I thought about her trying to get me to leave.

"Now is better. Micah and I were having a private talk before you got home. We need to finish our chat."

What? I thought Micah had come to see me. This did not compute.

"It's okay," Micah said. "He can stay."

Mom paused, looking back and forth between the two of us. "Tell you what," she said finally. "Let's you and I finish talking, and if you decide you want to share some things with Ham afterward, that's your choice. But for now, I'd like to have you all to myself. Okay with you?"

Micah nodded, his eyes cast down to his hands in his lap.

I couldn't believe I was getting the boot. Mom gave me a poky finger in the shoulder when I didn't get up. I glared at her. I got poky finger number two.

I unfolded myself from the chair and scooted it back.

"Thanks, son," Mom said.

Buster followed after me, meowing and scolding me for my recent bad behavior with the cheese. I closed my bedroom door, cursing myself that I'd never hidden a mic under the coffee table at some point. That would have come in extremely handy right now.

What were they talking about that Mom didn't want me to hear? I yanked off my shoes while a thousand crazy scenarios swirled in my head.

1. Micah's mother kicked him out, and he needed a place to stay.
2. He was getting bad grades at school and needed a tutor. He could tell I was really smart and wanted to hire me. He'd come to get Mom's permission.
3. He'd come to confess about stealing from the collection basket, and to pay the money back. Mom would be so impressed, she'd ask Micah to stay for dinner and a sleepover.
4. Something bad had happened to him, and he'd come over to tell me about it. But Mom had stuck her snoopy nose in it, and was poaching my chance to be a friend and hero to Micah.

I was good with numbers one, two, three. If it was number four, I was going to kill Mom. Seriously. She had no right to keep me out of this. Micah was my friend, not hers. Though the reasonable part of my brain knew that if Micah was in real trouble, my mom was the best person to talk to. Not an eighth-grade boy with very few street smarts like me.

I pressed my ear to the inside of my bedroom door. I could hear talking, but it was muffled. I looked around my room for a glass to hold up to the door, but for once, there were no dirty dishes in my room. Dang it! My eyes scanned the room for something else I could use. I spied a straw on my dresser and grabbed that. Stuck it in my ear and held it up to the door. Listened as hard as I could. I nearly gave myself an ear hernia. Nothing.

I got down on my belly and tried to listen through the crack in the bottom of the door.

And I was nearly annihilated by the smell of dirty socks near me. Dirty socks! A warning siren went off in my brain. What if Micah was going to come live with us starting tonight? Maybe he and Mason both. We only had two bedrooms in the parsonage, and I'd have to share my room. I started to freak. My room was a stinky, slobby boy mess. It used to be neater when I was homeschooled. Now with school, homework, and track practice, it was a wreck. My wet, sweat-soaked track clothes were draped over every surface, waiting for a weekend wash.

For the next few minutes, I became a human

Hoover, sucking up all the dirty trash, laundry, and evidence that a sloppy kid lived here. I found the rest of my cologne sample, rubbed it all into my hands, and waved them around. Buster started sneezing so bad I had to let him out.

I really needed to vacuum, but they would hear me, and Micah would think I was a big goober. Correction: Micah would realize I was a big goober. I put on a big, thick pair of socks and dusted the floor as best I could with my feet. I stripped the sheets off my bed and balled them up. I had to get some clean ones. Mom was better at church stuff than cleaning stuff. I hoped to God we had some. And truth be told, I couldn't even remember the last time I'd changed them. The linen closet was on the other side of the living room, so I'd have to pass Micah.

There was a loud rap on my door, and my head whipped toward it. My nerves felt like they'd just pulled an all-nighter at Starbucks.

"Ham?" Mom called from the other side.

I yanked the door open, way too hard. Easy, boy.

Mom started to say something, but then covered her mouth and nose with the palm of her hand. "What is that smell?"

"SHHH! Nothing!"

"Smells like Coco Chanel up and died in here."

I peered over her shoulder to make sure that Micah was still on the couch. And not hearing any of this. He was bent over, trying to get Buster to come up on his lap.

"I was coming to tell you that we finished our talk. We're all done. You can come back in, if you want." She gave me a once-over then. "But you haven't showered yet. And that perfume isn't going to cut it. Get in the shower."

"I was just getting ready to, but I needed to change my sheets."

She started to say something, and then seemed to stop herself. She moved past me and crossed the room. "I'm going to open your window so you don't suffer brain damage in your sleep."

I took a last peek at Micah to make sure he hadn't moved. He was still trying to pick up Buster. I moved back toward Mom. "I know you can't tell me exactly what you talked about because of the priest privacy thing, but can you at least tell me if we have any clean sheets?"

Mom gave me a confused look. "Do we have any clean *sheets*?"

"I mean, is he coming to stay with us? You know like how sometimes people in crisis come over late at night to see you? And then, sometimes, you have them spend the night? Because if he is, Micah can stay in my room. Or, he can have my room? But I'm going to need clean sheets."

"No, we are not inviting Micah to stay with us."

"Oh, okay. Well, can you at least tell me if he is okay? I haven't really gotten to talk to him all week."

"He's fine. We had an interesting talk. He mostly came over to ask me if he could interview me for a paper he is doing for a class."

"A paper? What kind of paper? About being a lady priest?"

"No, he wants to write about adoption. He said he is particularly interested in unmarried people who adopt babies."

I was shaking my head even before she finished her sentence. How the heck did he know I was adopted?

"Did you tell him you adopted me?"

"Of course not! He already knew. I assumed you told him. But it's not exactly a big secret around here. He could have heard it from anybody. Anyway, I told him to talk to you about it first. I'd only do it if you agreed to it."

I was still shaking my head, and she put her hands up in surrender.

"How about I invite him to dinner? We can at least feed the boy. I will make myself scarce at some point, and you two can talk about it."

I nodded and headed to find some clean clothes for after my shower.

She headed out my door, and called to him. "Micah?"

"Wait!" I said, grabbing the back of her sweater. "We don't know how to cook."

"We know people who do," she said. "That's close enough."

# CHAPTER TWENTY-SEVEN

Lucky for us, Deuce the Wonder Chef was home just looking for an excuse to do something with an eggplant he'd grown to the size of a shoebox. He'd figured out a "teen friendly" Italian feast for us in nothing flat. Mom had to convince him he had to eat with us, or no deal. In the end, we decided to eat at Deuce's house so he could cook in his own kitchen. Our knives were so dull, he'd said, even Jesus's own mother wouldn't be able to cut with them.

I thought we might have to work to convince Micah to stay and eat with us, but he pretty much jumped at the chance. I knew he didn't get a home-cooked meal too often, as in never, and that gave me a tight feeling across my chest. I wanted to learn how to cook so he and Mason could come over every night. Micah had showed me a picture of him on his phone, and he was pretty darn cute.

Micah was very curious about Deuce and his house. In fact, once we got over there, he acted like Mom and I were nearly invisible. He went bonkers for the place, and begged for a full tour. He stopped in the hallway to look at the pictures on the wall. They were mostly of Deuce and Mr. Flynn working on the cars, the house, the garden, and one of them at a baseball game.

After a moment, he turned to Deuce and said, "Who's the guy in all these pictures with you?"

Deuce wiped his hands on the dish towel he'd thrown over his shoulder. He paused a moment.

I butted in quick so Deuce didn't have to answer. "That's his best friend, Mr. Flynn. He died last spring."

Micah nodded, and turned back to study the photos again. "Sorry," he said. "I didn't know. He looks like a really great guy."

"It's fine," Deuce said.

I blew out the breath I'd been holding.

"Deuce!" Mom yelled from the kitchen. "Is your whatchamacallit in here supposed to be doing this?"

"Excuse me," he said, and hurried back to the kitchen. It was never a good idea to leave Mom unsupervised around electrical appliances. He called out over his shoulder, "Ham, go ahead and show Micah the rest of the house."

Micah headed toward the back, following the trail of pictures. He was a very curious kid.

I followed him, giving him space. I was happy just being in his wake.

He ran his fingers over a long table in the hallway, picking up a large polished shell. "Everything is so nice, so perfect. Deuce must have a lot of money." He sighed at that.

"Some, I suppose," I said, my hand following the path his fingers had just traveled.

He pointed to the only room with a closed door. "What's in there?" he asked.

"Oh, well, that's his office, kind of."

"I want to see," he said, his hand on the knob.

"Well, the door's shut. So, I'm not sure that's part of the tour."

"C'mon, he told you to show me the rest of the house."

Micah turned the knob and eased the door open before I even had a chance to respond.

"Oh, wow!" Micah said. "Check this out."

I followed him in, checking behind me to make sure Deuce wasn't coming.

Micah stood under the slick tandem bicycle that was mounted on the wall. It was as amazing as I remembered. It was a da Vinci, a top-of-the-line custom build, made just for Deuce and Mr. Flynn. Not long after they had met, Mr. Flynn and Deuce had started planning a coast-to-coast ride across the country together. It was something Deuce had dreamed about doing in prison, and it helped him get through his years in lockup. He wanted to see the whole country from its back roads. And Mr. Flynn had been super excited about the idea. I remember the two of them with their heads together over maps and atlases, charting their course.

"This is an expensive ride," Micah breathed, running his hand over the chrome-moly steel. "I had a stepdad for a while who was a cyclist, and he taught me a lot. These are all custom components. Probably Italian."

I'd stopped admiring the bike, and was studying all the oversized framed photographs that covered the entire wall around the tandem. There was Deuce and Mr. Flynn at the Golden Gate Bridge, where they started the trip, giant smiles plastered across their faces. And the two of them laughing at a roadside café behind giant cups of coffee on the Pacific Coast Highway. I couldn't remember the last time I'd seen Deuce that happy, but I was pretty sure it hadn't been since Mr. Flynn died.

Micah had torn himself away from the bike to look at the pictures, too. "Man, look at all the places they went on it."

"It was all one trip," I said, my voice quieter, like the one you used in church, or any place that felt—sort of holy.

"Why'd they get a tandem?" Micah asked. "You know, instead of just two separate bikes."

I made my voice even lower. "They were going to ride across the country on two bikes, but then Mr. Flynn got sick. Deuce decided that cancer wasn't going to stop them from taking the trip they'd planned for so long. So he talked Mr. Flynn into the tandem, so Deuce could, you know, do most of the peddling on the days that Mr. Flynn didn't feel good."

"Wow," Micah said, exhaling a breath, and moved across me to look at the rest of the photos. "Deuce is an amazing guy."

"Yeah, I know. So was Mr. Flynn." It still got to

me every time I thought about it. They really loved each other.

"If I had a bike this cool, I wouldn't just stick it up on a wall. I'd ride it," Micah said.

But Deuce hadn't. After Mr. Flynn died, he'd shut the door on all of this. I wondered if he even came in here anymore.

"Do you think he would let us ride it?" Micah asked. "I bet we could go super fast on it."

I shook my head. "I don't think it's for riding anymore."

"Boys! Dinner!"

Saved by the bell.

Micah moved to the door, and I put a hand on his arm. "Don't—" I started.

"I won't," he said. "I get it. I won't say anything to him about it. Geez, I'm not a moron."

I closed the door softly behind me. Not so Deuce wouldn't hear it, but so I wouldn't do anything to further disturb this silent tribute to their lives together.

Even though I'm sure the dinner that Deuce fixed was super delicious, it could have been roadkill for all I could tell. My mind was everywhere except eating. Micah was seated next to me, and had just slid his foot right next to mine. Just like he had at the dance. This time, though, it stayed there, holding pressure. I'd wondered what it meant since the first time. That he'd done it again now was still confusing. I knew it meant something, but I wasn't sure what.

"This is so good. I haven't had a real dinner for so long," Micah said. "I usually just eat cereal for dinner in front of the TV with—I mean, I don't usually get a real dinner."

He looked over at me, and his cheeks were pink. I knew he'd almost said "with Mason." I hoped to God that Mom or Deuce didn't ask about him.

"Your mom doesn't like to cook? Or, like Annie here, she doesn't know a roasting pan from a rotisserie?" Deuce teased.

Mom gave him a shocked look. "I do know how to cook. Ham and I are just very busy. We would rather spend our time expanding our minds, not our waistlines."

Micah grabbed the conversation then. "Hey, Ham, I talked to your mom earlier about adoption. I wanted to interview her for a paper for my social studies class. She said I should ask you. I think it would be really interesting to write about a single lady who adopted a baby."

I'd been so excited to have this time with him, I'd

almost forgotten that was why he'd come over in the first place.

When I didn't say anything right away, Micah continued, asking Mom, "I mean, did it take a long time to get a baby, since you were single? Is it easier for couples?"

"It's complicated," Mom said, shooting me a glance.

"Ham, did you ever wish you got adopted by a couple instead? You know, so you'd have a dad?"

I swirled my eggplant in fancy loops on my plate. Lifted one shoulder high, then dropped it. I was just on the verge of being a regular kid, and now this. I mean, it wasn't like I was dragged out of a dumpster, but that part of my life wasn't something I wanted to talk about, especially with Micah. If he'd found out somehow that I'd been adopted, what if he found out I was the semifamous local manger baby? There had been a lot of newspaper stories about me. Mom had kept them all. How long until Royce and Benny started calling me "Baby Jesus" or "Ham in a Manger"? And what if they found out about Buster, too? I hadn't even told Fey about that yet.

"I don't really think much about it," I said. A total lie. My first to him.

"Well, is it okay if I interview your mom at least?"

Micah asked. "You know, how it was for her?"

"Maybe you could find another family to talk to?" I suggested. "It's not a very interesting story."

Micah stared at me, the light fading from his eyes. I felt him slide his foot away from me. My stomach dropped.

"Can I get anyone dessert?" Deuce asked.

Mom started collecting plates. "I think we'll pass. I didn't realize it was getting so late."

"Of course! You three go on. I'll take care of all this," Deuce said.

"I'll stay and help," Micah offered Deuce. "I want to see the rest of your place. I bet the backyard is great, too. Do you have a pool?"

"Oh, Micah," Mom said. "It's getting late. Let's not overstay our welcome. We should call your mom to pick you up."

"I don't want to bother her," he said. "I'll just walk; it's fine."

"I can walk you home," I said.

"No thanks," he said. I felt a little whiff of frost blow toward me from his direction.

"Where do you live, Micah?" Deuce asked. "I can drop you off. I need to run out and pick up some coffee for the morning. No trouble at all."

"Could you just drop me off at the bowling alley? My cousin works there, and sometimes I go help her out. She can take me home when she's done."

"Sounds like a plan," Mom said. "Ham, why don't you go with the two of them? While Deuce is grabbing some coffee, pick up some cereal, will you? We're out."

"Sure!" I said. I'd hardly had any time alone with Micah tonight, with Mom all over us, and then dinner with everyone. I knew Deuce would let us talk in the car and not be all nosy. Though I hoped Micah wouldn't use the time to grill me for adoption info.

That case was closed.

# CHAPTER TWENTY-EIGHT

Micah and I waited outside while Deuce opened up the garage. The Mustang was draped over, tucked in for the night. Deuce climbed into his pickup truck and started the engine.

"Oh!" Micah said, sounding bummed. "I was hoping we could go in the Mustang. That is such a cool car! I'm going to ask him," he said.

"Not a chance," I said. "He hardly ever drives it. He mostly just works on it, and keeps it up."

"He drove you and Fey in it," Micah said.

"I know," I said, "I was surprised. Guess 'cause it was my first dance, or something."

"Huh." He walked away from me toward the end of the driveway.

I followed him. "Look, I'm sorry about your school paper and stuff."

"No big deal," he said, but clearly, it was from his tone of voice.

Once Deuce reached the end of the driveway, I opened the truck door and pulled the front seat up, so I could get in back. Micah slammed the seat back down, and jumped into the front seat. He acted like I wasn't even back there.

He asked Deuce lots of questions about driving a classic car. And other questions about his life. Like maybe he was going to write a paper on him, too. Deuce kept trying to draw me into the conversation, but Micah seemed way more interested in him. My armpits itched with nerves. I didn't understand why he was so bent out of shape about me not wanting him to write about my adoption. He didn't even care that much about schoolwork, I'd thought. Maybe I had done something at dinner that turned him off. I was pretty sure I hadn't burped, chewed with my mouth open, or spilled anything.

Maybe Micah had decided I was too big of a mama's boy to be friends with me. Though to her credit, Mom hadn't once called me "Hammy." My eyes narrowed. Maybe I was boring him to death, like Fey seemed to bore him. I couldn't bear the thought that he might start looking right past me, the way he did with Fey.

I needed to do something, anything to convince him I was a great friend to have. It was hard because I'd never figured out why he wanted to be friends with me in the first place.

Micah kept asking questions about the car, so I tried to chime in. "Hey, Deuce," I said. "What's the bore configuration on the Mustang's carburetor? Is that two-bore or four-bore?"

Deuce craned his neck and looked into his rear-view mirror like maybe the wrong kid had climbed into the back seat. What I knew about cars and carburetors could fit in a gnat's ear, and he knew it. I was just basically repeating a conversation from a movie I'd watched over the weekend, between two guys hanging over an engine.

"Uh, gee, let's see, four-bore. I've been meaning to have a look at it. Maybe you can help me with it."

"Sure thing," I said.

"And, if there's time, we can finish cleaning the rifles," Deuce said, playing along.

Easy there. Don't go overboard. I knew for a fact he didn't have a single firearm, and planned to keep it that way.

"You hunt?" Micah asked Deuce, still ignoring me.

"Not anymore. Fishing is more my thing."

"I love to fish!" Micah said. "Will you take me with you sometime? My stepdad and I used to go down to Lake Cachuma. I miss that."

"Sure, all three of us could go," Deuce said, shooting me another glance in the mirror. "Ham loves to fish. The last time he and I went, well, he definitely got the catch of the day. You wouldn't believe the fight that thing gave him."

Har-har. Last time we'd gone, I'd caught an old raincoat full of mud and more. Nearly fell out of the boat trying to reel it in.

I glanced over at Micah to see if I was earning any points, but he was looking out the window now. He didn't seem interested in hearing anything about me.

"Right here," Micah said as we approached the bowling alley.

"Wait!" I said, trying to delay things. "We still need to go to the grocery store. Micah, do you want to go with us? Do you need anything?" I pointed across the street. "There's a Trader Joe's right there."

Deuce made a quick left into the parking lot and pulled into a stall. "Would you two mind going without me? I need to make a call."

He was making that up, I bet, and I could have kissed him for it. He pulled out his wallet and extracted a twenty.

Micah plucked it from his fingers before I could take it. "I'll get it!" He was out the door in a shot. I raced after him.

He made a beeline for the one-dollar greeting cards and stood there reading a few, his lips moving over the words.

"Micah, are you mad at me or something?"

"Why would I be?" he asked, still not looking at me.

"I don't know, but you're kinda acting like something's wrong."

He shrugged. "The only thing 'wrong' is that I thought we were friends."

"Of course we're friends!"

He turned at last to look at me. "If we were friends, you'd trust me."

"What makes you think I don't trust you?" I was so confused.

"Well, if you trusted me, you'd let me talk to you and your mom about your adoption."

My face heated up. "I'm embarrassed about it."

"You don't think I'm embarrassed about my home life? But I've told you a lot about it. Because that's what friends do, Ham. There's more stuff I could tell you, but I'm not going to now because you don't think I deserve to know anything important about your life."

We had moved to the coffee section, and I reached up to get Deuce's favorite blend.

As I did, in one quick-fire move, Micah stepped behind me and shoved his handful of greeting cards into the waistband of my pants. Then he wrapped his arms around me and gave me a squeeze, pulling my shirt down around them.

I twirled back around to look at him, stunned.

"Thanks, Ham."

I wanted to say something. I wanted to protest. I wanted to tell him that I had money in my wallet and could pay for the cards. That he didn't need to steal them. Correction: I didn't need to steal them. But I had a feeling he was giving me a last chance with him. If I refused to take the cards out, he'd give up on me.

And I didn't want that to happen. At all. I could always send Trader Joe's the money anonymously to make up for it.

He hooked his thumb into one of my belt loops and led me to the checkout clerk, snagging a box of sugarcoated cereal on the way there. Mom would have a fit about that. I moved stiffly, but we reached the parking lot without any Goliath-sized security guards coming after us. Micah slipped an arm around my waist and claimed his goods.

"Thanks for the ride, Deuce," he said through his open window. "And for the fantastic dinner!"

"Well here, get in. I'll drive you across the street," Deuce said.

"No, that's okay. I can probably walk over quicker than you can drive. Good night, you two! Oh, wait! Here's your change." He reached into his pocket and pulled out Deuce's change, leaning over me in the front seat to give it to him.

"Don't forget you owe me a fishing trip!" he reminded him. Then he gave my leg a squeeze before he closed the door.

And a secret special smile, meant just for me.

# CHAPTER TWENTY-NINE

The next Saturday morning, while I was out running with Deuce, Micah came by and gave Mom a card, and one for Deuce, too. The same cards from Trader Joe's that I'd shoplifted. Micah wanted to thank them for having him over for dinner.

She handed me the card to read. My breath felt short as I took the card that already had my DNA on it—sweat DNA from being hidden under my shirt. I hoped maybe Micah mentioned in the card how much he liked me, and hoped to see more of me, of us.

But there was no mention of me at all.

"That was nice of him to do that," Mom commented. "Someone raised their boy right."

I picked up the envelope on the counter, as casual

as I could. But there was no return address on it.

"Something eating you, Hammy?" she asked. "You haven't seemed yourself the last few days."

You mean since I started stealing from Trader Joe's? I shrugged. "Guess I'm just worn out from track practice all week. Coach has been turning up the heat as we get closer to our first meet."

She piled dishes together in the sink to wash. "Did you and Micah have a falling-out about the interview he wanted to do? Is he upset with you?"

"He seems okay, I guess. Kind of normal."

It was me who wasn't feeling normal at all these days. And I'd been trying to figure out a way to talk to Mom about it. I had an idea, but it was risky. She might see right through me.

I paused a minute to get my thoughts together. Drew a breath. "Mom, did you ever think you might be a lesbian?"

She turned around, almost in slow motion, from the sink.

I plunged on. "I mean, you never got married, and you don't go on dates with men. Just made me wonder if you could be gay, but you didn't want the people at church to know. In case not everyone would approve."

"No, honey, I don't think I am gay. If I was, I would be happy with that, and would hope that the church would support me."

"But, how can you be sure you're not gay? I mean, have you ever gone on a date with a lady?"

She came around from the sink and slid onto the barstool next to me. "I haven't felt attracted to women. So no, I've never gone on a date with a woman, in the way you mean."

She was quiet after that, probably waiting to see what was going to come out of my mouth next.

"Deuce is gay, right?" I asked. "I mean, we never talked about it exactly, but he is, isn't he? He and Mr. Flynn loved each other that way. Right?"

"Well, I think that would be a good conversation to have with Deuce, not me," she said.

"Okay, I'll ask him sometime. It's no big deal. I just wanted to let you know if you ever want to go on a date with a lady, I don't mind. That's all. Coach Becerra isn't married, either. I thought maybe you could ask her on a date. She could even help you with your workouts." I scooted off the barstool. "Well, good talk, but I need to go do my homework."

"Ham?" she called after me as I hurried to my room.

I pretended not to hear and closed my bedroom door. I think I half hoped Mom would tell me she was gay, and then, exactly how she figured out she was gay. That would be hugely helpful to me. I was so mixed up. I could talk to Deuce about it, but I didn't want to make him sad thinking about Mr. Flynn. How were you supposed to know for sure?

I put a Supremes album on my turntable, and then dropped down on my bed. I picked up my phone and texted Micah.

ME: **hi mom and deuce got their cards that was nice of you—sorry I missed you**

His answer came quick.

HIM: **thx for helping me get the cards ☺**

I saw more comment bubbles coming, so I waited to see what he said next.

HIM: **i was gonna text you anyway—just heard from bij she has plans for you at practice Monday**

Uh-oh, this can't be good. I typed quickly.

ME: **what do you mean plans?**

HIM: **she wouldn't say but whatever it is don't back down you gotta show her who's boss out there**

ME: **will you be there?**

HIM: **course, dude, ive got you covered**

I was so relieved he wasn't mad at me that I barely

had time to worry about what Bijou might do to me at practice on Monday. I'd been right. The shoplifting had put me back on track with him. Even though I hadn't agreed to it. He had just made me his mule.

I wondered if it was a guy friendship thing. If you were going to be real friends, you had to prove it with some kind of initiation. I hadn't had to do anything for Fey to be friends with me. Was it because girls didn't require that? This wasn't exactly something I could ask Mom or Deuce about. They'd want to know what Micah had me do.

And, there was no way I could talk to Fey about it. She'd texted me right after the dance. She'd wanted to know if Micah had rigged the raffle so I'd win. I couldn't lie to her. I'd admitted that he had, and told her that was why I'd given him the gift certificate. He had promised he would give it back to Coach.

Fey didn't say much after that, but I knew she wondered why I'd pick a friend like that.

And now I didn't feel I could really talk to her about Micah. How I thought I could be a good influence on him. And, how he needed someone like me. Somehow, I knew that I'd see disappointment in her eyes. Not because I liked a boy instead of a girl, but because I'd picked one that would rig a raffle, and he'd still hang out with the girl who bullied me. It was hard enough for me to understand that.

All of it just made my head spin. My life had been way easier when all my friends were over sixty years old.

But the problem was that I couldn't go back to my former life. I'd officially passed the point of no return. Micah was on me like a rash.

One that I didn't want to go away.

I arrived at practice on Monday at the last possible minute. I didn't want to be there with Bijou and without Micah. She always came early now. He always came at the last minute. I knew she hoped I might just drop dead so she could take over the team. Even though Coach had told her that would not be the case if anything happened to me. But she was ready, anyway.

No Micah yet, though. Anxiety crept across the back of my neck.

"Hey, loser," she said, out of earshot of Coach Becerra, who was busy marking on her clipboard.

I ignored her and changed out my school shoes for my trail shoes. Tried to pretend she wasn't there.

"You do know you being captain is a total joke,

right? The captain should be the best runner, not the biggest kiss-up. And you—are not the best runner. I am. Everyone wants me to talk to Coach about replacing you."

I wasn't sure if that was true or not, but I wasn't going to let her keep at me. I was sick of it.

"Look, our first meet is going to go a lot better if you and I learn to work together."

She turned and gave me the full benefit of a sneering stare. "Our meet is going to go a lot better if you just stay home and play with your cat."

"Don't be stupid. The team needs both of us, and you know it."

She raised her eyebrows, not sure how to answer that.

"You're a really great runner," I said. "Don't blow it. Whatever game you've got planned for me today, let it go."

Coach Becerra's whistle blew, and she waved everyone over. "Let's go, people. Move it!" She studied the small group assembling in front of her, and glanced at her watch. "Where is everyone? Lord, this isn't a team, this is a train wreck."

I looked back toward the gym. Where was Micah? He said he would be here for me. I drew in a deep breath, bent over with my hands on my knees, and blew it out.

Coach shook her head in clear frustration. "Ham? Bijou? This is on you. Get your teammates to come to practice, or we will have to forfeit the meet. You got that?"

"YES, COACH!" Bijou and I shouted.

"Hope everyone got some good training miles in this weekend?"

I looked around and raised my hand. Then, Bijou's hand shot up.

"About what I figured," she said. "Well, the rest of you should have nice, fresh legs for the course today. We're going over to the Farrell Trail. It's got some nice rises, and it is just technical enough to make it interesting. We'll need to watch out for mountain bikers, so I want everyone to stick together. We're less likely to get mowed down if we run in a tight pack. This is not a race. It is training. Impress me by following directions. It's not how fast you run in cross-country, it's how *long* you can run fast. Training is learning how to pace yourself."

I glanced at Bijou, who was hanging on Coach's every word and fastening on her safety vest. She could change channels faster than anyone I'd ever met.

"We're going to drive up to give us more time on the trail." She pointed over to the big fifteen-passenger van nearby. "Load up!" She yelled over at Jet, who was in a smaller van. "Change of plans, Jet. We had some no-shows, so we can all go together."

"Shotgun!" nearly everyone except Bijou and me yelled.

"Everyone in back," Coach said. "Shotgun privilege on the way home for whoever impresses me today. Jet, you'll ride shotgun with me on the way over. Let's move out!"

I couldn't believe my good luck. I'd run the Farrell Trail with Deuce many times before. I knew it well. Knew when the steeps were coming, and which downhills would murder your quads. I was glad Coach thought we were ready for this. Or, maybe she wanted to show us how unprepared we were. I didn't know about the others, but I knew I was ready.

We gathered at the foot of the trail and waited for our instructions from Coach.

"First one of you to see, hear, or smell a cyclist coming, yell 'bike up' or 'bike back.' There's a few cars in the parking lot. Could be mountain bikers or nice old ladies. You STOP for everyone, bikes or hikers, and step off the trail until they pass. You all got that?"

"YES, COACH!"

"You hear my whistle, what do you do?"

"STOP AND STEP OFF, COACH!"

"Everyone have water?"

"YES, COACH!"

"Okay, then. We're taking the first loop of the trail. It's well marked. I want a ten-minute easy warm-up, and then Jet will set the pace. There will be some single-track trail coming up, so be ready for it. Single file, and give everyone a little bit of extra room today." She looked around to make sure we were all paying attention and then shrugged into a big backpack that carried our extra water, her phone, and medical supplies.

"Since we're short today, Ham, Bijou, you two run in the pack. Jet will lead us out, and I'll take up the back. Let's move out!"

Bijou took the lead spot behind Jet, cocky enough to assume she was the best runner. She was, except for me. I let another kid get in between us to save myself another kick in the shin like she'd given me before.

We finished our warm-up and the first hill appeared, as I knew it would.

Jet turned and yelled back to us. "That's the end of warm-up! Let's kick it up a bit. And remember," she teased, "sweat is your weakness crying."

I knew Bijou would take it fast, and I let her have at it. She'd pay for it later, and that was fine with me. I was saving my juice for where I'd need it.

"Bike up!" I shouted, beating Jet to the punch. I'd heard the telltale sound of loose dirt and gravel ahead. Whoever was coming was coming fast. We all jumped off the trail best we could and waited. It was a girl in pink cycling gear. She was flying! She caught some good airtime over a bump.

"Thanks!" she shouted to all of us as she sped by. Gravel and dust shot all over us in her wake.

"Good call, Ham!" Coach yelled. "Jet! Bijou! You two sleeping up there? You should have caught that!"

Bijou turned and saluted Coach, and then checked me out. Probably wanted to see how hard I was breathing and sweating. I was fine, but I poured some water over my head so she'd think I was suffering a little.

The trail leveled out after that for a while, and the vistas were long and wide. We all took advantage of it to pick up our pace. But we weren't fast enough for Bijou. She kept trying to come off the front, and Jet kept reeling her in. Bijou was like a racehorse at the gate itching to break off and leave us. I knew we had one more long and tough climb coming up before we hit the turnaround point.

The trail was loose and dry, lots of small rocks. I'd noticed when Bijou and I were stretching out that her shoes were really worn out, especially the tread on the sole. She'd have a tough trip down if she didn't slow down after the turn.

The team groaned and complained all the way up the last climb, panting, spitting, and slugging their waters down. Coach hollered at us from the rear. "People! Breathe! Pace yourselves! We are training, not racing! And relax! You *should* be out of breath."

Of course we all noticed that she didn't seem out of breath at all, even though she carried the team pack. I knew some runners and cyclists carried buckshot in their water bottles to make their workout even harder. Coach probably had her backpack loaded with buckshot. She was so cool.

"Okay, heads up! Turnaround coming—easy easy easy on the downhill, you hear me?"

"YES, COACH!"

And at that, Bijou bolted ahead of Jet, made the turn, and shot by us, a big grin on her face. "Try and keep up, *loser*!" she hissed at me.

Game on.

# CHAPTER THIRTY

Coach started shouting the minute Bijou whizzed by, and didn't stop when I jumped out of the pack, hit the turnaround, and raced by her, too.

"I'll get her, Coach!" Not exactly a lie. I was going after her, but not to bring her back. I wanted to bury her at the bottom of the trail. I knew I could do it. It seemed the only way to get her off my case once and for all.

"HAM! Get back here!" she shouted. "I don't need the both of you—"

After that, all I could hear was the sound of my feet hitting the trail, and rocks and debris shooting out around me. I could see Bijou in the distance, and she was moving fast. I threw more water on my head, and quickened my pace. She disappeared from view when she entered into the trees and the beginning of the single-track trail.

I came through those trees just seconds later, breathing hard and fast. She really was an amazing runner, but I was counting on her being stupid about it.

A sudden thrashing sounded behind me. I turned quickly to see a mountain bike coming down fast.

"BIKE! BACK!" I shouted as loud as I could, and jumped off the trail. As the biker passed me, I yelled "Runner up!" I sped up again, hoping they both had heard me. I came around a steep corner just in time to catch the unmistakable sound of *C-R-A-S-H*, metal vs. flesh vs. gravel, and skidding and swearing like I'd never heard before.

Bijou and the biker were both on the ground, under the bike. They were a tangled mess of limbs, and the biker was trying to clip out of his pedals.

"Just hold on!" he yelled as Bijou tried to wriggle out from under the bike that he was still clipped to.

"You two *okay*?" I huffed.

I surveyed the damage. Both of them were scratched up pretty good and bleeding with trail rash. "Okay," the biker said, moving his bike off Bijou. "There you go."

She put her hand out. I grabbed her and eased her up. She seemed dazed. She got up slowly like she wasn't sure she'd be able to stand.

"Did you hurt anything?" I asked as she tested putting weight on one ankle, then the other. And then, totally exasperated, I asked, "Did you two not hear me yell 'heads up'?"

The cyclist got up and checked his bike. "Man, my rim is dust." He shook his head, and then looked up at Bijou. "Sorry, kid. I tried to avoid you. You all right?"

"Where's my watch?" she said, looking around frantically. "Oh no! My uncle will kill me if I lose it!"

I scanned the dirt where we stood, then moved to the bushes close to where they crashed. I got down on my haunches to look, moving the prickly branches apart. "Don't see it here," I said, and turned.

Just in time to see Bijou tearing down the trail, leaving us both in a cloud of her dust.

"Oh man! That's cold!" Biker Guy hooted. "Run her scrawny butt down."

I launched myself like a missile down the trail. I leaned in and pushed hard. I spotted her ahead, tucked in tight, giving it everything she had. The downhill grew steeper, and her worn shoes cost her. I watched her slide, but she hung on to her footing. She was good.

We were both all lean arms and legs, flying through the dust, pumping wind and speed machines.

But if it was possible, I wanted this more than she did. She wanted it to prove a point.

I wanted it to prove myself.

I could almost reach out and touch her now. My lungs screamed for a single pocket of oxygen. I dug in as deep as I could, and with a final burst took the lead. Bijou's hair nearly burst into flames from the heat of me when I blew by her.

I could have yelled "Loser!" when I shot ahead, but I didn't. That wasn't me.

But that didn't mean that it didn't feel incredible to take that trail and *own* it.

I'd never seen Coach Becerra at a loss for words. When she, Jet, and the team caught up with us at the bottom of the trail, Bijou and I were shouting at each other. Well, Bijou was shouting. I was trying to get a word in edgewise.

"Think you're some kind of hotshot now? You're nothin'!" she yelled at me.

"Well, I am captain, and you better start running for the team! Not just for yourself!" My adrenaline was running high, and I let loose on her.

"I am running for the team! I'm the best chance

to win we have. You just got lucky today!" She leaned over and spat.

"Can it, both of you!" Coach barked.

She grabbed Bijou by the back of her safety vest and dragged her to a log to sit. She turned to Jet. "Check Ham. Make sure he's okay."

Coach pulled out her first aid kit, and quickly cleaned the cuts and scrapes on Bijou's legs and arms. She checked her limbs and joints. Gave her water to drink.

Jet gave me a good once-over. "I'm fine," I said, still huffing.

Logan clapped me on the back as he passed me. "You okay, Cap?"

I nodded.

The rest of the team did some quick cool-down stretches, and climbed into the van. I think they knew Bijou and I were about to get Coach's full fury. They wanted good seats to watch, and a place to rest.

Coach's voice was low but deadly when she began. "I don't know when I've seen such irresponsible behavior! You both did the exact opposite of what I told you to do. You two could have been badly hurt, and the biker, too. What the heck were you thinking?"

Silence, from both of us. We agreed on that, at least.

Coach sighed hard. "Bijou, I should take you to Urgent Care. I'm worried about that ankle."

Bijou shook her head, eyes down. "No, I just want to go home. I'm okay."

"Then I need to turn you over directly to a parent. Who's home?"

"No one. My uncle works at night. You can drop me off with him. He's the boss, so it doesn't matter."

"Okay, I'll take you there when we get everyone back to the school."

She eyed us both, still shaking her head. "How am I supposed to trust either of you again? You're my best runners, and you just set the worst example for the rest of the team. Was there any point to that?"

We both said nothing.

But she wasn't done. "When I take students off campus, I'm responsible for your safety. If I can't trust you, maybe we should do all our training in the back of the school from now on."

Coach just kept staring us down and shaking her head. "Neither of you has anything to say?"

Still silence from the both of us.

"Let's load up, then." She helped Bijou to her feet

and then led her to the van. Put her in the back.

Man, I'd never been in this much trouble in my whole life. I didn't quite know what to do. I started packing Coach's medical stuff back up for her. She came up next to me and finished the job. She slung the backpack over one shoulder and gave me a long look. "What was that all about?"

I shook my head. "I don't know. I couldn't get her to stop!"

I lowered my eyes, knowing I really hadn't even tried. I just wanted to win today. It was the only language Bijou understood. "I'm really sorry, Coach."

She pinched the bridge of her nose and closed her eyes. "Did you at least beat her to the bottom?"

I nodded yes.

"Well, there's that," she said. "Let's hope to God she learns something from it."

# CHAPTER THIRTY-ONE

Mom was waiting by the door when I arrived home covered in dust, sweat, and snot.

Coach had already called her and told her what happened.

"I'm totally fine, Mom," I said when she moved close to give me a full mother inspection and once-over.

"Coach Becerra said Bijou ran away from the team, and you went after her. Even though she told you not to. What happened out there?"

I collapsed onto our couch while Mom fetched a Gatorade. I peeled off my shoes and socks. They were soaked with sweat.

I took a record-long drink of Gatorade so I didn't

have to answer the question.

"Jesus will have to forgive me, but I swear I could strangle that child," she said.

"Mom, really it's okay. We'll work it out. It has gotten better. But I need to get in the shower. Can we talk about this later?"

"Okay, go get cleaned up. I'll throw some pizzas in the oven."

"Thanks, pizza sounds awesome."

I headed toward my room, digging through my gear bag for my phone. I'd texted Micah from the van, and hoped he'd texted me back by now.

I had two messages—one from Fey and one from him.

HIM: **heard you crushed bij on the trail jacob said she's in a rage**

ME: **WHERE WERE YOU?**

HIM: **got there late and you guys had already left in the van hey I gotta go**

ME: **k bye**

Fey had texted me to call her when I got home. I'd do that later. I was wet, cold, and hungry but still lit up with adrenaline. Beating Bijou made me feel strong and invincible. As if I could do anything. It made me feel brave enough to have a talk with Micah.

About us. I was desperate to know if he felt about me the way I felt about him.

But what if he didn't? What if he burst out laughing, or worse, what if he got mad about it? What if he didn't want to be friends after that?

But what if he did feel the same way? The chance of that was dizzying. I had no words for that. But my vinyl did. Lots of words. I set down the needle arm on my record player, and let the sound of the Temptations sing me some courage.

The next morning, I raced at the sound of last bell for first period. I hurried so I wouldn't be late. I had tried to find Micah during a morning break, but couldn't. It felt like someone was standing on my chest, and I couldn't quite breathe until I could see him.

"Everything okay with Buster?" Miss Emma asked as I hurried by her office with a quick wave.

"Sure, he's—" And then, I stopped.

In my tracks.

"He's not with you?" I asked, backing up into her office. He was always with Miss Emma in the morning for brunch.

"No, I haven't seen him," she said. "Was he in first period with you?"

"Yeah, but then he left to come here." My heart skipped a beat.

"Well, that's strange." She dropped to her knees and looked under her desk. "Buster?"

She reappeared, her glasses crooked. "He's not been here at all, Ham. His breakfast is untouched."

I hitched up my backpack, and tried to think. A shadow of dread rose in my gut.

"Ham, I'm sure he's okay. He probably just went home. Or, maybe Principal Strickland was here when he came, so he went somewhere else. Are you sure he came to school with you today?"

"Yes!" I remembered because he'd been super fussy with me when I'd shooed him out of homeroom and shut the door. He'd given me an earful. But he knew the way to Miss Emma's office and seemed headed there. It was his routine.

Every. Single. Day.

"I'm sure he's fine. You get to class and first chance when Principal gets back, I'll go look for him. I can't leave the office with no one here. He probably found a nice sunny spot somewhere."

She came around and put her arm around me and gave me a little squeeze. "Scoot! He's fine. Hurry, you'll be late!"

I was going to be more than late. I was going to be a no-show. I nearly yanked the door off the hinges as I left the admin building.

It was one thing to mess with a kid. Even to mess with him really bad. It was another thing entirely to mess with his cat. And this had the stink of Bijou, Royce, and Benny all over it.

I remembered Micah's text that Bijou was "in a rage." My heart sank.

I walked the entire grounds of Harvey Mellencamp. Twice. No Buster.

I ran home fast. Maybe he'd decided to come home for some reason. But he'd never done that even once since I'd started school. Fortunately, Mom was out somewhere or I would have been busted bad for cutting school.

I circled around the house calling him, checked all his favorite sleeping nooks, looked under all the beds. Nothing. His litter box was still clean, and he still had leftovers in his breakfast bowl. I pulled out a box of breakfast cereal and shook it. If he was anywhere in the house, that would bring him running. Buster would take a bullet for a box of Cheerios.

Still nothing. The house was like a tomb.

A terrible picture flashed through my mind of

Buster being abducted by Bijou and stuffed in a pillowcase or backpack. Or, worse, a closed box. Because Buster would not have let Bijou or her idiots pick him up and sling him over their shoulder. He would have fought to the death. Maybe he got away, I thought, my breath coming faster. He could be hiding from them somewhere; afraid to come out until he was sure they were gone.

I dropped onto the couch and squeezed my head between my hands. I should have guessed I would have to pay for humiliating Bijou on the trail last night. But I never thought she would go this far. And maybe she hadn't. I needed to slow down and think.

I wiped the sweat from my forehead. I had to do something. I couldn't just sit here and imagine awful things that could be happening to Buster.

*If* kids had done this, there wouldn't have been time for them to take Buster to anyone's house. They probably stashed him somewhere on campus. But my cat was completely un-stashable. He would be howling. Where could you hide a furious cat?

I had to get back to the school. Couldn't waste another single minute.

I ran back to school, my backpack banging hard against my tailbone. I thought about calling the cops, but I doubted they would respond to a missing cat or cat kidnapping, especially since I had no proof. I could call Mom or Deuce, but at best they'd just walk through the neighborhood and school trying to find Buster. Mom would make me go back to class.

I hadn't told either of them how bad my problems with Bijou were, and I didn't want to. In all the movies I'd watched about public school, the new kid (or geek kid) always did something amazing to win over the whole school. The kid never had his mama come and fix all his problems. There was no movie for that because it'd be just too pitiful.

If this was payback from Bijou, I couldn't go after her full barrel this early in the game. I had to be the fox. Maybe I needed to act like Buster's absence was no big deal.

I wondered if I could pull it off.

When I got back on campus, I went straight to a water faucet and drank long and deep. Then I dunked my head and face. I shook myself off like a dog. The wheels in my head turned faster than I could plan. I checked my watch. Ten more minutes until PE started. Perfect. Benny and Royce would be there. If they'd done this, it was probably the moment they'd been waiting for all day. Buster always came to PE.

Bet they couldn't wait to see my reaction when he didn't.

Maybe they even had some big finale planned for the day. Something they hoped would embarrass the snot out of me. But just embarrassing me wouldn't be enough for Bijou. I had to be ready.

It was showtime.

Things seemed pretty normal in the locker room. Just a lot of gross boys banging in and out of their lockers. I usually picked the same locker in a back corner to avoid the towel-snapping gauntlet. Lockers weren't assigned in the gym. You just picked the one you were going to use for the day and put your combination lock on it. Still, I opened the one I always used slowly, not sure what I might find.

Okay, that was one bad scenario down. Buster wasn't bound and gagged in my locker. I suited up quick and headed out to the field. There was always the possibility that Buster had just been pulling a Rip Van Winkle somewhere else earlier but would show up for PE. I scanned the bleachers and field, looking in all the usual places. Nothing. And he wasn't snacking under the bleachers, either.

The cold feeling in my gut dropped twenty degrees.

Our PE coach, Mr. Hancock, came out of his office and blew his whistle long and hard three times. He was always a little late from sneaking a few hits off a cigar in the parking lot by the gym. Three whistle blasts meant stadium running. He wasn't big on warm-ups. He liked to get right to the action.

I'd run up and down twice before Benny and Royce showed up, rushing from the gym, still pulling their shirts over their puny chests. Coach Hancock hollered at them. I knew we'd be running extra laps to make up for them being late. And I wondered exactly what they had been doing that had made them late.

I slowed on the steps so they'd catch up with me. They were looking at me and grinning. More than usual, it seemed. They slowed their pace. I slowed down more. None of this got by Coach Hancock. He yelled up at us from where he stood. "Pick it up, boys! Guerrero, Munson, Hudson! Move it!"

I picked up my pace but turned to shout at them over my shoulder. "Hey! You guys seen my cat?"

"Your what?" Royce shot back at me. "Your *bat*?"

"My cat!" I shouted. So much for my plan to be low-key about this. C'mon, Ham, easy does it.

Benny bounded up next to me with his long, gangly legs. Royce hitched on and followed him, with a kid named Liam on his tail. Benny shot an innocent smirk my way.

"Yes—my CAT! Have you seen him?" I asked again, huffing from the anger I was trying to manage.

"Yeah, saw him yesterday driving the school bus," Royce snickered.

I wanted to take him by the neck and shake him.

Instead, I tried to stay calm. "Did you see him today? He's not here. I have to find him. It's an emergency."

"Hear that, guys?" Benny yelled over his shoulder to Liam and Royce. "It's a kitty emergency!"

"OOOOHHHH!" They hooted.

"Guys! I'm not kidding!"

That made them cut up even more. "He's not kidding!" they cracked back.

"Get the lead out!" Coach Hancock yelled from the field.

We picked up our pace, and I gave it one last shot. "If you do see him, whatever you do, don't touch him. We just found out he's got a bad case of ringworm. And its super contagious to humans."

Their mouths opened, but this time nothing came out.

# CHAPTER THIRTY-TWO

Benny, Royce, and Liam steered me under the bleachers the minute Coach Hancock left the field after class.

"What does your stupid cat have again?" Royce got right up in my face.

"If you haven't seen him and touched him, don't sweat it," I said, and backed away.

Royce moved closer with Benny right behind me, so I couldn't escape. "I'm not saying I touched him, but I might know someone who did."

"What's the cat got?" Benny asked.

I wiped sweat from my face with my forearm. "Ringworm, only it's a mutant variety. The vet called my mom and told her we both need to get to the doctor and get this super antifungal vaccination."

"Like whoever touched him will get cat *worms*?" Royce asked, looking like he might be sick on the spot.

I knew ringworm wasn't actual worms, but they didn't need to know that.

"I saw it all go down, but I didn't touch him even once," Liam swore.

"Shut up, you two!" Benny said. "You're making this up," he said, right up in my face. You're trying to scare us."

"I'm not trying to scare anyone. We just got the lab test back today, and now I can't find Buster. I need to get him to the vet for treatment. I just thought I should warn you guys, in case you touched him. Ringworm is really bad, especially this beefed-up version of it."

"Bad like how?" came from Royce. "Benny, we gotta tell you-know-who—"

"SHUT YOUR MOUTH!" Benny yelled.

"The worms form under the skin and make this ring formation. They raise up and fill up with pus, like an acid pus."

"That's some bad shit!" Liam said.

Benny looked me over like he was measuring me for a coffin. "You just want your cat back. I know what you're doing!"

"Of course I want to find my cat. He needs to be quarantined!"

"Liar." Benny breathed his lunch into my face. "Big loser mama's boy is a liar."

"Whatever," I said. "I don't really care what you think." But even as I said that, I realized that as pitiful as it was, I did care.

I pushed my way out of the sweaty circle of them, but I had a feeling I would smell them all day, particularly Royce. That kind of stink sticks.

"Look, if you guys did something to Buster as a joke—ha-ha! Good one. You got me!" I threw up my hands. "But enough already. It's one thing to yank my chain, but to hurt an animal or hold him against his will is a felony. I don't know if any of you plan to go to college, but this will go on your record for life. You might want to think if it's worth getting in this much trouble."

I watched them shoot a worried glance at each other.

"And if Bijou has anything to do with this, Coach will kick her off the team."

Royce jumped in. "It's not a felony to take a cat. It's a practical joke."

"SHUT UP, ROYCE!" Benny yelled.

"Just get me my cat so I can take him to the vet. If I get him back before the vet closes, and he isn't hurt in any way, no hard feelings. I won't turn you in."

Royce and Benny started to talk at once, and Benny grabbed Royce by the front of his sweaty T-shirt.

"Not. Another. Word," he growled.

Benny let him go then, giving him a shove. "Get out of here! And you keep your piehole shut!"

"So what is it, Benny? You take Buster or not?" I asked, feeling flecks of spit fly out of my mouth.

"First, you tell me if he's really contagious with ringworm," he said.

"Doesn't work that way," I said. "Where is he? Is he *okay*? He's old—a kidnapping could give him a heart attack. I swear I'll beat Bijou into the earth if she hurts my cat."

"Bijou!" he said, and then shook his head. "You know what, loser? You worry too much about her. You've got way bigger problems than her—and you're just too dumb to see it."

"What's that supposed to mean?"

"You figure it out. I'm bored with all this," he said. He spat on the ground and started walking off.

I tried to digest what he'd just said. Who or what

*else* was I supposed to be worrying about?

Benny turned one last time toward me. "I did see your cat today, but I didn't touch him. He was sitting on the dairy-truck ramp by the cafeteria, watching the guy unload supplies. Who knows? Maybe he hitched a ride."

# CHAPTER THIRTY-THREE

Both Mom and Deuce agreed it wasn't likely the California Highway Patrol would set up roadblocks, and shake down all the dairy trucks on the highway. Nor would the authorities agree to put out an Amber Alert for Buster.

Mom had been on the phone with the school for the last half hour, trying to nail down all the delivery trucks that had been at the school that morning. They told her there'd been a dairy delivery late morning by the Knudsen Company out of San Francisco. After delivering to Harvey Mellencamp, the truck had stopped at a high school in Paso Robles. Then it had returned to its home base in the Bay Area.

I wasn't convinced that Buster had gotten trapped in the truck, but Mom thought that made more sense than kids catching and hiding Buster. She wanted us to rule that out first, before accusing my schoolmates. A dark, cool truck that smelled like milk and ice cream might have been irresistible to him. It's possible that when the driver came back to the truck with a load of empty crates, the racket might have scared Buster, and he'd hidden. Then he might have escaped the truck during the Paso Robles delivery, or he could be headed to San Francisco.

Still on hold with the Knudsen Company, Mom rummaged through the fridge. She wanted me to eat. She was big on feeding people during a crisis. Deuce came up from behind her and moved her aside. "Let me," he said.

"Ham, what sounds good?" he asked.

"Finding my CAT sounds good!" I nearly hollered. I was beyond wound up. I was ricocheting off every surface.

"You still need to eat something," he said. He riffled through the fridge, and then turned to frown at Mom.

"I know! I was supposed to shop today, and then *this* happened," she said.

"I'm not hungry," I said. "I'm going back to school to have another look."

Before I'd come home, I'd searched the entire

school grounds again. I stopped to tell Coach I had to miss practice. She could see I was shook, and made me tell her what was going on. She promised me the team would look for him during practice. Bijou wasn't there yet, either, which made me even more suspicious. I told Coach that if she showed up, to ask her to please call me. I left my number, even though I was pretty sure Bijou already had it.

I kept returning to my locker, hoping that Buster would appear there. Miss Emma was out searching, too, going through closed classrooms and closets, shaking a bag of treats.

There was absolutely nothing in the world that would keep Buster from me. He'd have to be hurt, sick, or captured. Each of those options was unbearable to think about.

"Sounds like there are people already checking the campus," Deuce said. "Let's get up to Paso Robles and check the high school. He may have jumped out of the truck first chance he had."

"Great! Let's go!" I said. "Mom, will you go to the school and look for him after you get off the phone?"

She gave me a nod, and then turned back to the phone. "YES! I'm still here."

"C'mon," Deuce said. "Let's go to my place and

grab some food. We'll eat on the road. I've got leftover roast and we'll make sandwiches."

Deuce paused in the doorway, eyes on Mom. Mine too.

She sighed and motioned for us to go on. "Yes, I can keep holding."

I'd texted both Fey and Micah about Buster, but hadn't heard back from either of them yet.

Deuce grabbed the back of my neck as we traipsed across the front of the parsonage. "You doing okay?"

I just looked up at him.

He pulled me closer to him as we continued to walk. "Yeah, I know. Sorry, dumb question. But Buster is a smart cat. He'll figure this out."

"But what if he can't? What if Bijou did something to him to get back at me? I wouldn't put it past her to have chased Buster into the truck herself. If she's hurt him in any way, she's going to be so sorry."

"Okay, okay—take a breath. Let's not worry so much about Bijou right now, all right? Let's keep our focus on getting Buster home safely."

Just as Deuce opened the door to his place, Fey shot out her front door and raced over.

"Ham! I just read your text! Sorry, I was at the dentist! Did you find him?"

I shook my head and bit hard on the underside of my lip.

Fey put her arms around me and gave me a very tight squeeze. "We'll find him!"

"Fey, come on in," Deuce said. "I'm just going to make some sandwiches."

I slid onto a barstool, and I brought Fey up to speed on the possibility that Buster had gotten trapped in a Knudsen truck. "So we're going to check the school that got the other milk delivery. Do you want to come?" I asked. I turned back to Deuce then. "I mean, if that's okay with you?"

"Of course!" he said. "Fey, do you want to check with your folks?"

"Let me just run over and ask them. Be right back," she said.

"Thanks, Fey," I said. Buster loved her a lot. It would be good to have her out calling for him with us.

"This will take me just a minute," Deuce said as he began pulling things from his fridge.

"Need help?" I asked unconvincingly.

"Sit!" he said. "Beer?"

"Sure," I said, not smiling this time at our regular joke.

He wiped the top of a can of Coke with his shirttail,

popped it open, and slid it down the marble counter to me. I caught it without looking.

"Tell me more about Bijou," he said. "What's her story?"

Shoulders up. Shoulders down.

"Ah."

I looked at him. "She's pretty rough."

"She been giving you a hard time even since you made captain?"

"Yeah, not quite as bad, but don't tell Mom. I don't want her to worry."

"Deal for now. But I want you to tell me."

I took a big swig of my Coke, grimacing at the bite of carbonation. "It's complicated."

He nodded as he sharpened a knife on his special stone. It was a religious practice with him, and had been for Mr. Flynn, too. I'm pretty sure their knives could split an atom.

"Give me a try? I'm not too bad with the complicated stuff."

I exhaled hard and dropped my forehead to the counter.

He laid a hand on my head. "It's gonna feel less complicated if you get it out."

"K—well, ever since she messed with me at the

creek that day and stole my bike, her friends have been all over my butt at school. And she didn't exactly just return my bike like I told you. She locked it to the principal's car door. I was in big trouble for that one."

Deuce raised his eyebrows as he pulled out bread. "Go on," he said.

"The two guys she hangs out with most, Benny and Royce, won't get off my case. They're always teasing me, and Fey sometimes, too. Bijou's really pretty horrible. Which is so confusing because—" I broke off, not sure I wanted to say more.

"What's confusing?" Deuce asked while he lathered mustard and mayo across the bread.

"Well, she and Micah seem really tight. Which makes NO sense. I mean, he and *I* are friends, so I don't understand why he would want to be friends with someone who's nasty to me."

Fey tapped lightly on the front door, which was partially open. Deuce called her in.

"I can come!" she said. She'd brought a jacket, two large flashlights, a towel, and a first aid kit. She reddened when I looked at all the stuff. "Sorry, I like to be prepared."

"That's really smart, Fey! Thanks."

She dumped her things on the counter, and slid

onto the stool next to me.

"Ham was just telling me about Bijou, and how her friends Royce and Benny have been giving you two a hard time," Deuce said.

Fey waved it away. "They're morons."

"Yeah, but I think they might have something to do with Buster being gone," I said.

Fey's eyes grew wide. "Are you kidding? They're awful, but do you think they'd do something that mean—that stupid?"

Deuce raised his hand. "We're not going there yet. First, let's see if Buster hitched a ride up north."

I nodded at Deuce. "I know. I know! But, Fey, if Royce and Benny did do something, it wouldn't have been on their own. Bijou would have to be behind it. They just do what she tells them to do. And since Coach won't let Bijou mess with me anymore, maybe this is the only way she could think of to get back at me."

"Back at you for what?" Fey asked.

I dug my hands in my hair and closed my eyes.

"What have you ever done to Bijou?" Fey asked again.

There was a loud rap on the front door, and we all turned, startled. Mom never knocked.

"Hello-o-o-o? Anybody here? Deuce? Ham?" Micah came bounding into the kitchen. "Hey, everybody! Ham, I got your message about Buster being lost. Poor little guy." He dropped his pack on the counter.

"Look, Micah, I know Bijou is your friend, but do you think there's any chance she has something to do with Buster missing?"

"*No* way, really. That would be so cold!"

Fey butted in. "So she didn't say anything to you about doing something to get back at Ham?"

Micah shook his head and raised his hands. "Sorry, I don't know anything. God, I wish I did. She's been blowing me off a little. I think she's kinda mad because Ham and I are such good friends now."

Hearing Micah call us "good friends" should have sent me over the moon and Mars, but right now, nothing mattered except Buster.

Micah started to unwrap the scarf around his neck, but then stopped midway. He looped it all the way back around quickly. Then he hopped up on the stool next to me.

"Something to drink, Micah?" Deuce asked.

"Coke, please," he said. "I nearly ran all the way."

Deuce popped a can and had it over ice and on a

coaster before he could blink.

"Thanks!" Micah said, taking a swig like he hadn't had any fluid in days.

When he came up for air, he said, "So what's the plan? I stopped over at your house first. Your mom said you two were working on it. She was on the phone with somebody about it."

"Mom's trying to track down the delivery driver who did the drop-off at Mellencamp today," I said. "There's a possibility that Buster may have gotten in the truck and gotten locked in. Benny told me he saw Buster earlier today on the ramp of the truck. So the three of us are going up to Paso Robles where the truck made its next stop. Buster could have jumped out then."

"I wish I could go with you guys! I need to get home, though. Promise me you'll call me with any news." He shot a pleading look at Fey then. "Will you please text me if he forgets to call me?"

"Sure" was all she said. Her tone was agreeable but cool.

"Okay, then," Deuce said. "We're all set here. Let me just check that the house is all locked up. And I want to grab one more flashlight for us."

"Deuce, can I use your bathroom first?" Micah

asked. "I need to wash my hands."

"Sure, go ahead," Deuce said, pointing toward the hall.

"Back in a sec," Micah said over his shoulder.

Fey, Deuce, and I packed up all the sandwiches and bottles of water.

"Do we need to get your cat carrier?" Deuce asked.

I loved that he assumed we would find him. "No, we only use that to take him to the vet. I think that would freak him out more. If—I mean, when we find him, he'll be fine in the car on my lap."

Micah came back into the kitchen, and Deuce asked, "Do you want us to drop you off at home, or the bowling alley?"

"No, I'm fine. Don't forget to let me know how it goes, okay? I'm here for you, Ham. Buster is okay. I have a really good feeling about it."

Micah pulled my head close to his and laid his forehead on mine for a moment. I could smell Mr. Flynn's cologne on him. He'd probably tried it out when he was in the bathroom. I hoped to God that Deuce didn't smell it. The smell made my heart wince.

When Micah stepped back and turned to go, I saw Deuce watching us. I wondered what he was thinking. Fey was checking the batteries on her flashlights. She didn't look up or say goodbye to Micah when he left.

I tried to sort it all, my jumbled mess of feelings about Micah and my fears about Buster's disappearance. It was all much too much.

While Deuce closed up the house, I could hear him muttering. When he came in, he looked distracted.

"Everything okay?" I asked.

"Yeah, I just can't find my keys to the Mustang. I wanted to get the big flashlight from the trunk. Never mind. I probably left them in a jacket pocket. Okay, you two. Let's get on the road."

I drew a deep, bracing breath. Fey came and squeezed my hand. I squeezed it back.

I made a mental vow to Buster.

*I'm coming, buddy. I'm going to find you if it's the last thing I do!*

# CHAPTER THIRTY-FOUR

The news from Mom, when it finally came, was bad. Worse than bad. The Knudsen dispatcher had tracked down the guy who made the delivery to Mellencamp, and had him call her. The driver told Mom that he hadn't seen or heard any cat in his truck all day. Mom told him that Buster was a bit of a Houdini and was a pro at hiding. The driver said he checked the back, front, and everywhere for us. No sign of a cat.

"I want to talk to him myself," I told Mom. I wrote the number down on my hand as she recited it and was dialing before I'd even said goodbye to her.

The driver answered right away, and I explained who I was.

"Sir, I know you looked everywhere, but did you check under your seats, too? Do you have overhead compartments in the back? Did you look there, too?"

"I'm so sorry, son, I looked everywhere. I even crawled under the truck to see if he might have climbed up in the engine. Nothing. My wife has a cat, and I know how attached you can get. I wish I had better news for you."

"Wull, did you stop anywhere else today besides the high school in Paso Robles? Any other places he might have had a chance to jump out?"

"Nope, I made a quick pit stop around Salinas. But I didn't open the back of the truck."

"But you can't be a hundred percent sure he's not there somewhere. He could have found a safe crawl space. He's probably totally freaked out," I said.

"Ham, let me talk to him," Deuce said, reaching for the phone.

I turned and stared out the window, feeling both hopeless and mad. I half heard Deuce asking the driver for details about exactly where he had parked the truck in Paso Robles.

Deuce and Fey just let me be for a while, and didn't try to give me any pep talks. He asked me once if I wanted to eat my sandwich; I shook my head. But as we neared Paso Robles, I asked him to stop at a grocery store. I wanted to get a box of Cheerios to shake for Buster. If he was there, he'd know for sure it was me calling him.

We pulled into the exact spot where the Knudsen driver had been parked at the school. I jumped out of the car, ready to tear up the school grounds. Deuce suggested that we let Buster find us vs. running around in circles. There was a picnic table near where we'd pulled up.

"That's a smart idea," Fey said. "Here, Ham, sit down. You can shake your cereal and call him, but I think we should stay put for a bit."

I nodded. They were right, and it was a good idea. If his favorite cereal didn't draw him in, hopefully the smell of roast beef and our voices would do the trick.

As Deuce put our food out, I checked in with Mom and Miss Emma. Mom was circling the neighborhood, and Miss Emma had promised to walk the school grounds again after all the evening school clubs finished up.

I wished I had Bijou's number so I could call and scream at her.

I shot Micah a quick text.

ME: **can you check with bijou and see if she'll tell you anything???**

No answer. He was probably too busy with Mason.

We sat for about half an hour while I just tore my sandwich into bits and pieces. Fey nudged me gently about eating, but I couldn't.

We sat for another ten minutes, and then the three of us took flashlights from the car. We walked the entire school grounds.

Twice.

We found an orange cat, a white-and-black cat, several squirrels, a raccoon, and a skunk.

But no Buster. It was cold and dark out, and he was alone. Probably so confused, too. I couldn't bear it. I didn't know if my heart would survive this blow.

When we finished our second loop and reached the car, Deuce and Fey both looked at me. I knew that they would keep looking all night if I wanted.

I started to shake, from a deep place inside me. I tried to hold myself still. I'd hoped so hard we'd find him here, disoriented and hungry but okay. But he wasn't here. He would have come running if he had been. So, if not here, *where*?

I knew he'd be scared. Just like I was.

I wiped my nose on my sleeve, and Fey moved up

close. She rubbed circles on my back.

"You must think it's nuts for me to be so upset about a cat," I said.

"Don't be silly. It's not nuts at all."

I thought back to where Buster had come from, and I wanted to tell Fey. Deuce already knew. I wanted so much for her to understand why Buster was more than my cat. He was a part of everything that was me.

I started, drew a breath, and stopped.

"What is it, Ham?" she said gently.

Deuce put his arm around me and drew me close. He read my mind. "Does Fey know the story of where Buster came from?"

I shook my head and swiped my nose again. Tried to stop the trembling from deep inside. I couldn't.

She leaned into the other side of me. "Where did you get Buster?" she asked, her voice soft.

"He came with me," I said. My eyes burned with tears I tried to hold.

"Came with you where, Ham?" she asked.

"He came with me from my birth mom."

Deuce tightened his arm around me. He and Fey waited until I could get the words out. A hot rock sat in my throat.

"He was—he was wrapped up in the manger with

me. She left me *and* Buster."

"*Oh*, Ham," Fey breathed.

I buried my head in Deuce. Tears made their way down my cheeks and neck. My shoulders shook.

He pulled me in hard against him, and put his chin on my head. Fey circled around, laid her head on my back, and held me tight. A circle of three.

I cried then for Buster—my witness, my champion, my first and oldest friend in the world.

=^..^=

MISSING CAT!
THIRTEEN-YEAR-OLD GRAY & WHITE MALE
ORANGE TIP ON TAIL
ANSWERS TO "BUSTER"
HAS A MISSING RIGHT EYEBALL
LOVES CHEERIOS AND DIRTY SOCKS
HATES COUNTRY MUSIC
$$$ GIANT REWARD FOR HIS SAFE RETURN $$$
CALL 805-555-2104 ANYTIME DAY OR NIGHT
NO QUESTIONS ASKED

# CHAPTER THIRTY-FIVE

I woke to the sound of Mom on the phone early the next morning. She was telling Miss Emma that I'd need to take the morning off from school. Maybe even the whole day. We planned to visit animal shelters around the county, and put signs up.

I'd hardly slept all night. I was so used to having Buster draped over my feet. Or curled up behind my knees. He'd turn on his motor and purr until we both fell asleep. After that he'd snore through the night like an old man. Not having him with me made me feel weightless in a bad way, like I might just float off into black space.

I'd finally gone into the living room and crashed there. Mom must have come out to check on me because when I woke up, I was covered with my Superman blanket. Didn't know we even still had it. I held it up to my nose. My throat burned, and I wiped my nose in the crook of my elbow.

"Hey, you," Mom said, coming into the living room, her hands wrapped around a cup of coffee. "Can I make you a hot chocolate? Or a smoothie?"

"Nah," I said, and scrubbed my eyes with my fists.

"Scooch over," she said, and plopped down on the end of the couch. She rubbed my leg a minute and took a long sip of her coffee.

"I can't believe you kept this blanket," I said, running my hand over it.

"It's what moms do."

"I hope he wasn't cold last night," I said, my voice small.

"He found a way to stay warm. I'm sure of that."

I hoped to God she was right. If he felt as bad as I did without him, I couldn't stand it. I guess I'd known that he wouldn't live forever, and someday I'd be without him. But I wasn't anywhere near ready for that.

"I heard you on the phone with Miss Emma," I said. "I don't have to go to school today?"

"I'll leave that up to you. If it would feel better to

stick with your routine, that's fine. But if you want to stay home this morning, or even all day, I can live with that."

I nodded and said, "I want to stay home. You'll take me to the shelters?"

"Of course. I have a light day today. Nothing that I can't reschedule."

"Thanks, Mom." I reached across the coffee table for my notebook. I'd made a sign in the middle of the night. I flipped to the page and showed it to her.

She nodded while she read it. "'Giant reward'? What did you have in mind?"

"Well, Deuce and Fey said they'd pitch in, and I've got birthday money I've been saving."

"Count me in, too. How about instead of 'giant reward,' you list five hundred dollars. Not that we can put a price tag on Buster. He's priceless. But that's what we can afford."

"I've known Buster even longer than I've known you, Mom."

"I know, honey. You two go way, way back."

"Why do you think she wrapped up Buster in the blanket with me?"

It was something we'd talked about before, but today especially, I felt desperate to understand.

"I honestly don't know. Why do you think?" she asked.

Another mystery of my life I'd always wondered about. It was strange enough to put your baby in a manger, and drive off. But to put a half-blind kitten wrapped in the blanket with him was really weird. "I guess we'll never know for sure. Did she do it for me, or did she do it for Buster?"

Mom nodded and took a sip of her coffee.

I exhaled. "Maybe she didn't want me to feel alone until you would find me."

"She did the best she knew how. And that's all we can ask of someone."

"Yeah, I guess."

We sat quiet for a few moments together. Mom kept petting my leg while I tried to imagine the possibility that I would never see Buster again. Even after my short time in public school, I knew it was not cool to be a boy with a cat. Boys had dogs. And as important as being normal was to me, I was a boy who loved a cat. It was that simple.

"Ham, we need to talk about Bijou before you go back to school."

"What's to talk about?" I said, stiffening.

"If she and her friends did, in fact, have anything

to do with Buster being missing, it's time for the parents to get involved."

I nodded. But I didn't like it.

"I agreed to let you handle this on your own, the scene at the creek and her taking your bike. But if you are right, this is escalating and I can't let it go on. It's not good for either of you, Ham. And her parents need to know what's been going on."

"She doesn't have parents," I told her. "Micah told me that she lives with her uncle who owns a bar and works late every night. I think Bijou is on her own, mostly."

"All right, I'll talk to Principal Strickland today and figure out the best way to set up a meeting with all of us."

"Please, Mom. Can't you just try and help me find Buster? I'll sort out the Bijou part."

"Here's the deal. Just so you remember. I'm the parent and you're the kid. You are in over your head with this girl. But let's just take this one step at a time. Today, we work on finding Buster. Okay?"

"Deal," I said, giving her a limp fist bump.

But that didn't mean I couldn't start making plans of my own. And I had to act fast before Mom set up a meeting with Bijou and her uncle. Once Bijou got wind of that, if she had Buster stashed somewhere, he could be in even greater jeopardy. Bijou had only promised Coach she'd watch my back.

Not my cat's.

Before we left the house, Mom and I called all the animal shelters between our house and San Francisco. Buster had an electronic chip, so if someone found him and turned him in, we would get a call right away. Next, we redid the "missing cat" sign to include the amount of the reward. We made enough copies for nearly the whole town of Muddy Waters. Mom had called the Church Ladies, and they were coming by to grab a stack to post everywhere.

There were a lot of lost cats at the Muddy Waters shelter, but none of them were Buster.

By midafternoon, Mom and I had done about all we could.

"Fey called," Mom said. "I just heard the message. Said you weren't answering your phone."

"I'll call her in a bit," I said, stirring the protein smoothie Mom was trying to get me to drink.

I glanced up at the clock. It was getting close to three. I tipped my drink back and sucked down as much as I could. It was terrible, but I needed fuel.

I hadn't had anything to eat in nearly twenty-four hours. I needed my strength for what was coming next.

"I'm going to go change for practice," I said, casual-like.

"You're going to practice?" Mom asked, looking both surprised and concerned.

"Well, yeah," I said. "I'm the captain, and there's nothing left to do about Buster right now. We just have to wait. And our first meet is next week. I have to go, Mom. I missed yesterday. Plus, I want to walk around the campus some more."

"Is Bijou going to be there?"

I shrugged and tossed back the rest of my smoothie. I scooted out my barstool and stood up. "Probably, but so will Coach. Nothing bad will happen."

"Hammy, I think it's great that you are being such a conscientious captain, but I don't think it is wise for you to see Bijou right now. I don't want you two getting into it."

"Coach Becerra will be there! Believe me, she's not going to let us 'get into it.'"

Mom didn't look convinced. I tried another tack. "Mom, I just want to go run. It'll make me feel better. I don't know for sure if it was Bijou. Could have been any of the kids at school who tease me. Or, something else entirely."

"Abraham Hudson, I want you to look me right in the eye and tell me that you're not going to practice just so you can have a showdown with her."

I put both my arms around her and pulled her into a hug, so I didn't have to look her right in the eye. "Don't worry!" I said, also avoiding the promise.

She held on to me too long, as she was prone to do. "Mom!" I fake-laughed. "You're going to make me late!"

"Go on, then," she said, giving me a swat on my behind. "If there is any news about Buster, I'll come to the track."

"Thanks, Mom," I said.

Mom showing up would definitely be convenient. Chances are we'd need a priest on hand to pray over Bijou's carcass. If she'd done anything to my cat, she was dead meat.

# CHAPTER THIRTY-SIX

I ran over to the school, keeping a slow and steady pace. I wanted to be warmed up and ready for anything that went down. But I knew that I had to be smart. I couldn't come in like Iron Man, but I sure wasn't coming in like Bambi, either. I had to remember that the goal was getting Buster back. I couldn't take a chance that I would make Bijou so mad that she wouldn't cooperate. Once I got Buster back, though, there was no telling what I might do to her.

Part of me half expected her to be a no-show. But when I reached the track, there she was cool as anything, doing trunk rotations and chatting with Coach.

"Hey!" I said to them both as I reached for my safety vest and threaded my arms through. Bijou just nodded in my general direction, but Coach gave me a kind smile. "Hi, Ham. Any news about Buster?"

I dropped down to the ground near Bijou and began my stretches. "Not yet, but I'm not giving up hope."

"Just keep the faith. Cats are very smart. If he's out there, he'll make his way back." Coach tossed me a bottle of water. "Drink up! I was just talking to Bijou about today's workout. I need to run back to the office for a minute. You two talk, and I'll let you pick where we train today. This will be our last hard workout, and then we'll start tapering down. I want everyone with fresh, strong legs for the first meet next week."

After Coach left, Bijou continued to ignore me, focusing on stretching. It gave me a minute to study her closely. Her legs looked really strong. Heck, she looked stronger all over. I suspected she'd been doing what Coach called "secret training." That's when you train above and beyond the workouts Coach already gave you. Like getting up early before school to run. But she wasn't the only one who had been doing extra workouts. So had I.

"You going to actually warm up or just watch me do it?" she said.

"What did you do to my cat, Bijou? I know you're involved somehow."

"I didn't do anything," she said, sighing with disgust.

"Yeah, you did. But that's water under the bridge. What comes next is more important."

"I hope it's deciding on today's workout because you're really boring me with kitty talk."

I pulled a wad of cash out of the pocket of my shorts. "Did you know there's a five-hundred-dollar reward for my cat?" I waved the money in her direction.

"I wouldn't, except the whole school has had to read your pitiful posters all day. They're plastered everywhere."

"This hundred bucks is yours now with four hundred more to come. Just get me my cat back."

"Hey, you're good with words! What's a word for 'beyond pitiful'?"

"Look, no questions. Just tell me where he is, or what you did with him."

The rest of the team came hurrying up but must have known there was a showdown in the works. They all kept a safe distance. But every one of them was watching us.

"Look, Captain Kitty-Cat, you're so dense you don't even know you have more than one person messing with you at this school. And you're about to be *minus* one, because you're not even worth my effort."

My heart sped up. My eyes narrowed. Was there really someone *else* who would mess with me like this? Wasn't that what Royce had hinted at?

"Tell me who it is, then, and I'll give you fifty bucks."

Coach returned to the track just then, and blew her whistle for everyone to round up. She looked down at me and Bijou. "On your feet, you two! What's the plan today?"

Bijou jumped up and shook her legs out. "I really don't know, Coach, because poor Ham is too worried about his cat to make a plan for today. But I think we should—"

I cut her short. I made my voice loud, and prayed it wouldn't crack in the middle. "Warm-up at the track, then stadiums, Rocket Park three-mile loop with five-minute speed intervals at miles two and three, then hill repeats at Purity Hill until people puke or ask you to call the paramedics."

Coach looked at her clipboard, and jotted down some notes. She nodded and then said, "Okay, sounds good, but everyone is going to hate you for this."

"Well, they can get in line," I said with a shrug.

"Bijou," Coach said, "tuck in tight behind Ham at the park and stay there. When I call the sprints, you take the lead. He'll round out the back and keep people moving. You two got that?"

"Yes, Coach," we said in near unison.

She jerked her head in our direction. "You two, stay—the rest of you, GO!"

As the team headed to the track for warm-ups, she pulled off her sunglasses and eyeballed us both. "Bijou, if you know anything about Ham's cat, or had anything to do with its disappearance, I want it out NOW."

Bijou spit into the dirt. "I told him, I didn't. And I'm telling you the same. I didn't take his cat."

"Did you tell any of your guys to take the cat?" I asked.

"NO!" Bijou looked at me then. "I'm allergic to cats. Wouldn't touch one with a ten-foot pole."

I tried to draw a full breath. She had to be lying.

"All right, then," Coach said. "If I find out different, Bijou, you're off the team. Now, if you two can manage to work together, we may have a chance at the meet. Your combined talent is our strongest asset.

If either of you go hot-dogging off on your own, we lose. I need to know that you can keep your personal differences aside. I don't want the team to blow up after we've all worked so hard. So—are we good?"

"YES, COACH!" we shouted.

"Then let's get out there!"

Bijou stood back and waved me on. "After you, Captain."

Bijou didn't stick around after practice. I saw her get into an old jeep with a decal for a place called the Alano Club. I'd never heard of it. Must be her uncle's bar.

The workout had been even harder than I thought it would be, but I knew that part of the weakness in my legs and lungs was stress. Like Coach had told her to, Bijou had stayed on me, her knees right behind mine. We fell into a kind of rhythm together. We pulled the team long and hard. Bijou and I almost became one single breathing machine. We didn't talk. We just did what Coach had told us. She'd been smart to let Bijou do the sprints. She was hungry to pull out from behind me and run all out. And I was the right person to take up the rear to round up and motivate our weaker teammates.

Coach Becerra wasn't the kind of coach to give out a lot of compliments, but I could tell she was happy with how the workout had gone when we finished. Everyone was drenched and breathing hard.

"Huh! Apparently, I have a team after all. Strong work—*everyone*. Ham, Bijou, that's what leading a team looks like. Now get out of here and get some rest."

I took my time to finish up before I headed home. I was more afraid to be greeted by bad news about Buster than hoping for good news. I coughed to clear my lungs and spit. Dumped some more water on my head.

"Hey, Cap!"

I whirled at the sound of Micah's voice as he came onto the track. I wiped the water from my eyes.

"Oh, hi!"

Coach had told me to tell him the next time I saw him that he was off the team. I was too tired to bring it up, though, and maybe she would change her mind. He was doing the best he could, but she didn't understand. I couldn't help him if he wouldn't let me tell her about his home situation.

"You looked beat," he said. "I brought you a Mountain Dew."

“Thanks.” I took a long slug. I hoped it wasn’t stolen, but it tasted so good that right then, I almost didn’t even care.

“I went by your house after my last period,” he said, “but no one was home. I didn’t see you at school today, so I figured you’d stayed back.”

“Yeah, my mom and I went to the animal shelters. But I couldn’t miss another practice.”

“I saw your posters around school. There was a whole army of ladies putting them up, and Miss Emma was making rounds all day, calling for Buster. A lot of people looking.”

I tried to dry myself with a small hand towel I carried in my backpack. I’d worked up the sweat of a team of horses.

“Oh, and Fey texted me. She asked me to tell you she was thinking about you, and wanted you to call her when you could. I don’t know how she got my number. She seemed really worried about you.”

“I’ll call her after I get home,” I said.

“I know you keep saying you two are just friends, but she *really* likes you,” Micah said. “Dude, she wants to be your girlfriend.”

He kept bringing this up, and I didn’t know what to say.

Micah gave me a searching look. "You didn't know? It's so obvious."

"No. And I'm not ready for a girlfriend, anyway."

"Well, if you were," he said, "would you pick her?"

"I dunno, I haven't given it any thought. I don't think of her that way." I took another long drink of Mountain Dew.

I remembered my plan to talk to him about us—my plan from before Buster went missing. Did he just give me an opening?

Micah took the hand towel from me. He walked behind and wiped the back of my neck and shoulder blades. I could feel his breath on me. My stomach started to spin, and I felt off-balance.

He came back around. Studied me a moment.

"You sure about that?"

"Yes, I'm—" But I couldn't finish my sentence. What could I say? *It's you I like like that, not her? You're the one I think about all the time?*

As if he'd heard my thoughts, Micah stepped in closer. Very close. I swallowed. He moved his lips close to mine. He hesitated. I gulped, and quickly looked around to make sure no one else was still at the track. His mouth landed slightly off-center of mine, and stayed just a moment. It was more a nudge than a kiss.

When he pulled away, we both dropped our eyes, and neither of us spoke. But we stayed near enough that we could feel each other's breath on our faces.

He said at last, "I've been wanting to do that for the longest time. Hope it was okay?"

I nodded, stunned, unable to make any words.

"Was that your first?" he asked as he stepped back.

"Huh?"

"First kiss? Was that your first?"

I put my head down and nodded, embarrassed that it was. Couldn't handle looking him in the eyes. I couldn't quite believe that he'd kissed me. I needed time to stop so I could just catch up a minute. I knew that if I could have a minute to think, some questions could be answered at last.

"Okay, then," Micah said, a small smile on his face. "Then, let's go."

"Where?" I asked, numb.

"To pick up Buster."

My head swam. "What do you mean—pick up Buster? You know where he is?"

"Yep. He's at Bijou's. He's been there the whole time. The story about the delivery truck was just to throw you off track."

I grabbed his arm. "Are you *sure*? How do you know?"

"I wrung it out of Royce today."

"Oh my GOD! I can't believe it. Buster's okay?"

"Royce says he's fine, but he won't stop meowing and trying to escape from her house. I guess her uncle is pretty fed up. Bijou told him Buster was the class cat, and it was her week to take him home. Her uncle fell for it. Can you believe it?"

"We have to go get him—now!"

"I know!" Micah said. "That's why I'm here. I'll take you."

"What do you mean—'take me'?" My mind raced through the logistics. Deuce wasn't going to want to take me to a showdown at Bijou's, not without Mom at least. And she was at the prison until around eight p.m.

"I brought wheels," he said simply.

"What do you mean? You don't know how to *drive*!"

"I didn't bring us a car, but I did bring wheels," he said.

I shook my head. "I don't understand!"

"They're not my wheels. I borrowed some from a friend."

He pointed over to the parking lot across from the track.

I shaded my eyes and stared. Then swallowed hard. Tried to make my mouth move.

"Is that *Deuce's* tandem?" I asked, incredulous. Though it was a stupid question. The bike was one-of-a-kind. I'd know it anywhere.

"Like I said, I borrowed some wheels from a friend."

I knew with a sick rush that by the way he said "borrowed," he meant stolen.

And he looked pretty pleased with himself.

# CHAPTER THIRTY-SEVEN

Like a sleepwalker, I stumbled toward the bike, my mind ready to explode with what I was seeing, and what that meant Micah had done.

When the questions finally came, they came rapid-fire.

"You STOLE the tandem???"

"What were you *thinking*?"

"Are you OUT of your mind?"

"Deuce is going to kill us both—you know that, don't you?"

This could not be happening. This was unbelievable.

Oh God. "You didn't scratch it anywhere, did you???"

"If you can calm down, Mr. Ungrateful," he said,

"I'll answer all your questions."

He pulled sunglasses from the top of his head, and put them on. He was wearing a long scarf like he had the night before. He tossed the scarf back around his neck where it had blown off.

"Look, I borrowed Deuce's bike because getting Buster back is an emergency. You have a bike, but I don't, so we needed the tandem so we could go together. You don't know where Bij lives, and I do. It's kind of hard to find. Plus, we'll get out there in no time on this baby."

"But how did you get it from his office?" I asked, hoping to wake up from this nightmare any minute now. "Was he *home* when you took it?"

"I'm not an idiot! Of course not. I saw keys on his side table last night, and I borrowed them. I had a bad feeling Bijou might have Buster, and we'd need wheels to get out there and save him."

As he said that, I had a sudden recollection of Deuce not being able to find his extra set of keys to the Mustang before we left for Paso Robles. There must have been a duplicate house key on there, too. Micah had stolen them when he used the bathroom!

I just stared at him, still not believing what he'd done.

"You broke into his house today and stole his

bike!" I was going to vomit.

"If it turned out I was wrong and Bijou didn't have Buster, I would have just quietly put his keys back. He'd never know. But here we are, Ham. We have a chance to go get Buster, and we need a way to get there. Bijou just left with her uncle. He takes her to his work so she can use his office computer for homework. If we can get out to her house now, we can just grab Buster and leave. And what's Bijou going to do about it when she discovers Buster is gone? Call the police and report a stolen cat has been stolen from her? She'll probably be relieved to have it over with. It was a joke that just went too far."

I felt like I might be having a brain bleed. How did this boy who just gave me my first kiss manage to make breaking into someone's house seem like a good plan?

"I pumped up the tires before I left, and lowered both seats so it would fit us better. I was able to ride it over here, no problem. With the two of us, we'll get there in no time. She lives out on Suey Road. It's only five miles from here." He laid his hand over mine, which was on the bike seat, where I was trying to steady myself.

I shook my head. "We need to call my mom. We need to call Deuce."

"Hold up a sec. Think about that. What's your mom going to say?"

I drew a big, shaky breath. "She'll tell us to stay still, not move so much as one inch, and she'll be here in twenty minutes."

"And will she take us to Bijou's place to get Buster?"

"Not if they're not home. She'll want to have a meeting at school and work this all out. She would not be in favor of us breaking into Bijou's house. And she would probably not want me to hang out with you ever again." Those last two words were like a punch to my gut.

"Exactly," Micah said. "And what would Deuce tell you to do?"

"Pretty much the same—"

"Ham, what is the Most. Important. Thing. Right. Now?"

"The two of us staying out of prison?"

"Funny, but NO! We need to get Buster while we have a chance. At least I didn't take the Mustang. I thought about it. I *do* know how to drive."

I exploded with a sound that I didn't even recognize.

"See what I mean? I *knew* you would never go for that," as if he was now absolved because he hadn't committed grand theft auto. "I'm trying to do things more your way. Borrowing a bike to rescue a poor old cat is no big deal. Everyone will understand, believe me!"

I covered my face with my hands.

"Look, Ham, I'm going with or without you. So, you coming or not?" he asked.

He reached into his backpack and pulled out a sling contraption. "And, look, I got this cat carrier thing. You slip Buster into here," he said, pointing to the opening. "Then these straps go over your shoulders. I'll ride in the front, and all you will need to do is hold Buster and pedal."

My mind raced. He was right. He was wrong. He was both. How could that even be *possible*? He already had a cat carrier? How did he always manage to make me start to believe he was right when he was doing all the wrong things?

I unfolded the sling fully, and studied it. The idea that I could have Buster tucked in there, safe with me, in a matter of minutes filled me with such hope and relief that I couldn't spend one more minute standing there.

"Okay, I'm in," I said, and breathed out hard.

Micah clapped me on the shoulder and smiled. "I knew you would be!"

"Wait! We don't have helmets," I said.

"Which is why we are going to be extra careful," Micah cautioned. "I didn't see any helmets in his office or garage."

I shook my head. "And look, these are those clip-in pedals! We don't have clip-in bike shoes."

"I did fine on the way over," he said. "You'll get used to it. And we both have our trail shoes on. The treads mostly keep your feet from slipping off."

This was such a bad idea. Still. I grabbed my hoodie out of my gym bag, and pulled my sweatpants over my wet shorts. Then I tossed the bag into the bushes. I couldn't ride and carry Buster and my gym bag.

Micah considered his backpack a minute. "I don't want to leave this here. I have some important stuff in it. Here," he said. "Can you wear it? If I wear it, it will be in your face on the bike, and in your way."

"Sure," I said, taking it and putting my arms through the straps. It was heavy, and packed to the limit. "Geez! What do you have in here?" I asked.

"Some new school clothes I had to pick up for Mason. Sorry about that."

"It's fine," I said, and looked around. "It's getting dark. Please tell me the lights work at least."

Micah clicked the front light on. The beam was

strong and bright. Then he snapped on the flashing back light. "We're good."

"Well, come on, then!" I said. "It's getting darker by the minute."

"Ham, could you stop trying to steer from back there? You're making the bike wobble! You just pedal."

I shivered under my sweatshirt. My track clothes were wet and clammy against me. I probably stunk to high heaven. I wanted my cat. I wanted a scalding shower.

"Sorry!" I said over his shoulder.

I still couldn't believe what Micah and I were doing—riding a stolen tandem on our way to break into a classmate's house. I wanted the life back where Mom was my teacher, Deuce thought I was the best kid in the world, Fey was my after-school and weekend friend, and the Church Ladies watched my back.

Even as I thought that, I knew that having met Micah, there was no going back to my old life. Not after having just been kissed—or nudged, I should say. Not with these crazy, wild feelings I had for him. But I had to do something to help him stop ~~bending~~ *breaking* the law when he felt like it. And just as soon as we rescued Buster, I would get right to work on that.

Micah downshifted, and the bike came to a shaky stop. We tilted hard to the right. My feet slipped off the slick metal pedals, and hit the ground. Micah and I righted the bike before it hit the curb.

Some guy from a car yelled at us as he passed by, "You need to be in helmets, you two!"

Micah gave him a salute, and then turned and said to me, "Sorry. Saw the red light at the last minute."

"S'kay, just let me know when you're going to stop, or turn, or anything. It's hard to see back here."

"Okay, we're almost out of town. It's a straight shot after that with no more stop signs. We can pick up some good speed on Suey Road. I can't wait to see how fast we can get this baby going."

A beat-up red sedan pulled up next to us, filled with what looked like a bunch of high school students. They rolled down their windows on the side next to us. Country music blasted from their radio.

"Aw, aren't they sweet?" a girl shouted from the back seat.

"Hey, cuties," another girl called. "Want to come party with us?"

"Forget it, girls," the driver yelled. "Can't you tell? That's true love right there. They don't want to party with *girls*."

The whole car started making gross kissing noises at us.

Micah turned, and I could see his furious glare at the car. He raised his hand in a bad gesture. I grabbed his arm and pulled it down. "Ignore them!" I shouted.

They gunned their motor then, and as the light turned green, left us in their dust.

We tried to start back up, but both our feet kept slipping off the pedals. Which were not pedals at all, but small metal discs not much bigger or thicker than an Oreo cookie. Trying to keep our feet from sliding off was hard.

The bike leaned hard right and crashed on its side against the curb.

"Okay, just stop," I said. "Let's catch our breath." I tried not to think about how badly we'd just scratched the bike as we lifted it back up under us. It was too dark now to tell.

"I wish I had some duct tape. We could tape the pedals to our shoes," he muttered.

"Yeah, well, except if we started to tip and go down, we wouldn't be able to get off the bike."

"Ready?" I asked. I got my foot in position, steadied the bike under me, and watched him do the same. "On three—*one—two—three*!"

We both hopped back on our seats, feet where they were supposed to be, and moved back into the bike lane. I tried to see up and around Micah's head so I knew what was coming. Looked like we had a pretty decent straightaway out of town.

A single cyclist zoomed up behind us. He yelled, "On your left!" and then sped ahead of us. "Helmets, guys!" he called once he got around us.

"Sorry!" I shouted up to him.

Micah's backpack felt heavier and heavier as the blocks went by. The straps cut into my shoulder blades. I felt like I was carrying bricks, not new clothes for a little boy.

I tugged at the straps when Micah hollered over his shoulder, "Okay! Suey Road—taking a LEFT!" He steered us out of the bike lane and into the middle traffic lane. "Going for it—light's yellow!"

Cars blasted their horns as Micah took the left in front of oncoming traffic. "Faster!" he shouted. I pedaled as hard as I could, and tried not to look.

He whooped and laughed as we cleared the intersection and hit Suey Road.

"Micah!" I yelled. "That's not us being extra careful without helmets. Remember?"

"Sorry," he said. "I knew we'd make it. We're

really getting the hang of it now. We'll be able to go a lot faster. There's less traffic here."

"And less light!" I said. "Let's just get there in one piece, okay?"

In addition to it being darker on Suey Road, there wasn't a marked bike lane. On our left were houses with big unkept yards. To our right was a narrow dirt shoulder that dropped down into a wide concrete ditch. There were some cars parked on the shoulder, and Micah wove in and around them.

I didn't like riding in back, especially not being able to steer. I remember hearing Mr. Flynn talk about how hard it was not to jerk the handlebars when you're on the back. You have to trust the front guy. He steers, he strategizes, and you pedal.

Lights from a car crept up behind us. I yelled for Micah to move us over. We were too far out in the middle of the road. He turned to look at the car behind us, and then steered us out of their way.

Once they passed us, I could feel Micah picking up the pace, pedaling faster. His head was bent down, and he fiddled with the tiny cycling computer on the handlebars. "Come on, let's crank it up! Let's try for twenty-five miles per hour. We'll get there in no time flat if we do."

Another car came up from behind us again, flashing their headlights on and off. Micah moved us over so they could get around us. Instead they pulled up next to us. I recognized the red sedan. They'd switched from country music to pop.

"*There* they are!"

"It's the LOVEBIRDS!"

Micah stayed intent on building our speed, and kept motioning for them to pass. We ignored them.

"Ohhhh!" The driver yelled across the passenger side. "I think the baby queers want to be alone."

Micah turned then, and yelled, "SHUT UP!"

The girl in back said, "Let's go, Jake. Leave them alone."

But Jake edged toward us again.

"Please drive *ON*!" I pleaded, waving them away from us with my hand.

The guy riding shotgun laughed and said, "Uh-oh! Little gay boy is getting cranky!"

Micah sat up tall in his seat. He pulled his phone out of his pocket and shouted toward their car. "Hey! Move up, will you! I need a good shot of your license plate for the COPS!"

But they stayed in place alongside of us, so Micah pushed us faster. When we were right ahead of them, he turned then in his seat, and started taking pictures of the car.

So it was only me who noticed the large dark pickup parked on the shoulder in front of us.

"MI-*CAAAH*!" I shouted.

Too late, he turned back around, wrenched the handlebars, and squeezed the brakes. The bike shimmied, shuddered, and then slammed sideways into the back of the pickup. And as metal hit metal, I heard the sound of air being forced from our lungs as Micah and I flew off the bike.

And then, a godforsaken silence.

# CHAPTER THIRTY-EIGHT

My eyes shot open from white-hot pain, searing my shoulder and ribs. I blinked to focus. Turned my head toward Micah. He was sprawled a few feet from me, looking dazed. There was blood on his mouth. I tried to reach for him, but a wave of dizziness washed over me. "Micah! You *okay*?"

"Uh . . . yeah . . . think so . . ."

"Your mouth is bleeding!"

He put his hand to his mouth. "My jaw," he mumbled. "I must have bit my lip." He tested his teeth with a finger, then eased up onto his elbow, and looked at me.

"Are you all right?"

"I *think* so," I said. I still had two arms and two

legs. I ran my hand over my head. It was still in one piece. But I felt like I'd fallen off a cliff.

"Where are those *idiots*?" Micah asked. He winced as he turned his trunk to look behind us.

"Huh?"

"Those jerks who nearly ran us off the road!"

"I dunno. Gone, I guess." I pulled myself into a sitting position. Tried to pull my arms out of Micah's backpack, but it hurt like hell. I breathed through another blast of dizziness.

"Oh no!" I moaned.

"What?" Micah said. "What *is it*?" He got on all fours and came toward me.

"The bike! Look!"

Deuce and Mr. Flynn's tandem lay on its side, partially hidden under the truck. But I could see the front wheel folded like a taco, and the spokes were broken.

"Oh man," Micah said. He eased up to his feet, and limped over. He pulled the bike up and out. Even the frame was bent.

I had to close my eyes. I couldn't bear to look anymore.

"Guess we won't be riding home," Micah said. He blew out a gust. "Oh man, Deuce is going to kill us." He ran a hand over the back side of the pickup then.

"Well, the truck did better than the bike, but the owner is not going to be happy with these scratches."

I was still stuck on his saying that Deuce was going to kill "us." Even though Micah was the one who had burgled Deuce's house and stolen the bike. But he was right. I was in this up to my neck.

He leaned over me, held out a hand to help me up. As he gripped my hand and pulled, the pain in my shoulder was brutal. I let out a sharp cry.

"You're hurt!" Micah said.

I bit down hard on my lower lip to fight the pain. "A little. I jammed up my shoulder. It'll be okay. But we need to call and get some help."

What I didn't tell him was that it was hard for me to get a full breath. I tried to find a comfortable way to sit so I didn't pass out.

"Here, let me get my pack off you." He tried to ease the straps off, but I cried out again.

"Leave it!" I begged.

"Right, okay, we did need help, but let's think a sec." He cursed under his breath. "Okay, here's what we have to do." He wiped the blood off his mouth with the bottom of his shirt. He felt his teeth again.

I held on to my shoulder, waiting. For what, I wasn't sure. We needed help. Checked my legs again.

They still moved. I could feel quads, knees, calves, and ankles. Thank God.

"Here's what needs to happen. I need to get out of here."

I stared at him. He was going to leave me?

"If I stay here, when the police come, they're going to want to call my mom. I can't let that happen."

"But—" I started.

"I mean, we have to let the cops know about the accident, and about those jerks who ran us off the road. And you need medical help."

"They didn't run us off the road," I said. "You weren't looking where you were going!"

"I know! Because they were chasing us, and then they called us, you know, *queers*!"

Micah looked incensed about that.

"Oh," I said, my voice small.

"This is all their fault! We were just minding our own business, trying to rescue Buster." He rubbed his jaw, and tried to roll his neck.

"You sure you're okay?" I asked. "You need to see a doctor, too. I can tell you've hurt your leg."

"I'll be okay, but I need to get out of here." He ran his hands through his hair, then pulled his hoodie up over his head.

"Where are you going to go?" I asked, still dumbstruck that he was going to leave me here.

"Home eventually. I can catch a bus. But, look, I was *never* here, Ham. Do you understand?"

"No!" I reached for his hand, but he pulled it away.

He wiped his nose in the crook of his elbow. "I feel terrible that you hurt your shoulder." He sighed hard. "And, that we wrecked Deuce's bike, but that can be fixed. He's gotta have insurance, right? And I'm sorry we couldn't get Buster tonight."

Buster! I remembered all of a sudden why we'd even been doing this.

"Okay," he continued. "You have your cell phone, right?"

I patted the pocket of my sweats. I tried to lift my shoulder to move my hand to my pocket. I was speared by another bolt of hot pain.

"Here, I'll get it." Micah reached into my pocket and pulled it out. He looked over at me with a frown. "Bad news. It's dead."

I'd been on the phone so much about Buster, and I'd forgotten to charge it before I went to bed last night.

"Well, call my mom, or, maybe the police? I can't think right now. Just call someone, okay?"

"I would, but I don't want the call traced back to my phone. They trace 911 calls. Remember, I was never here. You're going to have to take the hit for this."

I breathed out hard, and it hurt so bad I had to grab my side.

"I promise I'll make this up to you. I know things look terrible right now, but your mom and Deuce will totally understand that you went into his house and borrowed the bike. But they wouldn't understand if I did it. You'll get in so much less trouble than I would."

"Right," I said, trying to find a more comfortable way to sit. There wasn't one.

"I'll find a pay phone. I promise I'll get you some help. Just try and relax, okay? You don't look too good."

"Just go and call for help," I said, trying to hold it together. I fought a tsunami of nausea.

Micah studied his backpack, still on my back. "I wish I could get that off you. I could empty it, but I don't have anything to put all the stuff in. And I've gotta walk a couple of miles, probably."

I nodded, too weak to tell him how stupid it was to even worry about that right now.

He touched his chin and lips. "Am I still bleeding?"

"Just a little."

He pulled his scarf down to wipe his mouth. He had a big nasty scratch across the front of his neck. He rewound the scarf around it. "I'll take care of it all when I get home. Okay, let's go over this one more time. You need to get the story right and stick to it."

"I got it," I said, waving him off. "Go." I was seconds away from heaving, and I didn't want him to watch.

"You'll say that *you* borrowed the tandem to go pick up Buster from Bijou," he started.

"Why would I take Deuce's tandem, instead of just riding my own bike? That doesn't make any sense!"

"Right," Micah said, considering that. "Oh, I know! So, you needed my help getting Buster from Bijou, so you took the tandem so we could both go. And I was supposed to meet you outside the school, but then I had to go pick up Mason. You decided to go without me, and took the tandem anyway. It would have taken too much time to go back home, to get your own bike."

"And I suppose I broke into Deuce's house," I said, dropping my head into my hands and groaning.

"Yeah, but your mom and Deuce will totally understand why you had to do that, right?"

I had no idea whether they would or not.

"Someday this will be one of those funny stories," he said.

Great, just what I needed. Another "funny story" from eighth grade. Like the one about Buster coming to my class the first day to wash my face.

My poor Buster. I was so mad he was at Bijou's, but so relieved he was alive. Maybe I could convince the cops to stop and get him on the way to the hospital. Yeah, probably not.

Micah leaned down and gave me a soft pat on top of my head. "Hey," he said. "Do you think you can stand up? We need to get out of the road, at least. Can you make it across the street?"

I gave him the arm that hurt less, and he pulled me up. He steered me across the road, and sat me down on the curb. Then he went and gathered up the bike and brought that over and laid it near me.

"Good. That's better! There's more light here. The cops will be able to find you, and no one will, like, run you over while you're waiting."

"Great!" I said sarcastically.

"Oh, and here," he said. He pulled keys out of his pocket. "Here's Deuce's keys."

I didn't reach for them. I sat mummified, my hands

holding my shoulders and rib cage together. Trying not to move anything.

"Oh, right." He crouched down and shoved them into my pocket for me. "All set now!" he said.

I waited until he was about a half a block away. I stopped fighting the rolling nausea. I threw up all over my track shoes. The ones that used to belong to the team captain. But now belonged to the kid about to get in the biggest trouble of his life.

# CHAPTER THIRTY-NINE

I thought my head would split right in two as the siren grew closer. I wondered how long I'd been out here. My nasty track clothes felt like they had grown attached to my skin.

I tried to answer the officers' questions best as I could. Yes, I was alone. Yes, I knew two people usually ride a tandem. Yes, that was my puke. When the lady cop asked if I could stand, I tried. I nearly collapsed from the pain this time. She helped set me back down and promised me an ambulance was on the way.

"Let's get this backpack off you," she said. "It looks heavy."

"He—I mean, *I* already tried. I can't move my shoulder right now."

“Can I cut the straps?” she asked.

“No!” I didn’t think Micah would want his backpack ruined. Though that should be the least of my worries right now, considering the mess he’d left me in.

“Well, let me get a bag out of the car. I can at least empty it for you. And I’ll try to call your mom again.”

“Uh, great, thanks,” I said, staring at my vomit-covered shoes. I was a stinkin’ mess.

When she left, the other officer stooped down to study the bike. I’d already told them when they first arrived how I’d accidentally plowed into the back of the pickup.

“This is a heck of a bike—wow, it’s a da Vinci. Custom-built?”

“Yeah,” I said.

“Is it yours?” he asked.

I shook my head. “It belongs to my neighbor.”

“Does he know you’re out riding it in the dark by yourself? Without a helmet?”

“It wasn’t dark when I left,” I said, trying to avoid his questions.

The lady officer returned then, and unzipped my pack. She pulled the contents out, and I sighed with relief to have that weight off my back.

She came around to the front of me, holding up two leather jackets, with price tags dangling from them. "These yours?" she asked.

I stared at them, trying to make sense of it. Micah had said he'd bought his little brother some clothes for school. But these were adult jackets.

"Yeah, uh . . ."

She studied the price tag on one. "Expensive jackets. Do you have the receipt for these?"

"I . . . um . . . no, I guess I don't . . . no, no receipts, ma'am."

She cocked her head at me. "Where did you get them?"

*Stick to the story,* Micah had said to me. But he didn't tell me the story included taking a rap for shoplifting.

"Ma'am, did you get ahold of my mom yet?"

"Not yet. She's not at the prison, so she must be on her way home. I'll swing by there once the ambulance gets here."

The other cop cut in. "Son, I'm going to need the name and phone number of your neighbor who owns this bike."

Oh no. I swallowed. "His name is Deuce, uh, Deuce Jewett, but please, *please* don't call him."

"Does he know you took his bike out?" the lady cop asked.

"No, but he'll understand if you let me explain it to him first. No offense, but he doesn't like to talk to the police."

"Hmm," she said, her eyes darting to the other cop.

He stepped away from us then, and spoke quietly into the radio on his shoulder. But I thought I heard him say Deuce's name.

Little bright lights began dancing before my eyes, and my stomach rolled. The street tilted.

And that's the last thing I remember before I passed out, the pain shooting my eyeballs into the back of my head.

There was a soft hand on my forehand when I opened my eyes. Mom stared down at me. "There's my guy," she said.

"Mom!" I reached for her hand. My mouth was dry and fuzzy.

"Easy," she said. She held up a glass of water and gently put the straw into my mouth.

I was pretty sure I hadn't had a drink of water in like a year.

"Mom! Buster is at *Bijou's* house. He didn't go in the delivery truck. I have to go get him." I tried to sit up, but one arm was bound to my side, and everything hurt so bad.

"One thing at a time," she said. She put a cool hand against my forehead. I sighed. It felt like heaven.

"You're grounded until the day you die, you know."

I nodded.

"The police are somewhere hovering about. They need to talk to you. You ready to talk?"

"Do I have to?" I whispered.

"Well, it seems you've been on a crime spree since I saw you last. Yeah, they need to talk to you. How about first you tell *me* what happened?"

"What do you mean, 'crime spree'? I just borrowed Deuce's bike—"

"No, you seem to have stolen Deuce's bike. You did not have permission to borrow it or ride it. How did you get into his house? You don't have a key."

"I know where he hides a key," I said, my face flashing with color. Too late I remembered that I had a set of Deuce's keys in my sweatpants. Which they seemed to have taken away from me at some point.

"Interesting," she said, and shook her head.

"I'm sorry about all of this, Mom." She did not

need this kind of stress in her life. She needed less stress.

"You also had about three hundred dollars of stolen property in a backpack you were wearing. Which I know for a fact is not yours. You only took your gym bag to school today. Your backpack is on the dining room table. Whose backpack is it?"

"Wull, um," I said, and then stopped. There was no explaining any of this.

"Ham?" Mom prodded, her voice now getting stern.

"Water," I said, trying to give myself a minute.

She put the straw to my mouth. I downed the remainder, and tried to think through the fog for some reasonable explanation. I'd promised Micah I wouldn't rat on him, but I never thought it would be this complicated covering for all the stuff he'd done.

"I—I—I needed those jackets to get Buster back. Bijou has him, Mom! She told me at practice that she wanted the five-hundred-dollar reward, plus a couple of new jackets for Royce and Benny because they helped her."

I colored again as Mom's eyes drilled into mine.

"You ready to tell that load of baloney to the cops?"

"It's the truth!"

"My son broke into our dearest friend's house, stole a tandem bicycle with immense sentimental value, and rode it by himself on a shoplifting spree. Then wrecked it on the side of the road? All this after track practice?"

I nodded.

"I've taught you better than this," she said. "You know that. Stop lying to me right now. Who was with you?"

I stared at my lap. I couldn't bear to look her in the eyes.

"Okay, then, I'll have you try to sell that to the police. You're getting quick at this lying thing, but you're terrible at it." She went to the door and stuck her head out. She came back with the man cop.

"This is Officer Mendoza. He has some questions he needs to ask you. Tell him the truth, Ham, for God's sake." She turned and looked at the officer. "He's going to be X-rayed pretty soon. They think he's broken his collarbone, and maybe some ribs. But until they need him, he's all yours, sir."

The cop pulled up the visitor chair and sat down, lifting his utility belt so he didn't sit on all the weapons strapped to it. I swallowed. Hard.

"How old are you, son?"

"Thirteen, sir."

"Can you tell me what happened after your cross-country practice today? Your coach confirmed that you were there, and had quite a workout."

"Right, but I heard that this kid on my team was the one who had stolen my cat. I needed to get out there to her house quick to get him. She's kind of hard to get along with, so my friend Micah was going to go there with me. So I made a very bad decision to borrow—"

"Steal—" Mom interrupted.

The cop shot a look at her, clearly not wanting any parent participation in my confession.

"Right," I continued, "so I made a very bad decision to steal my neighbor's tandem. I know where he hides his house key, so it was easy to get into his place. And then Micah couldn't come with me after all. So I ended up riding out to the girl's house by myself. It got dark, and I crashed into a parked truck on her street."

Mom harrumphed.

"Ma'am?" The cop gave her a warning glance and continued. "Did you stop anywhere on your way to the crash?"

"I did not, sir," I said.

He scribbled notes at that, and I looked at Mom. She just put her head in her hands.

Oh God, what if she had a heart attack from all of this? I would never forgive myself.

"Mom, are you okay?" I asked. "Maybe you should wait outside."

"I'm fine," she said. "I wouldn't dream of missing any of this adventure of yours."

"Son," the cop went on. "If you didn't stop anywhere on your way to get your cat, how did those jackets get into your backpack? Did someone give you the backpack to hold for them?"

"No! No one gave it me. I just forgot that I stopped to steal some stuff."

"I see," he said, and nodded encouragingly. "Where exactly did you stop?"

I squirmed a bit in my hospital bed. I had no idea where Micah had taken them from. Maybe he hadn't even stolen them. Maybe the receipt was in his pants pocket. But he had lied to me about what was in the backpack, so I felt pretty certain he had taken them without paying. "Some store on Broad Street. I can't remember the name right now."

"Where did you park the tandem while you went shoplifting?" he asked.

"Right out front," I said. "I didn't have a lock for it, so I wanted to keep an eye on it."

"How long were you in the store?"

"I dunno, maybe twenty minutes. I didn't try stuff on or anything. I just shoved them in my backpack."

"And no one in the store noticed you doing that?"

"No, the girl in the store was on her cell phone the whole time," I lied. But it did seem possible.

"Okay, son. Last question, at least for tonight. "The girl who called the accident in said that there were two males riding the tandem on Suey, not just one."

I swallowed. "A girl called it in?"

"Yes, she said that she and her friends were teasing the two of you, and as they drove off, they saw you two crash the bike."

The girl from the red sedan called it in? Micah never called the cops?

I licked my lips and reached for the water again. Mom refilled the glass from the small pitcher on my bedside table.

"Ham, can you explain why she told us there were two people riding the tandem, not just you, as you've said?"

"Maybe she needs glasses?" I offered. "And it was pretty dark out there."

Officer Mendoza continued. "We've spoken to your neighbor, Mr. Jewett, and he confirmed he is the owner of the tandem. We're sending someone to his house now so that he can show us the bill of sale for it. Ham, I want you to think long and hard about this next question before you answer it."

I nodded, glad for the chance to have some time to figure out how to answer it, whatever it was.

"Was Mr. Jewett the other person on the bike with you?"

My mouth dropped open. Huh?

The cop looked over at Mom. "Did you know that your neighbor is a felon? We just ran his background."

"Yes, I know that, and still I would trust him with my life, and my son's life," she said. "Deuce would not take my son out shoplifting, or riding in the dark without a helmet. And he absolutely would not leave him in the street injured!"

Mom looked at me to back her up.

I hesitated a moment. Would telling them Deuce was with me be a safer way to keep Micah in the clear? Maybe I could explain that Deuce had left me only to go get help.

"Ham?" Mom said.

"Wull, right. Deuce is a totally great guy, sir."

"Noted," Officer Mendoza said. "Please answer my question. Was Mr. Jewett the one who stole the jackets you had in your pack? And was he on the tandem with you when you crashed?"

My mind was spinning at warp speed. If I could just talk to Deuce, maybe he wouldn't mind covering for Micah. He was very understanding. Especially if he knew why it was so important.

"Abraham Hudson, you tell this officer right now that Deuce had nothing to do with this!" Mom said, as angry as I think I'd ever seen her.

"Ma'am, please, I'm going to have to ask you to leave the room if you can't let me handle this."

I looked at Mom, and then looked away. "I'd like to take the Fifth," I said at last.

# CHAPTER FORTY

Officer Mendoza ran his hand over his buzz cut.

Mom took the Lord's name in vain.

"Aren't I supposed to get a phone call? May I please call Deuce?" I asked, looking back and forth between them. "I have to talk to him."

A man in hospital scrubs came into the room just then. "Excuse me," he said. "I need to take this young man to X-ray."

Mom backed out of his way. As I was wheeled away, she gave me a look that I'd never seen before. It was worse than mad. I had let her down so bad. I didn't think there was even a word for that kind of disappointed.

I tried desperately not to think about how Deuce

was feeling about now. I knew he'd be upset about the bike being wrecked. But he'd be relieved that I wasn't hurt too awful. And like Micah said, the insurance would take care of all the damages. He'd be sore at me, for sure, for how stupid he'd think I'd been, even though the stupid belonged mostly to Micah. Didn't it?

I wished hard there was a way I could let Mom and Deuce know that I was trying to keep Micah and Mason from having to go into foster care. Or, to keep Micah from going to Juvenile Hall—what would happen to poor Mason then?

Mom didn't even come with me to X-ray. She was that upset with me.

After all the god-awful stuff that had gone on, X-ray was a piece of cake. The worst part was when they had to cut my Harvey Mellencamp T-shirt off me. Fey had bought it for me at our school's first pep rally. I couldn't lift my shoulder for them to take it off, so they sliced it off.

"How's your shoulder feeling?" Mom asked after they wheeled me back into my room.

"Hurts," I said, nervous about being in the room alone with her right now.

"Want me to call the nurse for you?"

"Nah." I licked my lips. "Did you talk to Deuce yet? Is he really mad?"

"He's very upset," she said. "You could have been hurt much worse than this." She paused and then continued. "I didn't tell him that you just about threw him under the bus a few minutes ago with Officer Mendoza."

I dropped my head. I couldn't meet her gaze.

"Can you imagine how it feels for him to have the cops at his house, having to prove the tandem is his? And, even worse, being asked if he'd stolen a couple of jackets, and then abandoned you after a crash?" Hurt lined her face.

I knew that this was Deuce's worst nightmare. I swallowed hard. How did everything get so messed up?

She slid a chair over to the bed next to me and sat down. "Ham, I need you to listen to me. You have a very short window of time here to think about what you're doing. It is a very noble thing to stick up for your friends when they are in trouble. But it is a very stupid thing to try to cover for them when they've done something very wrong. You are in way over your head. Didn't I teach you to tell the truth? That's what you need to do right now. Please!"

"I know you don't understand. But I promise you I

am doing the right thing," I said.

"No—you are not. You have to trust me on this one. Just tell the officer when he comes back the whole truth, who you were with, who took Deuce's tandem, and who stole those jackets."

The door whooshed open, and Officer Mendoza came back in.

"Okay, we've talked to Mr. Jewett. He has a solid alibi for the time frame in question. But he does want to proceed with pressing charges for breaking and entering, and the theft of the tandem."

"*What?* Deuce wants to press charges against me?"

The officer nodded. "Well, he wants to press charges against whoever broke into his home and took his tandem. From all you've told me, that would be you. Am I correct?"

My head pounded unbearably.

"You are also facing additional charges of shoplifting. But we'll let the judge sort all that out at your hearing."

Fear curled its snaky fingers around the back of my neck.

"Ma'am, once Ham is released here, you can take him home to get some rest. But tomorrow, you'll need to take him to the Juvenile Services Department so that he can be processed on these charges. Until then, you'll need to assume full responsibility for his supervision."

"Absolutely," Mom said, the color draining from her face. "You have my word that we will cooperate fully. And, he will remain under my direct supervision."

Mom walked Officer Mendoza out then, probably having questions she didn't want to ask in front of me. Or, maybe, trying to explain to him that I was usually a model boy and excellent citizen.

While she was gone, I tried to sort out all the things I needed to do. First, I needed to call Micah and make sure he was okay. Maybe he never called the accident in because he was hurt, and collapsed somewhere on his long walk home.

Then I needed to convince Mom to take me to Bijou's to get Buster. But if we went there now, and Bijou and her uncle weren't home, I knew Mom would not let me break in to get him.

But I could call Bijou at her uncle's bar, and tell her I knew she had Buster. She could meet us there and give him back. If she would, and that was a big IF.

I wanted to call Fey, who was probably sick with worry. She would have seen the cops come to Deuce's house, and maybe she even knew that I was at the hospital.

I had to talk to Deuce, too, and explain as much as I could without telling him about Micah. If he'd even be willing to talk to me tonight after all he'd been through.

I searched around the room to see if my clothes were there, so that I could get to my phone. Then, I remembered that the battery was dead. Maybe Mom had her charger in her purse and would let me use it.

When Mom came back to the room, she had the doctor with her, who'd come looking for her. He told us that I had a collarbone dislocation that was stable, and a couple of busted ribs. There was nothing to do but keep them immobile, and try to manage the pain. He touched me on the good shoulder and told me I wouldn't be able to play any contact sports for a while.

"Does that mean cross-country?" I said. "We have our first meet this coming weekend."

He gave me a sympathetic look and said, "Son, you are not going to feel like running for at least a couple of weeks. Take my word on that."

"But if I could handle the pain, *could* I?" I asked.

He looked at me, then over at Mom. He shook his

head as he signed something on the chart at the end of my bed. "Cross-country is too jarring a sport. I'm afraid you're benched for a bit."

"But I can't be benched," I said, near breathless. "I'm the team captain!"

He reached over and shook my hand, then Mom's. "I'm so sorry" was all he said. The door closed behind him.

I couldn't take it all in. And, I didn't know which was worse, missing the chance to run in my first meet, or letting Coach and the team down. It was a blow. A *big* one.

And here it was. After just a couple months of public school, a massive wrecking ball had just swung into my life and flattened nearly everything good about it. Nearly everything good about me. I was copping to crimes I didn't commit. I was lying to my mom like I never had before. And worst of all, I stood by and let the police think that Deuce might be involved in tonight's crime escapade.

How could so many terrible things happen just because I wanted to get my cat back?

An image of that wrecking ball flashed across my mind then, and Micah's name was etched on it in big black letters.

But that couldn't be right! Micah had been trying to help me with Buster, and trying to protect Mason. Deep down, he was kind and good. It wasn't his fault that he didn't have a parent who did their job with him.

I had fallen hard for him. I liked him so much, and with feelings that I now knew for sure were more than friendship. He must have liked me that same way, or he wouldn't have kissed me tonight. But I was so mad at him that the kiss, my very first, would always be linked to the night when everything went so wrong. There wasn't a single Motown song that would be able to help me remember the kiss without remembering lies and betrayals, his and my own.

I wanted Micah to be my boyfriend—didn't I? Somehow, this giant mess would get sorted out. He'd realize after tonight that I was true blue. He'd be so grateful that he'd stop hanging out with Bijou, and he'd try harder to be nice to Fey.

He owed me at least that after the worst night of my life.

# CHAPTER FORTY-ONE

It was late by the time Mom and I got home from the hospital. Once we'd gotten into the van, I'd asked her if we could go by Bijou's house, or her uncle's bar, so we could get Buster back. Mom looked like I'd just asked her if we could stop at the airport and take a shuttle to Mars.

I decided to stay quiet the rest of the ride, letting her catch her breath and calm down.

The cops were still at Deuce's house when we pulled up. My stomach dropped like a stone. I put my hoodie up and lowered myself in the passenger seat. Mom glanced over at me and raised an eyebrow.

"Yeah, awkward as heck, isn't it?" she said. Then she patted my arm to soften her words. "C'mon, let's get you inside."

My right arm was in a sling, and the sling was held in place against my chest with a big elastic band to keep it from flopping around while I moved. I had to use my left hand to open the car door, and then slid slowly out of my seat to the ground below. I drew a big breath and looked across the street. Cops were unloading the tandem in pieces from their back seat and trunk. They handed them all to Deuce. Like a broken corpse.

Mom came up to me and watched.

"Should I go over there?" I asked, looking up at her. "He sees us."

She gave Deuce a wave and steered me into the house. "Let's all get a good night's sleep before we tackle that."

Mom carried a clear plastic bag from the hospital that held my wet track clothes. My phone should have been in the bag, too. "I'm going to throw these in the wash, and then we'll see about getting you fed and settled."

"Um, while you do that, can I have my phone? It's dead and I want to charge it."

"No, sir. I'm keeping your phone for now."

"But I need to call—" I started.

"There is no one you need to call. I will call Fey and let her know you're home and okay. And now

Deuce knows you're home."

"Great, thanks. But I wanted to let Micah know I'm okay, too."

"Not tonight," she said, and I could tell by her jaw that she meant business.

"He'll be worried about me, Mom."

She pulled my phone out of the wet mess of my stuff. She tucked it into her back pocket. "Why would he be worried about you? He wasn't there when you got hurt, was he?"

She had me, and she knew it.

"You need a shower. The nurse showed me how we can wrap your arm and sling in a big plastic bag so you don't get it wet. I'll help you with that. I'll make you some quesadillas while you're in the shower." She dropped the bag on the counter, and picked up our house phone. "This is going into my bedroom, and it's going to stay there for now."

If my mom ever got tired of being a priest, she'd make an excellent prison guard.

"Okay, Mom," I said. "I know I don't deserve any consideration right now, but Buster hasn't done anything wrong. Can't you just go get him? Please?"

"Shower, and then we talk."

* * *

Despite having a giant garbage bag wrapped around my trunk, taking a shower had never felt so good. The drying off and getting dressed was miserable, but I would learn to manage. Whatever they'd given me at the hospital for pain was wearing off.

My hair was still wet and spiked in several directions when I came out to the kitchen bar.

I hadn't been able to put a shirt on, so I just had the damp towel wrapped around my shoulders. I collapsed onto a stool and watched Mom finish making my dinner.

"Thanks, Mom, it smells really good."

She passed me a plate with two large, stuffed quesadillas and a side of salsa.

I noticed she was drinking a glass of wine, which she didn't do too often. I'd heard Deuce telling her a little red wine was good for her heart, and she seemed to be taking him up on it tonight.

She didn't come sit with me, but instead just stood and watched me from the kitchen.

"I just called Principal Strickland, and told her what happened tonight. She gave me the name and number of Bijou's uncle."

I stopped mid-chew. Oh God, she told the principal.

"Turns out that I know Bijou's uncle, Mr. McGuire. We have a number of common connections. He assured me that Buster is not at their house. Apparently, Bijou is severely allergic to animal dander of any kind. He also said that while his niece was a little 'rough around the edges,' she would never do anything that might hurt or frighten an animal."

"But Micah said she had him! He wouldn't make that up. I mean, he was going to go there with me and rescue him. He had to have known for sure."

Mom just nodded, her fingers splayed around her wineglass. "Confusing, isn't it? Why do you suppose he said that, then?"

"I guess Royce lied to him about it," I said. But Micah had seemed so sure. It didn't make sense.

Mom continued. "I also had Principal Strickland give me the contact information for Micah's family. I think it's time that we all sit down and get to know each other."

"What do you mean by 'we'? Me, you, and Micah?" I asked, nearly choking on a piece of shredded lettuce.

"And his parents," she said.

"Parent, not parents. I told you he just has a mom, and she works two jobs. I'm sure she doesn't have time for a meeting."

"You've been busy trying to handle things on your own, Ham, and I have tried to respect that. But now that the police have gotten involved, the parents need to be involved."

"But you told me you *wouldn't* bust him for stealing from the collection basket. Are you going to tell his mom?" I dropped the quesadilla in my hand. "Please don't! You'll ruin everything."

"What will I be 'ruining'?"

"Well, for one, he's sort of like, you know—" I broke off, trying to find the words. I felt a wild panic at the thought of this meeting.

"Sort of like, what?" she asked.

I exhaled hard and pushed my plate away. "He's kind of like my *boyfriend*, Mom!"

"I see," she said, setting her glass down on the counter. "I know that you like him very much, Ham. What about him? Does he feel the same way about you?"

"Yes! Yes he does, Mom." I almost blurted to her that he'd kissed me tonight, but it felt like the most private thing in the world. I wasn't ready to tell her or anybody.

She nodded and her face looked soft, tired soft.

"Mom, he's so nice. You'll really like him once you

get to know him."

She came out of the kitchen then, and stood next to me. She raked her fingers through my wet hair and then laid her cheek on top of my head. She was quiet for a long moment while we just breathed each other in.

"Had enough to eat?" she asked finally.

"Yeah, thanks. Am I going to go to school tomorrow?"

She pulled the damp towel off me, and replaced it with my Superman blanket that still hung over the back of the couch. "Tomorrow is Friday, so I told Principal Strickland you were going to take a three-day weekend. She understands. You're probably going to be even more sore tomorrow. And you and I have some business to take care of with Officer Mendoza."

Unless this entire day could just magically disappear. Like maybe God would let you erase your one worst day. I'd pick this day hands down. Even though it meant erasing Micah's kiss. But I had to believe he would kiss me again.

A boy could hope.

You'd think after all I'd been through, sleep would have taken me out with one of the cartoon sledgehammers.

Instead, the day played itself over and over, like a vinyl record that kept repeating the same song. One that you never wanted to hear again.

None of it added up.

And it didn't look anything like my life. Least not what it looked like pre–Harvey Mellencamp.

I wondered if Mom was awake, too. I hoped she knew how much I loved her. How much I needed her. I hoped she wasn't regretting she ever found me in her Nativity scene.

And then, there was Micah.

For all these weeks I'd been irresistibly pulled toward him. Like Isaac Newton's apple to the ground, like magnet to metal, or a whale to the surface. It wasn't always a good feeling, either. Sometimes it felt desperate. I hadn't thought too much about where he and I might be headed. At first, I'd thought that I liked him so much because he was the first boy who ever wanted to be friends with me.

But then, my feelings began to shape-shift. I knew now that how I felt about him was how most boys felt about girls. Did liking another boy that way make me gay now and gay forever? Had I always been this way, and I just didn't know it?

Did I really want to be Micah's boyfriend? Did he

want to be mine? I'd finally just started to fit in at school. Did I want to do something else that would make me stand out? I remembered how mad he'd gotten when those kids in the red car called us "baby queers."

My mind returned again and again to our kiss. Why had he done it? Did he know how I felt, and wanted me to know he felt the same way? He'd said he'd wanted to for a very long time. Had he felt that same instant gravitational attraction that we learned about in science class?

Or, worse, and I hated to think this—and it was probably because I was dead tired and every part of my body hurt—but, did he kiss me to distract me from the fact that he'd broken into Deuce's house and stolen his bike?

Sleep didn't save me—it threw me deeper into the darkness.

# CHAPTER FORTY-TWO

Mom brought the house phone back out the next morning and handed it me. "I'm giving you your ONE phone call," she said.

My heart leapt. "Thanks, Mom!"

"You're going to use that to call Coach Becerra."

Heart landed at my feet with a thud.

"I'm sure she's already heard from Principal Strickland about what has happened to her team captain. Still, it's your responsibility to let her know yourself." Mom glanced up at the clock and said, "If you call now, you can probably catch her before the first bell at school."

I sighed, and even that made my ribs hurt. "I'll call her in a little bit. I need to think about what I'm going to say, okay?"

"I have a call in to Officer Mendoza to find out what time he'd like us to meet him at Juvenile Services. And I left a message for—" She stopped as the phone she'd just put in my hand started to ring.

"I'll take that," she said, and moved into her office.

I sat on the couch with a few T-shirts, older ones, and our sharpest scissors. Mom had shown me how and where to cut the material so I could manage wearing my shirts while I had an arm in a sling plastered across my front.

Mom hadn't closed her office door, so I half listened to her while, in my head, I practiced my talk with Coach that I dreaded making.

*Hello, Coach Becerra, it's Ham . . .*

"Yes, thank you so much for calling me back!" Mom said to her caller.

*I know you probably heard the news already, but I wanted to tell you myself . . .*

After a minute, Mom said, "Oh! You've talked to Principal Strickland, too. Excellent—"

*I had a bike accident last night, and I won't be able to run for a while.*

"I'm relieved to hear that . . . ," Mom said.

*Coach, I was thinking you should let Bijou be the team captain for the meet and practices . . .*

"How about we meet here at the parsonage? Would three thirty work—"

Wait, I thought, distracted by what Mom had just said. Officer Mendoza was coming here?

"You'll pick him up from practice and then bring him with you?" Mom asked.

Now, wait a minute! WHO is getting picked up from practice?

"Fine, and I look forward to meeting you and the judge."

Officer Mendoza was going to bring a judge with him? A cold sweat broke out on my neck. Was Mom arranging to hold Juvenile Court here?

She came out a moment later, and tossed the phone back to me. It clattered to the floor at my feet.

"Oh, sorry. I guess you're going to have to learn to catch with your left hand."

"We're having COURT here in our house at three thirty?" My voice sounded shrill.

She gave me a funny look, and shook her head. "No, we're having Micah and his parents over then. I told you I was going to arrange a sit-down with all of us."

"Who is this judge, then, and why is he coming?"

"Judge Tuttle is Micah's father."

* * *

Coach Becerra came by the parsonage during the school lunch break. She'd heard the message I'd left her, and came by to see how I was doing. She also brought me my weekend homework assignments.

Mom used the time I was with Coach to go across the street and talk with Deuce.

I'd have given anything to be able to eavesdrop on their conversation. What if Deuce never forgave me? What if he decided he didn't want to live in Muddy Waters anymore? Now that the police had been all over him and his very private life, what if he just wanted to leave? I couldn't lose Deuce, too.

Coach settled in an armchair across from me. "That," she said, gesturing to my sling and bandages, "looks pretty miserable."

"Yeah," I said. Mom had been right. Everything did feel worse today. I was sore to the bone. I wondered how Micah felt. He'd been limping when he left me on Suey Road last night.

After Coach explained my homework and got that business out of the way, she sat back in the chair and gave me a long look. "I know everything hurts," she said. "But I hope you know how incredibly lucky you are not to have been injured worse. Promise me you will never get on a bike again without a helmet."

"I promise," I said. "I know, it was stupid."

"This whole thing seems so unlike you, Ham. Principal Strickland filled me in on the details."

"Are you going to kick me off the team?" I asked, my heart thudding.

"I certainly wouldn't kick you off the team for being injured," she said. "As far as the rest of what went down last night, I suppose it depends."

"Depends on what?" I asked, already afraid to hear the answer.

"Depends on you," she said. "I don't think we've heard the whole story about what happened. And until that all becomes clear, I can't really say what I'll decide to do."

I dropped my gaze and squeezed my fingers in the sling. The nurse had told me to do that so they would have good blood flow to them.

"Coach, I really hope that you'll let Bijou be the team captain while I'm gone. And even after, if I don't get to come back," I said, the words red-hot in my throat. "I know she hasn't always been a model team player, but there isn't anyone else on the team who cares about it as much as she does. It's the one thing she and I have in common. The team means everything to us."

"I know," Coach said. "I see that. I'll have a talk with her later today. But I'm going to forfeit this first meet, all the same. You, Bijou, and Micah are the strongest runners. With you out of commission and Micah unreliable, we don't have a chance. We simply don't have enough legs to compete this time."

"I'm so sorry, Coach," I said, my voice unsteady. "I'd give anything to do yesterday over."

"I know, Ham. And even though we don't have the luxury of do-overs, we can do what we need to do to make things right in the aftermath."

I shook my head. "I can't make this better. I can only make it worse."

"Worse for who?" Coach studied me, her face thoughtful. Then she glanced at her watch. "I have to get back to school. Will we see you on Monday?"

"Yeah, I'll be back. Thanks for bringing my homework and everything."

"You're very welcome." She stood up to gather her things, then turned back toward me. "Do you remember when you first joined the team, and you and I were talking about making friends?"

I wiped at my nose with my sleeve. "You told me how important it was to find a good friend, and then watch their back at all times."

"Right, but what else did I say about that? You're leaving something really important out."

I frowned, trying to remember.

She slung her pack over her shoulder. "I said a good friend would have your back as well."

# CHAPTER FORTY-THREE

By three fifteen that afternoon, I was sweating like I'd just run the Farrell Trail while being chased by a hungry bobcat. To distract myself, for the last hour I'd been on my computer staring at cat photos at all the shelters in the county. Since Buster had an electronic chip, and we'd called all the shelters already, he wouldn't be in a photo lineup of unclaimed cats. The expressions on the cats' faces were more than my heart could bear. I'd finally logged off and went to my room.

To wait.

I stared into my vinyl collection, but there was simply no music that could make any of this better.

Someone named Judge Tuttle, who was allegedly

Micah's dad, was coming. But Micah never talked about having a dad who lived in Muddy Waters, or was involved in his life at all. I half wondered if Mom had called the wrong family. Maybe it would be a strange boy named Micah who I'd never met, and his head-scratching parents arriving at our door.

I didn't know that Officer Mendoza was coming, though, and my breath quickened when his official patrol car pulled into the driveway. I peered at him through my bedroom window. I steeled myself as best I could on legs made of jelly.

A few moments later, a shiny silver BMW pulled in behind the patrol car. I watched as the passengers unloaded and headed up to the door—a man in a suit and tie, a woman in a suit but no tie, and regular-dressed Micah, dragging his heels like he'd rather be anywhere else. Who were these people he was with?

Mom had set up coffee, tea, and snacks on the counter, and showed everyone to their seats. She'd had to put out a couple of extra chairs. Micah and I each took one of the extra chairs and sat, looking everywhere but right at each other. I did notice when he came through the door that he was still limping. He had a swollen, busted-up lip. And that big scabbed-over scratch on his neck.

After Mom made introductions and welcomed everyone, she turned the meeting over to Officer Mendoza. I was super grateful she hadn't made everyone hold hands and say a prayer to start. And I was still trying to figure out how the woman in the business suit, who was introduced as Micah's mother, could forget to feed her kids. She looked like someone who was on top of everything she did.

Officer Mendoza had a big folder with him, which he placed across his large knees. "I really appreciate everyone being here. Now, I've had a chance to talk to everyone already, except you, Micah. Your parents and I spoke this morning on the phone, and I met the reverend at the hospital last night."

Micah stared back but didn't say a word.

"Right," Officer Mendoza said. "So, I wanted to get us all together so that we can sort out what happened yesterday afternoon and last night. As it stands now, we have evidence of some crimes that were committed, but it's unclear, at least to me," he said, looking around the room, "who all was involved in these infractions."

He opened his folder then, and said, "If it is agreeable with all of you, I'd like to start with what we know for sure."

Everyone nodded in agreement, except me, and except Micah. But Officer Mendoza went on anyway. "We know for a fact that someone broke into Mr. Jewett's house across the street sometime late yesterday afternoon."

He stopped then, and pulled a small padded envelope from the folder. He reached in and pulled out Deuce's house keys. "I've confirmed that these are Mr. Jewett's keys, which he said had been missing for at least two days. These keys were found among Ham's things at the scene of the accident."

My face burned.

Officer Mendoza looked at me, then Micah. "Who took these keys from Mr. Jewett's home?"

"I did, sir," I said, shooting a glance at Micah. He just stared ahead.

"I see," he said. "Ham, now, you told your mother you used the key Mr. Jewett kept hidden outside to gain access to the house. Why would you have used a key Mr. Jewett kept hidden outside if you already had his house keys in your possession?"

*This*, back to bite me. "Er—uh, I can't really remember," I said. "I was in a big hurry." I certainly couldn't say what Micah had told me about having the keys. That he'd considered taking the Mustang, too. No way I was going to cop to that.

"All right," he said, "we'll move on. The next fact is that Mr. Jewett's tandem bike, valued at approximately twelve thousand dollars, was taken from his house, ridden by one or more riders, and ultimately crashed on Suey Road."

I noticed both Judge Tuttle and Mrs. Tuttle were taking notes in official-looking folders of their own. Mom wasn't taking notes, but she kept looking at Micah. Chances were good she was praying hard that he'd stop lying.

"Who rode and crashed Mr. Jewett's tandem?" Officer Mendoza asked.

"I did, sir," I said.

Micah remained silent, though everyone seemed to be looking at him now.

Officer Mendoza, in particular, was staring hard at him. "The young lady who reported the accident said there were two boys on the tandem. Micah," he said, "do you have anything to say to that?"

"Nope," he said, and folded his arms across his chest.

Judge Tuttle cleared his throat loudly. Micah unfolded his arms and said, "No, sir, nothing to add to that."

Officer Mendoza held his gaze. "Micah, can you

explain your obvious injuries? Your parents said you came home last night with a bloody lip, and you seem to have hurt your leg."

"I'm fine—it's nothing," he said. "I was late to cross-country practice yesterday, so I went for a run on my own. I tripped over a log in the park behind the school."

"Uh-huh," Officer Mendoza said.

He pulled out some photos from his folder and held them up. "These are the photos of the unpaid merchandise that was found in the backpack you were wearing, Ham. There were two jackets valued at one hundred sixty-nine dollars each. We have determined that they came from Lucky Dudes clothing store on Broad Street. We also confirmed they were stolen, and not purchased."

He looked straight at Micah again. "Who took these jackets?"

I raised my hand. "I did, sir."

Officer Mendoza didn't even look at me. He kept his eyes locked on Micah.

"Interesting," he said. "We checked the CCT at Lucky Dudes from yesterday afternoon. I have a screenshot here of a young man stuffing one of the jackets into his backpack." He raised the photo and showed it around the room. “I’ll defer to the parents for formal identification, but in my opinion, this is not a photo of Ham Hudson.”

Mom reached over to take the photograph. She glanced at it a moment, then handed it over to Judge and Mrs. Tuttle.

Judge Tuttle cleared his throat again, and nodded toward Officer Mendoza. “This is our son in the photo, not Reverend Hudson’s son.” Mrs. Tuttle nodded, her face now drained of color.

Officer Mendoza pulled up another photo. “This is the backpack that Ham had when the stolen jackets were recovered at the scene. Reverend Hudson has already confirmed with me that this is not Ham’s backpack. Judge, Mrs. Tuttle, can you look at this and determine if this is your son’s backpack?” He stretched over and handed it to them.

Micah sat up in his seat at that, and broke in. “*Don’t* bother, they wouldn’t know what my backpack looks like. They just give me money. I do my own shopping.” His face darkened as he spoke.

His mother put a hand on his arm, and he yanked it away.

“Look, fine,” he continued. “That’s me stealing a jacket in the picture. But I did it for Ham.” He turned to look at me, finally and fully. Then he looked over at my mom. "No offense, Reverend, but you guys don't have a lot of money. I wanted Ham to have a nice jacket. So I took two. I was going to let him pick the one he liked best. And then take the other one back."

I watched Mom take a long, steadying breath through her nose.

"You *stole* jackets as a present for me, Micah?" I said, my voice hot now. "You told me that it was new school clothes for Mason in your backpack."

Judge Tuttle interrupted, setting his glasses on top of his head. "Who is Mason—another boy?"

I looked at him, shaking my head in surprise. "Mason is Micah's little *brother*—your son?" How could Micah's parents be *this* neglectful?

Mrs. Tuttle put her hand across her eyes a moment, then closed her folder. She laced her fingers together and sat up even straighter. "Micah doesn't have a little brother, Ham. He's an only child."

*"What?"* I said, dumbstruck, my head whipping in Micah's direction. "You lied about having a little brother?"

Micah stared back, lifted one shoulder, then dropped it. Slunk back down in his chair.

I looked at Judge Tuttle. "Do you live with Micah and Mrs. Tuttle?"

"I certainly do," he said.

I couldn't stop my head from shaking back and forth. Like I was trying to keep the truth from landing in my brain. "Mrs. Tuttle, does that mean you're not a single mother working two jobs?"

Mrs. Tuttle turned to her son. "Micah! What on earth have you been telling people?"

Judge Tuttle slammed his folder shut and dropped it to the floor. He brought his hands together in front of him. "Officer Mendoza, Reverend Hudson, if you don't mind, can we take a break for a few minutes? My wife and I would like to speak to our son in private."

# CHAPTER FORTY-FOUR

Twenty minutes or so later, we all sat back down together in the parsonage living room. This time, though, Mom motioned to the couch for me to come sit next to her.

Both Judge and Mrs. Tuttle looked drained, like maybe they'd both been mugged since we saw them last.

Micah looked the same.

Judge Tuttle tried to sort himself out a bit. He straightened his tie and ran his hand over his hair. Mrs. Tuttle had her arm around the back of Micah's chair. But she stared at the carpet.

"Officer Mendoza, Reverend, Ham, perhaps we can start over. I think things have become much clearer in the last few minutes."

Officer Mendoza sat back in the armchair. "I'm all ears."

Judge Tuttle nodded and turned to his son. "Micah, please tell Officer Mendoza what happened yesterday." His voice strained. "The truth, all of it this time."

Micah squirmed a bit in his seat, and then blew out a gust of air.

"I borrowed Deuce's keys the day before yesterday when I was in his house. Then yesterday, I let myself in so I could get the tandem."

I could almost feel Mom cringe next to me at the way Micah described what he had done. Like he'd been a choirboy on a charitable mission. It made me cringe, too. The truth was that he *stole* Deuce's keys, *broke* into his house, and then *robbed* him.

The room was dead quiet. Mrs. Tuttle wiped at her eyes.

Micah stopped for a second, and searched our faces. He seemed surprised. Like he wondered why no one was giving him an understanding nod. "Look, I just wanted to ride the tandem with Ham. You're all making such a big deal about it."

When we all just stared back at him, he said, "I

wasn't planning on wrecking it! That was an accident. Some kids in a car were hassling us really bad, and I took my eyes off the road for just a second. I wanted to get a picture of their license plate." His eyes darted to mine then. "Tell them, Ham, how those kids made us wreck the bike."

I shook my head no.

"They called us *queers*!" he blurted. He began to look desperate that none of us got what he'd been through.

Mom looked at Officer Mendoza and the Tuttles. "Is it okay if I ask Micah a question?"

When they all nodded, she turned to Micah. "You said you just wanted to ride the bike?"

"Yep," he said, and then before his father could correct him, he added, "I mean, yes, Reverend."

Mom nodded. "But Ham thought you had taken the tandem so the two of you could go to Bijou's to get his cat back, right? You told him that was where Buster was."

Color flashed on his cheeks for a moment. "Yeah, I did," he admitted. "I knew otherwise he wouldn't go for a ride with me."

I broke in, incredulous. "You made that up, too? Buster was never at Bijou's?"

He shrugged again.

"But you brought that cat sling so we could bring Buster home on the bike. Why did you bring one if you knew Buster wasn't there?" This didn't add up at all.

Micah lifted his eyes to mine, and this time his look was almost imploring. As in, can we just leave it alone?

As I stared back, I noticed again the long scratch on his neck. Which I realized wasn't fresh at all. It wouldn't have a big scab on it yet if it had just happened last night.

My body flooded then with heat and adrenaline, like a booster rocket firing up for launch. I knew why Micah had a big vicious scratch on his neck. And I knew why he just happened to have a cat carrier handy in his backpack.

I jumped to my feet, hands curling into fists. "Micah! Where is my cat? What have you *done* with Buster?"

# CHAPTER FORTY-FIVE

Micah and his real-life parents, Judge and Mrs. Tuttle, lived in the swankiest neighborhood I'd ever been in. I picked at my hangnails while Mom drove with tears nearly falling into her lap.

"It's okay, Mom." I didn't want to start crying, too, but the thought of getting Buster back, for sure this time, was almost more than my nerves could handle.

"I know, honey," she said, wiping at her eyes. "It's just an awful lot to process."

She reached over to squeeze my hand, and we didn't let go.

After Micah admitted that he was the one who had taken Buster, things had happened very fast. Officer Mendoza decided that it was time to take Micah down to Juvenile Services to finish the rest of the interview. The Tuttles led Micah to the car, and I could hear him trying to explain things. "I wasn't going to keep his cat, Mom! Honest!"

The Tuttles' housekeeper was waiting for us when we arrived, and led us out back to the guesthouse, which was just about as big as our entire parsonage. Micah had been keeping Buster in their guesthouse so his parents wouldn't find him.

"Mom?" I asked. "Can I go in alone? He's probably pretty freaked out."

"Of course, son. I'll wait out here."

I stepped into the cool air of the guesthouse, and closed the door softly behind me.

I walked across the tile entry onto the plush carpeting of the living room. I sank into a leather armchair.

"Buster?" I said, my voice soft. "I'm here. You just take all the time—"

Buster came at me like a shot. He launched himself onto me. I drew him close while he stomped over my lap and chest, chirring and meowing. He threw himself into me over and over, as if he wanted to stick himself to me for good.

Hot, giant tears fell at last and into his fur, and

he licked at my face. "I'm so sorry, so, so sorry!" I said. I couldn't imagine the terror he'd been through, wondering where he was. And wondering how to get back home.

When I finally called for Mom, she joined us on the chair, and laid her head onto his. His purr was nearly deafening.

"Oh, my sweet boys" was all she said, over and over.

I'd been so wrapped up in my own grief; it hadn't really hit me that Mom loved Buster just as much as I did. Losing him had ripped her as well. She hadn't just adopted me but Buster, too.

"I just called Deuce," she said finally, stroking Buster's ears. "He knew we were having a meeting. I wanted him to know that Micah had finally confessed."

I sighed into Buster's fur. "Do you think he'll ever forgive me about the tandem?"

"You can ask him when he gets here," she said.

"He's coming here?" I sat up at that.

"He's bringing the cat carrier. We weren't sure if we would need to take Buster to the vet after this, to have him checked out."

"You're fine, aren't you, boy?" I asked him. I gave

him a full checkup, and he seemed none worse for the wear.

"That's nice of Deuce to come help." I gulped. I didn't know if I was ready to face him.

"This is his family, too, you know," Mom said.

Buster wouldn't let me put him down for even a second as I stood at the window waiting for Deuce. Even though trying to hold him with just one arm was awkward and kind of painful. But I didn't care. I didn't want to put him down.

When Deuce pulled up in his truck, my heart began to boom in my chest. I couldn't bear having him mad at me. I stepped outside as he pulled the carrier out of the back, and headed toward us.

"Hey, kiddo," he said. He came over and gave Buster a good head rub. "If you aren't a sight for sore eyes."

"Deuce, I—" I started, but he pulled my head toward him, and laid it against his chest. "I'm so sorry," I said in a husky whisper.

"I know you are."

"I don't know how, but I promise I will pay you back for wrecking the tandem."

"Oh, I know how you'll pay me back," he said.

I looked up, and tried to wipe my nose with my sleeve. "You do? How?"

"Labor," he said. "You're going to help me put it all back together, piece by piece, dent by dent."

I shifted Buster in my arm, where he'd been crushed against my collarbone. Best pain I'd ever had.

"How you holding up?" Deuce asked. "Your mom told me about everything Micah put you through."

I knew Deuce was really asking, not just being polite. My heart felt sprained, swollen, bruised. They always say a bad sprain is worse than a clean break. I could vouch for that. It was.

"I guess I got in over my head, you know?"

"I can see that," Deuce said. "He's quite the charmer."

"I really like—or I guess, I liked him so much." I looked up at him, hoping he could see what I wasn't saying.

"I know you did. And first loves are magical. It's hard not to lose your head completely."

I tried to swallow over gravel lodged in my throat.

"Was Mr. Flynn your first love?" I asked, my voice almost a whisper.

"No, he wasn't my first love, but he was my very best love. And my last love," he said, his voice rough.

He pulled his baseball cap off, wiped his head, and put it back on. "My first love was a boy named Kenneth, and I would have happily jumped off a bridge if he'd asked me to."

A small smile found my mouth.

"Young love can hurt an awful lot," Deuce said. "Especially when that person disappoints you. I remember."

"Can I ask you something private? I almost asked Mom one day, but I didn't think she would know the answer."

"Sure, what is it?"

"Does liking Micah that way mean I'm going to always like boys? I mean, how do you know for sure if you're gay for good? When did you know for sure?" I asked.

"Here, let me take him for a minute," he said, reaching his arms out for Buster, who seemed happy to go, as long as he could still keep me in his line of vision.

Deuce continued. "If you knew the answer to that now, would it make a difference?"

I thought about it a long minute. If I knew for sure I was gay, would I just add it to my list of things to worry about? Or, if I was certain I was straight, would that make me happier?

"I'm guess I'm not sure what kind of difference it would make," I finally said. "It's kind of a hard thing to know just with your head."

"Your mom has taught me a lot about what she calls the 'divine mysteries' of life. Some things are only known by your heart. And your heart may not give you advance notice or understanding," he said, his voice soft.

That sort of made sense. It was hard to understand my feelings for Micah with just my brain. But my heart knew him the first moment I saw him. And it was my heart feeling the big loss of him now.

"Let's you and I keep talking about this, okay? But I think we should get this little fella home."

I reached out and took Buster back, and reveled in the familiar feel of him next to me.

"And I know your mom would want to talk to you about it, too. I've told her a lot of my secrets over the years. She just keeps coming back loving me with all her might."

"I know," I said. "It's her superpower."

Deuce laughed. "That it is."

He swung open the door of his truck and climbed in. "I'll see all of you back at the house, okay?"

"Deuce, just one more thing," I started, talking to him through the open window of his truck. "It's partly my fault that the police thought maybe you'd been on the tandem with me, and maybe even stole those jackets."

My throat burned, but I had to say it. "I had a chance to stand up for you, and I didn't." I swallowed hard. "I should have told Officer Mendoza right away that he was wrong."

Deuce didn't interrupt but waited.

"It's the one thing about this whole terrible mess that I wish I could undo. And because I didn't speak up for you, the police came to your house. Which I know must have been the most awful thing to happen to you."

The shame of it all burned so deep and hot I could barely stand it.

Deuce shook his head. "No, the most awful thing was hearing you'd been in an accident. That was the worst part for me."

My sigh was ragged. "I don't understand how me just liking a boy could lead to such a mess for everyone."

"I know," he said. "Life and love are messy. You do your very best, and stay close to the people who love you."

He started his engine, and then reached through

the window to place a gentle hand on my shoulder. "And, double bacon cheeseburgers make most everything better. I'll stop on the way and grab us some. One for your mom, too? A special treat?" he asked.

"Absolutely!" I said. "And some extra bacon for Buster."

# CHAPTER FORTY-SIX

The next morning at eight there was a loud knock on the front door. I ignored it.

Another knock, louder and longer.

I put the pillow over my head. Buster burrowed under it with me.

Then the doorbell, loud and piercing.

I couldn't imagine who would come this early, unless it was an emergency situation for Mom. I heard her bedroom door open, and she yelled, "Coming!" as she headed to the door. She banged into the coffee table like she always did when she was in a hurry.

She cursed like she always did when she hit it.

I lifted the pillow up from my head so I could hear who it was at the door. I heard Mom's voice first, then a girl voice. But it wasn't Fey's.

"Ham!" Mom called toward my door. "You have a visitor. Get dressed and come on out."

Mom must have invited her in because then I heard the front door close, and then more talking. There wasn't anyone I wanted to see that early on a Saturday morning, but I was stuck. Mom had already invited her in.

I threw on a pair of sweats, and one of my cut-up shirts that I could get over my sling and body bandage. Buster rolled onto his back and yawned, watching me. I swept the hair out of my eyes, then pulled open my bedroom door and peered out.

Bijou sat on the arm of the couch, talking to Mom. She looked up, casual-like, when I came out. Like there was nothing completely weird about her coming to my house.

"Uh, hi," I said.

"Hey," she said back.

"Uh, Mom," I said, "this is Bijou, from my team."

Mom smiled. "Yes, we were just getting acquainted. Bijou, can I get you anything to drink, or maybe to eat? I can scramble some eggs really quick."

"No thanks," she said, and rubbed at her eye. "I'm just here for Coach. I mean, she and I talked, and I came to take you out for a walk."

"You came to walk me?" I said, confused.

"Well, yeah, you can't run yet, but you can't just sit around. You'll get all soft. We're going for a long walk, a fitness walk."

Bijou sniffed and rubbed her eye again. "Oh! I forgot. Your cat! I'm super allergic to cats. I'll wait on the porch while you go get your shoes."

She let herself out quickly, and Mom and I just looked at each other, both kind of stunned.

"I don't believe this," I said. "But I guess this means I'm not kicked off the team, at least."

Mom nodded. "Coach called last night to check on you. She'd been in touch with Micah's parents, too. She knows Micah confessed."

Mom followed me into my room as I went after some socks and my shoes. She'd washed the vomit off them, but they were still a bit damp. After I got my feet shoved into them, Mom leaned over and tied them for me. This one-handed thing was going to get old.

She studied me. "You feel okay about being alone with her?"

"I do," I said, surprising myself. "I mean, look at me." I gestured toward my shoulder and chest. "Can't get much worse!"

Mom opened her mouth, but I stopped her. "I'm just kidding. She won't mess with me, promise. Especially since Coach assigned her to give me a workout."

"Okay, then, well, have a good time?"

I gave Buster a quick rubdown. "Keep him inside, okay, Mom?"

"You bet," she said.

"Oh, and if Fey comes over before I get back, get her to stay, will you? I really need to talk to her about—" I paused. "Well, about everything."

"Yeah," she said, nodding. "You do."

As Bijou and I hit the pavement, she fiddled with a giant sports watch. She pulled a piece of paper out of her shorts and handed it to me. "Here, hold this while I get us set up."

"Pretty cool watch," I said. "Is it new? I know you lost yours out on the trail," I commented, studying the paper. I recognized Coach's scribbled shorthand.

"Nah, I never had one. And, uh, never lost one. Yeah, I punked you on the trail."

I nodded, not surprised at all.

She flicked her wrist. "Coach lent this one to me. So I could time us. Okay, read me the splits."

As I read them off to her, she quickly entered them

into the watch, nodding when she was ready for the next number.

"Okay, that's it, right?"

"Yep, that's all of it," I said, handing the paper back to her.

"Good. So, we're going to warm up while we walk from here over to the track. We'll do some walking splits on the track, where the surface is softer, and then to the big grassy area where it's flat. No uneven surfaces until you start getting better, Coach says. You're supposed to let me know if anything starts hurting, then we slow down. Take a break if we need to."

"Okay," I said. "And thanks, this is really, uh, I guess, nice of you."

"It's not 'nice.' I'm just doing my job as assistant captain."

We walked another half block, and then she turned sideways to look at me. "Coach said you told her I should be the team captain while you're out."

"You're the best and obvious choice," I said.

"I know that, but it still surprised me you said that. My uncle used to play ball in the minor leagues. He told me the best person on the team is the one who thinks about the team first, and themselves second. I know Coach has said that like a million times, but it kind of sunk in when he said that."

"I'm sorry that we had to forfeit the first meet. That's all my fault."

"Stuff happens," she said.

We just walked then for a bit, falling in sync with each other like we had that day on the trail. Even though we were different, and we didn't like each other, it seemed like our bodies had a common language of their own.

"Is it weird living in a church?" she asked, surprising me.

"I suppose it would be, except that's where I've always lived. It doesn't seem weird to me at all."

"I live in a trailer now," she said. "I suppose that would be weird to some people."

"I guess," I said.

"I used to live in a regular house with my dad. But now he lives—you know." She pointed with her chin in the direction of the prison.

"You live with your uncle now, right?"

"Just until my dad gets out," she said. "A few more years."

"Right."

"My uncle knows your mom. He runs a place called the Alano Club. It's like a dry bar for people to go to hang out without drinking. He says your mom comes out there sometimes and meets with guys she helped when they were inside. He likes her. Says she's good people."

"She is," I said. "I'm lucky."

"You mean lucky that she found you?"

I shot a glance over at her.

She kept her gaze ahead. "My uncle told me about your mom finding you in her Nativity scene. And how she adopted you."

I took a swig from my water bottle. This was not a talk I ever expected to be having with Bijou. And I wondered why she hadn't ever teased me about it at school. Or, if that was coming next.

"There's worse things than being left by your birth mother in a manger," she said.

"Like what?" I asked, curious.

"Having your birth mother keep you when she can barely take care of herself, let alone a baby. My mom called it quits on me and my dad both when I was in kindergarten. Who knows where she ended up"

"Wow. I'm really sorry," I said.

"You know, I saw you and your mom a few days before school started at Target. My uncle gave me money to buy one new outfit for school. Not his fault, that's all he could afford. I saw you two there laughing and talking about all your new stuff. It rubbed me the wrong way. Then when you showed up at the creek that day, and I recognized you as the Target kid with the great mom, I guess I took it out on you." She stopped, winded from the longest I'd ever heard her talk.

"That was the first time I'd ever gotten new clothes," I said. "Until I started public school, I'd always worn clothes from the charity boxes. I hated it."

"God, I hate that stuff, too."

We'd reached the track, and Bijou called the first split. We increased our pace, still eerily locked in sync.

"Even when you can start running again, we're still short a runner on the team."

I looked at her, puzzled a moment.

"Micah won't be coming back for a long time, maybe never," she said.

"Oh," I said. "You heard what happened?"

"Small-town life," she said. "I've heard most of it. Since his dad is a judge, I doubt Micah will spend much time in juvie. They'll probably make some kind of deal to send him to a special program. Or, maybe one of those military schools."

My pace slowed, and then I had to stop. To try to catch my breath. It had just hit me that I might never see Micah again. Ever. My head knew he was a liar and a thief. But my heart still raced at the thought of him.

Bijou stopped alongside me. Put a hand on my back. "Hey! You okay?"

"Just give me a sec," I said, my voice uneven.

"That's another reason I didn't like you," she said. "I fell for him, too."

# CHAPTER FORTY-SEVEN

Buster stopped coming to school with me after he was kidnapped by Micah. I wondered, at first, if he was scared of public school kids now like I used to be. Or, maybe he just figured that I'd grown up enough in the last few months and I could handle school on my own. But he still waited every day on the living room windowsill, and he always did a happy dance when he saw me coming.

After all that had happened with Micah, Mom wanted to have a BIG talk with me about lying, and friendships, and "some other things," which probably meant the way I felt about Micah.

I was still pretty gutted after it all happened, and it was hard to talk. I mostly listened to Mom, and nodded a lot. I promised her that I would write about it in my journal, and talk to Fey about it. I noticed that some of her recent sermons had been about some of the stuff she knew I was confused about. Moms will do just about any sneaky thing they can to get a word in edgewise. But I really didn't mind. I knew how lucky I was to have her.

"Anybody need a refill on their iced tea? Or more chips?" I asked. Fey and Frida had come over, and we were getting things ready for our Saturday gig. Frida was the granddaughter of Mrs. Dort, and had come to live with her grandma for a year while her parents got divorced. Fey and I had begged Ms. Becerra to let Frida be in our homeroom when she started at Harvey Mellencamp. Like Fey and I had been, Frida was really happy to have friends at a new school.

Fey and Frida had hit it off right away. Fey loved collecting and categorizing nature, and Frida liked to write poems about it. For about a half second when Frida first started hanging out with us, I worried that I'd feel left out. But with real friendships, seems like there is always room for more people. And it meant that sometimes I could have lunch with the cross-country team without worrying Fey would sit alone in the cafeteria. It was hard to believe that

Bijou and I were eating together on purpose.

She and I hadn't become best buds or anything, but we both were committed to the team, and getting Coach Becerra to trust us again. Bijou and I were learning to trust each other a little bit. Mom hosted a couple of barbecues at the parsonage for the whole team, and made a special point of making Bijou feel welcome. She even took her shopping for bras, which I guess her uncle never had. Mom didn't tell me that, but I heard her talking to one of the Church Ladies about it. They'd all chipped in to buy her some "proper undergarments."

"More chips, please!" Fey and Frida said at the same second, and we all laughed.

"Coming right up!" I said, gently lifting Buster off my lap, and heading toward the kitchen.

The letter had come that morning, and it was still on the counter. Micah had addressed it to Mom, but inside the thick envelope, there was a letter for her, one for Deuce, and one for me. Micah was in Utah at a school for kids who had the kind of problems he had. His letters to us were full of apology, and hopes that he'd see us all again someday. He'd also sent the $100 gift certificate from the raffle, and asked that I give it back to Coach. He'd never turned it in like he said he would. He was sorry about that, too.

I hadn't told Fey or Frida yet, but I needed to. I wanted to. That's what friends do. You tell them stuff, even if it's hard to talk about.

"I got a letter from Utah today," I said as I opened another big bag of tortilla chips.

Fey's head whipped around to look at me. "Micah?"

Frida looked up, curious. "Oh, is he the one who—"

"Yep," Fey muttered. "What did he say? I mean, do you want to talk about it?" She got up off the floor, and came over to where I was standing.

"It's an apology letter. Feels sort of like someone at the school made him write it."

"You okay?" she asked, her voice soft.

Shoulders up. Shoulders down.

"You going to write him back?"

I shook my head, and felt the heat behind my eyes that still came sometimes when I thought about him.

Fey and I had had a very long talk about everything that had happened—the crush, the crash, and even the kiss. She had just listened, and didn't make me feel like I'd been an idiot. I think the hardest part had been telling her about my true, secret feelings for Micah. I worried how she would react. I still remember Micah saying that Fey liked me as more than a friend. If that was true, I didn't want to say anything that would hurt her.

When I had told her, Fey had taken my hand and held it. She'd said there was absolutely nothing wrong with liking a boy, just that I had liked the *wrong* boy.

The wrong boy had stolen my heart, and even my cat. But being Micah's friend, and sort of secret boyfriend, had made me think about what kind of person and what kind of friend I wanted to be. Deuce told me once that every single person has a private list of mistakes that they have made. Even some "doozies," he'd said. The key to a good life is to do better next time, he said.

"Here they come!" Fey said, spying out the front window.

"How many?" I asked.

"Looks like three today," Frida said. "But one more might be coming. I'll get the towels!"

Fey, Frida, and I ran a Saturday hair salon for the Church Ladies. It was Frida's idea for all three of us to do it, so it didn't take up my whole day. Plus, we could do more ladies at one time. For the rinsing part, Mom let us use the old baptismal font in the church, because the bowl was huge, and it had great water pressure. We just had to put towels all around it, and clean up really well, which we always did. It even had a little padded kneeler for them in front of the bowl. Mom always smiled when she saw us doing rinse-outs, and called our Saturday salon "Souls in the Bowl."

Mrs. Minelli, Mrs. Paschal, and Mrs. Martinez settled themselves on stools at the kitchen counter while Frida poured them iced tea. Fey draped them with towels, adding plastic clips to hold the ends together. We were getting fancy these days.

"Oh! There she is!" Frida said, and we all turned to see Mrs. Dort coming through the front door.

Frida ran to give her a hug. "Hi, Nana! You came! I'm so glad."

"I promised you I would," she said, and dropped her bag on the couch, after pulling out a box of hair dye.

Mrs. Minelli spun all the way around to look at her. "Nancy Dort, what in *heavens* are you doing here?" She spied the box in her hand. "Surely you're not—"

"She is!" Frida said with a happy laugh as Mrs. Dort plopped down on the empty stool next to Mrs. Minelli.

Mrs. Minelli stared at her, speechless.

"But you've always said coloring our hair is a terrible vanity!" Mrs. Paschal started.

"Oh, I imagine I've said a lot of things I've come to regret," she said with a sigh, sliding her box of dye toward me.

Mrs. Minelli gasped as she studied Mrs. Dort's box. "That's the same color I use!"

"And why not? You're my best friend. Now we'll look like sisters," she said, patting Mrs. Minelli's hand.

I turned at the sound of a long, plaintive meow.

"Be right back, everyone," I said.

"Go ahead," Fey said. "We'll get started without you."

I gave her a smile and went to find Buster. He sat in the hallway, looking up at the attic opening. He meowed again when he saw me, then got to his feet and started turning in quick circles.

Since he'd come back home, Buster had needed a little more comfort and reassurance than usual. I'd been taking him up to the attic, so he could get into the manger. That always settled him down. I looked up at the attic and then back toward the front room. I needed to get back to the Ladies, but once Buster had an idea in his head, he kept at it.

An idea formed in my head, too. I pulled the ladder down from the attic and headed up, Buster on my heels. I pulled the manger out of the corner and he leapt in.

"Hey, buddy, how about we take this downstairs? Then you can get in it whenever you want. How would that be?"

The manger wasn't heavy, but it was awkward. I'd mostly healed up from the bike crash, but I did get sore twinges now and then. I went back to the ladder and knelt down at the opening.

"Fey!" I called. "Can you come here a sec?"

She came into the hallway, spied the ladder, then looked up. "Oh! There you are!"

"Can you help me bring something down?" I asked.

"Sure, should I come up?" she asked, testing the bottom rung of the ladder.

"No, I'll just hand it to you. Hold on." I apologized to Buster as I scooped him out. I lowered the manger carefully to Fey, who waited with her arms up.

"Got it?" I asked.

"Yes!" she said as she took it, then lowered it to the floor.

I came down with Buster tucked under one arm,

fussing and chirping at me.

"Hold on a sec," I told him.

Fey's eyes were wide as she looked at me. "Is this—?"

"Yeah," I said, and dropped Buster gently into it. He began turning circles to get the towels just right.

I lifted the manger with care and carried it into my bedroom. Fey followed me. I set it down in the space next to my turntable. It fit perfectly.

I stepped back, and let out a big, deep breath. Buster finally had it just right and flopped down. He began to purr with his eyes at half-mast.

"Better, buddy?" I asked, getting down on my haunches and scratching the top of his head.

"He really likes being in it," I said, turning to Fey. "I usually take him up to the attic to get in it, but why not just have it down here for him?"

Fey came over and squatted next to me. She ran her fingers over the raw wood. "It won't be hard for you to see it all the time?" she asked.

I considered that a minute, and then shook my head. "It might have before," I said, "but now? I think it's just right in here. And look how happy it makes Buster."

Fey leaned down and kissed his head.

"Guys?" Frida called from the hallway. "Where *are* you two?"

"In here," we called. We stood up and turned around.

Frida appeared at the door, looking frazzled. "Okay, everything's *mostly* fine, but Mrs. Minelli wanted to show the Ladies the hats she's knitting. So she moved all the bowls out of the way."

"Uh-oh," Fey said.

*"Right!?!"* Frida exclaimed. "Now I don't know which color goes with which of the Ladies."

Fey and Frida hurried out to the kitchen, talking over each other. I turned to take a last look at Buster, curled round like a doughnut. He thought the manger was a perfect place to be. A great place to return. He hadn't turned himself inside out questioning why he'd been left there that dark and cold night. He'd just leaned into the warmth of the baby next to him. And he'd never stopped.

I headed back out to the kitchen, to my friends and my army of Church Ladies—leaning into that warmth, and the wonderful chaos of it all.

And I sent a silent thanks to the woman who left me in the best place of all.

# ACKNOWLEDGMENTS

# ACKNOWLEDGMENTS

I am indebted to those who lent their love and expertise to me during the writing of Ham's story. I am deeply grateful to my agent, Erin Murphy, and editors, Kristen Pettit and Elizabeth Lynch, for their tender and enduring patience with me as I worked and reworked these pages.

Robin LaFevers, YA author extraordinaire, handed me a spade, and urged me to dig like a feverish archaeologist to find the story's very core. It is to her credit that Ham's journey was illuminated and deepened. I owe her a kidney and a spa date, for sure.

Special thanks to national champion tandem cyclists Jill Gass and Julie Kaplan, who helped me with the hardware and logistics of a tandem cycle riding, and crashing. Lucky for me, Jill is also a critical care nurse. She gently pointed out that my first version of the crash would have left both my characters dead. Ham, Micah, and I are in your debt, Jill!

Lastly, a big thank-you to Arlene Golant, who simply believed I could do it.